DARK REBEL'S RECKONING

THE CHILDREN OF THE GODS
BOOK NINETY-THREE

I. T. LUCAS

Dark Rebel's Reckoning is a work of fiction! Names, characters, places, and incidents are products of the author's imagination or are used fictitiously and are not to be construed as real. Any similarity to actual persons, organizations, and/or events is purely coincidental.

Copyright © 2025 by I. T. Lucas

All rights reserved.

No part of this book may be reproduced in any form or by any electronic or mechanical means, including information storage and retrieval systems, without written permission from the author, except for the use of brief quotations in a book review.

Published by Evening Star Press, LLC.

EveningStarPress.com

ISBN: 978-1-962067-68-3

1

MAX

The rotors thudded above in a steady rhythm and the fuselage vibrated with every push of the wind, creating a concerto of sounds that represented safety.

At least in Max's ears.

Still, even though the mission objectives had been achieved and all team members had made it out alive, the sense of urgency refused to abate. Most of the enemy soldiers had been eliminated, humans and Doomers alike, and the compound was going up in smoke behind them. However, he was well aware that they wouldn't be out of danger until they crossed the border into Turkey, and that was despite Yamanu shrouding both helicopters.

Mental manipulation and illusions didn't fool equipment.

Not that Turkey was friendly territory. It used

to be a progressive country, but it had been slipping into the abyss of darkness for over a decade. Corruption was rampant, and with the right connections and enough money, anything could be arranged, and the chances of betrayal were high.

Max couldn't allow himself to relax until they were all on the jet and out of Turkish airspace.

The country had a formidable air force, and as a NATO member, it had all the latest jets, radar equipment, and armaments, and they were all in working condition. Yamanu's shrouding wouldn't help them against all that.

The infiltration had been even uglier than Max had feared, but they'd come out on top despite Drova and Yamanu getting hit.

Yamanu was already fully healed, his body repairing the damage in minutes, but Drova would take more time. The Kra-ell didn't heal as fast as immortals.

Although looking at the six women they'd rescued, the four humans were in better shape than the two immortals.

The damn so-called doctor, who was in a body bag in the cargo area, must have concocted a sedative that wreaked havoc on immortals. Kyra and Fenella were experiencing occasional moments of clarity, but they didn't last long.

Max was afraid even to hypothesize how the

Doomer had managed that with no medical training.

Hopefully, no lasting damage had been done to them, and Bridget would be able to fix whatever was wrong with the two females.

As turbulence jostled the helicopter, Max braced his forearm against the cabin wall and tightened his hold on Fenella. Across from him, Ell-rom held on to the unconscious Kyra, and sitting next to him, Jasmine held on to her mother's limp hand.

Max wished he could trade places with either of them.

His instincts demanded that Kyra belonged with him, and he wanted her in his arms, but he couldn't say that without sounding like a lunatic.

There was something special about her.

Perhaps he liked the warrior type? The lionesses?

In the past, he'd been attracted to damsels in distress, but Kyra was now both. The lioness had been captured and had become a damsel for him to save.

He glanced down at the woman in his arms and wondered what kind of person Fenella had become since the last time he'd seen her. For all he knew, she was a rebel as well and as ferocious as Kyra.

Otherwise, she probably wouldn't have been locked up in the same place.

She must have joined the Kurdish rebellion.

Since Kyra had been so insistent on getting her free, she had to know Fenella. Then again, she could have met her in the prison, and the two could have become friends.

Did Kyra know the other four women they had rescued?

Those women had also been drugged and abused, but they weren't in as bad a shape as Kyra and Fenella—the two immortals who should have fared better. The humans were understandably shell-shocked, and even though Jasmine had tried to convey reassurances and had given them water and energy bars, none of them had said a word so far. At least they were well enough to sit on their own, strapped for safety on the narrow bench of the military aircraft. The two immortal females, on the other hand, had to be carried and held and weren't showing signs of getting better.

What had been done to Kyra and Fenella to bring them to such a state?

Was it chemical or mental?

And how had Fenella become immortal and ended up in the same prison as Kyra?

She hadn't been immortal when Max met her half a century ago—he was sure of that—so the only logical explanation was that she'd been a

Dormant, and he'd unknowingly induced her transition.

Fenella had been on the pill, so they hadn't bothered with condoms, and her transition must have been uneventful, so she hadn't been hospitalized.

Max had only been with her twice before realizing that Din was in love with her, and after his best friend confronted him, hurling accusations, Max hadn't kept in touch with Fenella.

He could only speculate, but he imagined that she'd freaked out after realizing she was changed, not understanding how and what had happened to her.

That was probably what had prompted Fenella to quit her job at the pub and go backpacking on a self-discovery trip to the East. She must have been either searching for answers or afraid of being found out, so she'd continued moving from place to place.

Remembering how he'd found her, chained up and delirious, Max felt a swirl of emotions seizing his gut—shock, guilt, and relief.

It was surreal.

Now she was in his arms, and he owed her answers. Maybe even more than that.

He should call Din and let him know that he'd found her.

What was he going to tell him, though? How

would he even start that conversation? The guy had been his closest friend until Fenella had come between them, and now he needed to tell him that he'd found his girl half a world away from the Scottish pub where the three of them had first met.

Knowing Din, he would say that he was no longer interested and that Max could keep Fenella for himself. That was what he'd said over fifty years ago when Max had offered to stay away from her.

With a sigh, Max leaned his head against the grimy cabin wall.

From across the cabin, Jasmine gave him a searching look and then returned her gaze to her mother.

Kyra's hair was stuck to her clammy face, and her skin was pale. At first, he'd thought it was because of the cold, but she was wearing his thick sweater and was wrapped in blankets on top of that. Besides, as an immortal, she shouldn't be as sensitive to temperature fluctuations.

Jasmine's worried expression echoed his concerns, but she said nothing—just rested her hand on her mother's shoulder.

As Kyra stirred in Ell-rom's arms, Max tensed. He hated the thought of her opening her golden eyes only to gaze at another male's face, but there wasn't much he could do about it. After all, he couldn't just put Fenella on the floor and demand Kyra be handed over to him.

"Twelve?" Kyra murmured.

"We've got her," Jasmine said. "Max is holding her. If you turn your head that way, you'll be able to see her."

Kyra's heavy-lidded eyes darted toward Max, hovering over his face for a split second, but there was no recognition in them.

When she shifted her gaze to Fenella, a soft sigh escaped Kyra's lips. "Safe," she murmured, and then her eyes drifted closed again.

What an amazing woman she was, worrying for another when she herself was in such a bad state.

Feeling that she was the focus of everyone's attention, Fenella blinked her eyes open. They were dull from sedation, but recognition bloomed in them, and she parted her lips, trying to speak.

A wave of pity coursed through Max.

Fenella, who once had so much youthful energy, zest and spunk, had been reduced to this fragile shell, and that was despite being immortal.

"Whe...?" Her voice was a mere croak when it finally came out. "Max?" Her throat seemed to close around his name.

"Yes, it's me, in the flesh, and you are not dead, and you're not dreaming, either. You and I are alike. We don't age."

He expected her to ask how, but instead, she asked, "Where?"

"We're in a helicopter," Max said, leaning in so she could hear him above the roar of the rotors. "You are free."

Fenella's eyes fluttered. "Are you real?"

Her mind must still be foggy, and she either hadn't heard what he'd said or hadn't understood.

"As real as you are, and I'm taking you to safety. No one is going to hurt you ever again."

He would make sure of that.

As a resident of the village, she would be protected.

Fenella exhaled shakily, and the tension in her face melted into exhaustion. Her eyelids drooped, and she slumped against his chest again.

"How does she know you?" Jasmine asked.

He chuckled. "Remember the woman I told you about? The one who you reminded me of? This is her. Her name is Fenella, and evidently she was a Dormant and I induced her transition."

As another wave of turbulence jolted them, the pilot came on the com, "We're about to cross the border into Turkey."

Max breathed out. "Copy that. Any sign we've been spotted?"

"So far, it's quiet."

He closed his eyes, letting the hum of the rotors wash over him.

In the darkness behind his lids, he could almost see the mission in fragments—the infiltration at dawn, Jade's savage strength, plowing through the corridors with her Kra-ell warriors who had been unstoppable in their bloodlust and fury. Yamanu and Drova getting shot. The metal doors behind which terrified detainees had cowered, not trusting that their salvation had arrived.

Max had barely had time to thrall the released male prisoners to forget details about their rescue and instruct them to walk toward the town. Hopefully, they would find people willing to help them and direct them toward the Kurdish rebels so they wouldn't get recaptured.

Across from him, Kyra suddenly twitched, and her eyes shot open in panic. "My pendant?" she rasped, voice barely audible. "Did you get it?"

Max raised an eyebrow. "What is she talking about?"

"Syssi saw it in her vision," Jasmine said. "An amber pendant." She leaned over her mother. "I'm sorry, but you didn't have any jewelry on you, and there was nothing in the room you were held in."

A tear slid down Kyra's cheek. "He took it," she murmured.

"Who?" Jasmine asked but got no answer.

A spasm of despair crossed Kyra's face, and as she slumped back again, another tear rolled down her cheek.

One of the guards must have taken the pendant, and there wasn't much Max could do about it other than to get her a new one, but he was pretty sure it hadn't been just a piece of jewelry. It must have meant something to Kyra for her to cry over it.

Jasmine caught his eye and gave him a brief nod, but he wasn't sure what she was trying to communicate. He and Jasmine had gotten closer during this mission, and he'd changed his mind about her.

She was a surprisingly resilient young woman, and he admired how unshaken she appeared despite the carnage she'd just witnessed. Then again, she might be putting on a brave face for the sake of her mother and the other young women they had rescued. She was the only female team member on this helicopter, and the others looked to her for cues about what awaited them at their destination.

The truth was that Max had no idea.

He just knew they couldn't leave them behind to suffer even more abuse, and he wasn't sure they could leave them in Turkey either. Not until they could figure out why they had been taken and what had been done to them.

Max had a feeling that it had to do with Kyra and Fenella being immortal. Maybe the scumbag doctor thought he could turn these young women into immortals as well, and the big question was why he would think that.

The clan had yet to figure out how to identify Dormants, and there was no way the Doomers could know who could be induced to become immortal and who could not.

Well, they would know soon enough if the Doomer had discovered something the clan had failed to do despite centuries of effort. Once they revived him, Max would be the first in line to incentivize the minion of darkness to tell them everything he knew.

2

KIAN

Kian shifted his gaze from the proposal he was reviewing to glance at the clock at the corner of his laptop screen, but only a couple of minutes had passed since he'd checked it last.

Yamanu had already notified him that the team had boarded the helicopters, but it had been only to say that everyone made it out okay and that they had Kyra. The rest of the details would have to wait until they arrived at the airport in Turkey.

It shouldn't be long now.

Kian was anxious to hear about the mission, and his mind kept wandering, making it difficult to concentrate on the acquisition proposal he was trying to digest in the meantime.

When his office door opened, he smelled the cappuccino first and Syssi's perfume next. Her favorite was a nothing-special Lancôme fragrance available in every department store, and even though he'd gotten her some of the fanciest and most expensive perfumes in the world, the simple stuff was still her go-to scent.

"No news yet?" She put one cup before him and sat down with the other in hand.

"They got Kyra, and everyone is okay, but that's all I know. I'm waiting to hear the rest of the details."

"So am I." She took a sip of her cappuccino. "I'm amazed that Kyra was really where the vision showed me she would be. It doesn't happen often that my foretelling is so accurate. I'm curious to find out how she got there and whether she's immortal like we suspect."

Kyra had looked as young as her daughter in Syssi's vision, but the news segment playing in the background had indicated that what she was being shown had been of a recent event, and not from the past when Kyra was young. But since the woman's face was covered in bruises, Syssi couldn't be sure it was her. On the other hand, the doctor looked the same as he had in another vision that had seemed to be from the past.

Kian took another sip of his cappuccino before putting the cup down. "You know I trust your visions."

She smiled. "I know, but it was still going out

on a limb, and it involved sending a team halfway around the world to search for her."

Syssi's modesty never failed to amaze him. She was a powerful seer who had provided crucial information at critical times, and yet she was still surprised at what he was willing to do based on her visions.

Kian reached for her hand across the desk. "The frequency of the visions indicated urgency, and the stakes were higher than just finding Jasmine's mother, either as a potential Dormant or already an immortal. The Fates directed you, showing you what we needed to locate her, and hopefully, Kyra will point the way to finding Khiann. After all, your visions about her started when you beseeched the universe to show you whether Khiann was still alive and buried in stasis somewhere in the Arabian Desert. If she's really the key to finding him, then it was all well worth the effort. I'm just glad that the gamble paid off and we found her."

She gave his hand a gentle squeeze. "Thank you for your unwavering belief in me. I can't wait to hear all the details and find all the missing puzzle pieces."

Kian glanced at the clock again. "It shouldn't be long now."

For several moments, they sipped on their

cappuccinos in companionable silence, and then his phone finally rang.

Kian accepted the call and pressed the speaker button so Syssi wouldn't have to strain to hear Yamanu on the other side.

"Go ahead. I'm here with Syssi, and we are both eager to hear your report."

"We've got Kyra, as I said before, but we also took five other females. Are you ready for a bit of shocking news?"

Kian exchanged glances with Syssi and mouthed, "Five more?" He then turned to Yamanu. "We are listening."

"First, I want to tell you that you were right about Kyra, and she's immortal. She looks like she's Jasmine's age. Regrettably, she's in no shape to tell us what happened to her."

Kian frowned. "What's wrong with her?"

"She's been drugged. As an immortal, she should have burned through the sedative or whatever else they pumped into her by now, but she's still loopy. The other immortal female is in a similar state, and we are worried about them."

"What other immortal female?" Syssi asked.

"That's the shocking news I mentioned. The girl that Max kept talking about, the one who caused the rift between him and Din. Her name is Fenella, and he found her locked up in the same place. In fact, it was Kyra who insisted we free the prisoner in cell twelve, and that was where we found Fenella. Kyra must have realized that Fenella was like her. Aside from both being immortal, they also look a lot alike."

"Wow." Syssi leaned back. "That's indeed shocking. Now, I'm not sure which one the Fates wanted us to find. Maybe Fenella is the key to finding Khiann, especially if she resembles Jasmine and Kyra. Maybe she's the one I was supposed to see."

"There is more," Yamanu said. "We rescued four young women in addition to Kyra and Fenella. They are human, and they've also been drugged, but not as badly as the two immortals. Max thinks they might be Dormants and that the doctor was trying to turn them, or I should say rather the Doomer who called himself a doctor. I'm willing to bet that he has no medical training. Max put him in stasis, and we have him with us. Once we revive him, we will know more."

Syssi shook her head. "I saw the so-called doctor in my visions, but I didn't see Fenella and the additional four women."

"Tell us about the mission," Kian said.

"It was rough, boss. We encountered heavy resistance, and as I said, the so-called doctor was a Doomer, just as Syssi suspected. Drova and I were both shot at one point. I'm fine and she's recovering, but that complicated things for the team. I couldn't shroud the attack and Drova couldn't compel because she also lost her loudspeaker. She managed to compel those who were within earshot of her, but after getting injured she couldn't concentrate enough to produce compulsion. Max did a great job, the Kra-ell were magnificent, Jasmine was a trooper, and Ell-rom helped as much as he could. Given the fucked-up start of the mission, it has all ended well. We planted explosives and burned down the entire compound to boot."

"How many Doomers did you encounter?" Kian asked.

"At least eight in addition to the doctor. Max thinks he's one of Navuh's commanders, but we didn't recognize him as one of Navuh's adopted sons, so perhaps he recently climbed up the ranks. He's an evil piece of shit, given what he was doing to these women, even more so than the average Doomer. Reminds me of Sebastian."

The sadist who had tortured Carol had been dealt with by Dalhu, himself a former Doomer, which was poetic in a way, and Carol had not only recovered but had also turned her life around. Yet Kian's fangs still elongated at the mere mention of the vermin's name.

He pushed the thought aside, clearing his mind as best he could to deal with the situation at hand.

"Syssi had a vision about Kyra's captivity, so we expected she'd be in bad shape." Kian rubbed his jaw to loosen the tightness. "But given your description, it seems that the sedation was specifically formulated for immortals, so we might be dealing with a new kind of drug. Bridget will want to run tests."

"I hope they will improve during the flight back home," Yamanu said. "The four human girls are in better condition physically—they can at least walk with support—but they're traumatized. The question is, what do we do with them?"

Kian pinched the bridge of his nose. "Naturally, we can't leave them behind if there's even a small chance that they're Dormants. Bring them back. I'll have Julian meet you at the airstrip to check them and the Doomer for trackers. If they're clean, we will take them to the keep."

"The keep?" Yamanu sounded incredulous. "We can't take them there. We have Doomers and pedophiles in the dungeon."

Kian chuckled. "You should know that I would never put six traumatized women in the dungeon. I meant to bring them to the penthouses and the Doomer to the dungeon. Kyra can come to the village, but I want to find out what the deal is with the other five before I allow them in here."

"Of course," Yamanu said. "They need clothing. The poor things are all wearing tattered shifts and nothing else. We wrapped them in blankets so they wouldn't freeze on the way. I can call Mey and ask her to arrange for clothing and all the other things women need, and she can accompany Julian to the airstrip so the ladies can change there. The sooner they have decent clothes, the sooner they will start to heal, at least psychologically."

That was something that would've never occurred to Kian, but Yamanu's emotional intelligence far exceeded his.

"I'll talk to Mey," Syssi said. "I'll help her with the shopping."

Regarding his wife's gentle and kind face, Kian realized that the women would benefit from being greeted by someone like her. Mey was also a kind and considerate soul despite her stint as a Mossad agent. "I think it would be a good idea for the two of you to go with Julian. The females will feel less threatened if they see other women greeting them when they arrive. I'll also tell Julian to take one of the nurses with him. Maybe both."

"I'd love to help in any way I can," Syssi said.

Kian nodded. "Anything else?" he asked Yamanu.

"No, that's a wrap," the Guardian said. "I just wanted to call you before we are airborne in case you didn't want us to take the other girls. We can talk more once we are in the air."

"Call me if there is any change in their condition."

"I will."

"Safe travels." Kian ended the call and placed his phone face down on the desk.

"Five more women—one of them a likely immortal," Syssi mused. "And none of my visions hinted at that, unless I was shown Fenella and thought that it was Kyra because they look alike."

"That's possible." Kian let out a sigh. "The Fates want to keep us on our toes."

She chewed on her lower lip. "I don't like that they were all so heavily drugged. I'm worried about what was done to them."

"I'm worried as well," Kian admitted. "I'll call Julian and tell him to get the van with the portable scanner ready. We have about eighteen hours until they land at the airstrip. That's plenty of time and not enough. There is a lot of prep to be done."

Syssi pushed to her feet. "I'll call Mey, but you should also call William and have him prepare earpieces for the girls who don't speak English. He needs to program them with Farsi and Kurdish."

"Good idea. I'll do that right away."

3

KYRA

As Kyra drifted toward awareness, she first registered the luxuriously soft warmth she was cocooned in. It felt like a down blanket, and she wondered how she knew that. She'd never enjoyed such decadent comfort—at least none she could recall. She was also lying on a narrow but surprisingly comfortable surface, with a wonderfully fluffy pillow under her cheek and the blanket tucked snugly around her shoulders.

Was this how paradise felt? Had she died and gone to heaven?

No, it couldn't be heaven. No aches and discomforts should exist in paradise, and she still felt a little dizzy, a little hazy, and a lot hungry and thirsty.

A gentle vibration under her told her that she was in a moving vehicle, and then the hum of engines supplied the other clue. She was in an airplane, and given that she was so comfortable, it had to be a first-class cabin.

Again, she wondered how she knew that.

Kyra had never been on a plane—at least not that she remembered—but she'd seen first-class fully reclining seats in movies and commercials.

As a rustle on her left drew her attention, she turned as stealthily as she could to see who was making the noise and was relieved to see a woman. She was holding up a mobile phone and was either reading or watching something. Carefully, Kyra shifted to get a better look, and the woman turned to face her.

When their eyes met, Kyra's heart skipped a beat. The woman's eyes were identical to her own—the same amber-brown hue with flecks of gold swirling around the irises. It was like looking in the mirror.

A wave of dizziness threatened to pull her under, but she refused to surrender to it, realizing that she'd seen those eyes before and had reacted the same way as she was now.

"Good morning." The woman smiled. "How are you feeling?"

Kyra licked her parched lips. "Who are you?" Her voice came out in a hoarse whisper.

"My name is Jasmine." The woman reached into a compartment between their seats and pulled out a bottle of water. "You must be thirsty." She offered it to her.

"I am." Kyra tried to lift herself to a sitting position, but it was nearly impossible with the blanket holding her imprisoned and the difficulty of maneuvering on the narrow platform.

"Hold on," Jasmine said. "I'll lift the seat so you'll be more comfortable." She pressed a digital display, and the seat began to retreat and lift simultaneously, stopping when the back was elevated to a semi-reclining position. She then twisted the cap off and handed the bottle to Kyra again. "Do you think you can hold it?"

Freeing one arm out of the blanket, Kyra was surprised to find that she had someone's sweater on. The sleeve was so long that a large section dangled over her hand.

"Let me help you with that." Jasmine put the bottle on the platform dividing their seats and reached over. She folded the long sleeve several times until it cleared Kyra's wrist. "That's better." She handed her the water once more.

Kyra's hand shook slightly as she closed her palm over the smooth plastic and brought the bottle to her lips. Some of the water spilled over her chin, but she couldn't care less, and once she took her first sip, she nearly moaned in relief and kept drinking until Jasmine's hand landed on the bottle, and she tugged it away.

"You shouldn't drink that much all at once. You'll feel nauseous. Give it a few moments to settle in your stomach."

There was logic in Jasmine's words, but Kyra still eyed the remaining water with coveting eyes. "Is there anything to eat?"

The smile that bloomed on Jasmine's face was a sight to behold. "You seem much better, and the answer is yes. I'll warm up a meal for you."

"I'll do it." A man who was sitting across the aisle pushed to his feet.

He seemed familiar, and Kyra realized that he'd been the one who had carried her out of the cell and then sat with her in his arms during the helicopter ride, but he wasn't the one who'd given her his sweater.

The garment smelled of gunpowder, blood, and sweat, but underneath it all was a pleasing male scent, which was a very odd thing for her to register.

Kyra hadn't met any males whose smell, or anything else about them, had appealed to her, not even her fellow rebel fighters.

Oh, dear God. They must think I'm dead! She had to find a way to let her comrades know she was alive.

Jasmine frowned. "What's wrong?"

Kyra opened her mouth, intending to say that she needed to call her friends, when it suddenly occurred to her that she didn't know who these people were and whether she could trust them. They'd saved her, and she also remembered now that they'd saved Twelve as well, but she didn't know why, and what they were planning to do with them. It was much more important not to endanger her friends than to let them know that she was okay.

"I'm confused and uncertain. Why do we have the same eyes, Jasmine? Are we related?"

Another beautiful smile illuminated Jasmine's face. "We are. I'm your daughter."

Kyra's heart slammed so hard against her ribs that her next breath stuttered, and a blackness nipped at the corners of her vision, threatening to pull her under.

My daughter? She nearly caved to the overwhelming downward swirl, but she fought to stay awake, clenching the blanket in her fists to anchor herself.

"Impossible," she finally managed to say. "I would have remembered having a child."

Jasmine's face fell. "You don't remember being married and giving birth to me?"

She had a husband?

"I don't remember anything before the asylum," Kyra whispered. "But I dreamt of a little girl with dark hair and brown eyes with flakes of gold swirling in the irises. I thought I was dreaming of myself as a girl or of a sister or a cousin who looked a lot like me. I never dared to even entertain the thought that she could be my child." She swallowed. "I thought I couldn't have children."

Jasmine frowned. "Why did you think that?"

"I don't get monthly periods like other women."

Jasmine's eyes filled with understanding. "You can have children, Kyra, just not easily. I have so much to tell you. So much to explain about what happened to you."

4

MAX

Fenella stirred on the narrow seat next to Max, her eyelids fluttering, and then her eyes were open, but clouded with confusion.

"Hey," he said softly, not wanting to startle her. "You're safe. We got you out."

She looked at the down blanket covering her then lifted her eyes to the jet's ceiling and turned to look at the small window, and then back at him. "You must be a hallucination. There is no way you are here."

Max was glad that she was at least thinking clearly now and not imagining that she was dead and seeing him in the afterlife. He'd already told her that he was like her, immortal, but he wasn't surprised that she didn't remember their conversation. She'd been loopy from the sedatives.

"It's me, and yes, I know that I look the same as I did fifty years ago. So do you." He smiled. "Ever wondered how come you didn't age?"

Her eyes widened with fright. "What happened to us? Who did that? Why?"

He chuckled. "Those are not the kinds of questions I can answer with one-word replies. You will have to be patient." He reached for a bottle of water. "I'm sure you are thirsty." He removed the cap and then remembered that she couldn't drink while lying down and brought her seat up. "Have some water." He handed her the bottle. "Small sips."

She wrapped her hands around the bottle, and as she took a small sip just as he had instructed, her eyes closed, and she groaned. "God, this is so good."

As she took another sip and then another, Max wondered whether he should take the bottle away from her like he had seen Jasmine do to Kyra, but he didn't have the heart. Fenella was now gulping the water down, and he had a feeling that she would fight him if he tried to take the bottle away.

Instead, he shook his head. "If you can't hold the water down, just try not to puke all over me."

She glared at him over the bottle but kept on drinking until there was nothing left. "I guess there is no chance you will give me another."

"Sorry." He assumed an apologetic expression.

"You are really not supposed to drink so much all at once."

"Why?"

He laughed. "You are still just as feisty as I remember. I'm glad they didn't manage to beat it out of you."

Her momentary bravado vanished in an instant, and the look of fear on her face cut him to the core.

He took the empty bottle and set it aside, then clasped her hand, which had been steady before but was shaking now. "You are safe, Fenella. I won't let anything happen to you."

She shook her head and averted her eyes, which started leaking tears.

"Look at me," he said more firmly than he'd intended.

When she did, he forced his voice to soften. "I meant what I said. I'm taking you to a safe place where you will be surrounded by others who are like us. The bad guys will never get to you again. I mean it. Never."

She nodded. "I trust you. I don't know why, though. You were a shitty boyfriend who dumped me without a word and never even bothered to find out what happened to me."

He winced. "It was just a summer fling, Fenella. I never promised you anything."

He hadn't made any promises, but he'd inadvertently given her the greatest gift imaginable, exposing her to a great danger at the same time.

"Is there anything to eat?" Kyra asked across the aisle.

Fenella's eyes widened, and when Jasmine responded in the affirmative, she squeezed his hand. "I'm starving. Any chance there is more for me?"

He smiled. "Of course. I'll warm up a meal for you."

"Thank you." She let go of his hand. "I'll just close my eyes until you return. If I fall asleep again, wake me up."

"I will."

Max made his way to the galley where he found Ell-rom heating up a packaged meal. "Your girl is also hungry, I assume."

"Fenella is not my girl, but she's hungry." He pulled a tray out of the refrigerator. "Good thing that Kalugal ordered meals based on the headcount without accounting for the Kra-ell warriors, so we've got plenty extra for the women."

The five pureblooded Kra-ell were probably still bloated from the amount of blood they'd drunk from the humans and immortals they'd killed. They wouldn't even need the artificial blood they'd brought for the trip.

He opened the heating oven and added

another tray. "I just hope they don't puke everything up. We have no idea what was done to them." Max leaned against the counter. "They could probably use a shower and a change of clothes, but we don't have anything for them to change into."

The jet had a shower, but the water was limited, so Max had only washed his hands and face to conserve as much as possible for the women, who needed it more. The others had done the same.

Ell-rom pulled out the two heated meal trays and handed them to him. "I'll check with the pilot. Maybe they have something stored for emergencies."

"I doubt that, but it's worth a try."

Kalugal might have kept a change of clothing on board for himself and Jacki, but that wouldn't meet the needs of six women.

Balancing the trays, Max returned to where Kyra and Jasmine were sitting.

"Delivery." He smiled at Kyra as he put the tray on the table next to her seat. "I'm glad to see you are feeling better."

"Thank you." She returned his smile, and his heart skipped a beat. She really had a beautiful smile.

"I'd love to stay and chat, but I need to deliver this to Twelve, whose name is Fenella, by the way."

Kyra's head whipped around. "Where is she?"

He pointed with his free hand. "Two seats down across the aisle."

She leaned over, and when she saw Fenella dozing off in her seat, a sound left her throat that was a cross between a sigh and a sob.

"You should bring Fenella over here," Jasmine suggested. "She can take Ell-rom's seat while she's eating. That way she can hear what I'm about to tell my mother. She doesn't know how she turned immortal either, right?"

Max nodded. "She doesn't, and I'm very thankful to you for offering to explain the birds and the bees to both of them at once. I'm not good at that sort of thing."

"Of course." Jasmine removed the aluminum foil from the dish for her mother. "But you should stick around and help me. You know much more about the clan's history than I do."

"Gladly." He set one tray on Ell-rom's vacated seat, then walked over to Fenella.

When he put his hand on her shoulder, she opened her eyes. "Is the food ready?"

"It is, but I'm moving you to the seat over there so you can share the meal with Kyra."

"Kyra? Who is she?"

"A fellow prisoner. I assumed that the two of you knew each other."

Fenella shook her head. "I didn't know any of the other prisoners."

"Well, she knew you, or rather about you. She insisted on us freeing the prisoner in cell twelve, which was you." He offered her a hand up. "Do you think you can walk over there? It's only a couple of steps away and you can hold on to me for balance."

"I think so." She took his hand, but as soon as she tried to stand, her legs buckled.

He caught her, cursing himself inwardly for even suggesting that she walk on her own. She was in no state to do that. Besides, what she was wearing wasn't suitable even for the relatively warm cabin.

Grabbing the down blanket, he wrapped it around her and lifted her into his arms. "Maybe after you eat something you will have enough energy to walk." He forced a smile, offering reassurance.

He carried her to the seat, settled her in front of the tray, and then took the seat beside her.

Kyra smiled at Fenella between bites of pasta, her eyes warm. "It's nice to finally meet you in person."

Fenella echoed the sentiment, but then her brow furrowed. "Max told me that you were the one who told him to get me. How did you know I was there? I didn't know who the other prisoners were."

"That's a long story." Kyra swirled more creamy

pasta on her fork. "And right now, I'm too hungry to tell it."

"So am I." Fenella lowered her gaze to the tray. "This smells divine."

"Here, let me help you." Max removed the foil, letting the steam escape before unwrapping the utensils and handing Fenella a fork. "Dig in."

5

KYRA

Kyra shifted in her seat, the taste of warm pasta lingering on her tongue as she savored each bite. Even the disposable fork felt luxurious in her hand compared to the cold metal utensils she vaguely remembered from the prison.

So much of her imprisonment seemed like a bad dream, a nightmare, and in a way, she was grateful for not remembering much of it. Hopefully, those memories would remain locked away along with the memories of what had been done to her in the asylum.

She glanced across at Fenella, who seemed more vibrant now that she'd eaten. The woman was still gaunt and looked tense, but her eyes no longer looked dead, and there was a new spark in her gaze—a cautious curiosity.

Was that how she looked to others as well?

Kyra hadn't spent as long in captivity as Twelve—Fenella was her name, she reminded herself—so she should look a little better, but she was still apprehensive of what she would see in the mirror once she had a chance.

Speaking of which, she probably should visit the restroom, but she didn't trust her legs to carry her there. Besides, she was afraid to leave the comfortable seat and the soft blanket draped over her, mostly because she didn't fully trust that the nightmare was truly over.

What if all of this was an induced hallucination?

What if she dispelled the illusions and discovered that she was still in that prison cell?

Glancing around, Kyra focused on details that she couldn't have imagined to reassure herself that she was indeed free and that this was real.

The cabin wasn't big, but it was luxurious, like something belonging to a billionaire or the president of a multinational conglomerate.

Since Kyra couldn't remember ever flying on a plane, she had no point of reference, but she'd seen movies and commercials, so she knew what a regular cabin looked like as opposed to the interior of a private executive jet, and this was definitely the latter and not the former.

Large plush seats sat in pairs on either side of a

narrow aisle, and overhead, discreet lighting lent the space a cozy warmth. Even the carpeting underfoot felt impossibly soft.

Fenella smiled tentatively at her. "Hi," she said. "Have we ever met before?"

"I don't think so."

The woman chewed on her lower lip. "How did you know I was in cell number twelve?"

"As I said, it's a long story, and I'm sure what Jasmine is about to tell us is much more interesting than that."

She was almost sure now that she could trust Jasmine and could tell her about her rebel friends, but after a lifetime of being cautious, she preferred not to rush. Satisfying Fenella's curiosity was not a priority.

She turned to look at her daughter—the daughter she still could hardly believe she had—and felt a mix of awe and remorse. That first moment of recognition in the helicopter had been overshadowed by her drugged haze, and yet the memory still tugged at her heart. She'd looked at Jasmine and seen her own eyes, her own features, and had discovered that she was a mother.

Someone had robbed her of motherhood because she was absolutely certain that she would never have left her child voluntarily.

The thought brought about a spike of fury, but Kyra pushed it down to be dealt with later. Right now she wanted to enjoy the company of the daughter she'd just discovered and learn from her as much as she could about her past.

The man who volunteered to bring her meal returned with a small stack of clothing in his hands and stopped by Jasmine's seat, looking unsure. "That's all I could find, and that's not enough for six ladies."

"We'll look at it later. You can put it over there for now." Jasmine motioned at a seat across the aisle. "I want to introduce you properly to my mother." She smiled. "This is Ell-rom, my mate."

"Thank you for carrying me," Kyra said.

He dipped his head. "You are welcome."

It took her a moment to realize that the sound had come from a small, teardrop-shaped device hanging from a string near his throat.

"What's that?" She pointed a finger at the device.

"Ell-rom is still learning English," Jasmine explained. "He can understand what we are saying thanks to the specialized earpieces he's wearing, and the device you see around his neck translates what he speaks back to us."

"That's amazing," Kyra said. "Is that a new thing in America now? Translating equipment?"

Jasmine shook her head. "Actually, it's proprietary technology, not something you can buy in stores."

When Kyra lifted her gaze to Ell-rom, he smiled. "I'm happy to see you are getting better."

"Wow. This is truly extraordinary." She turned to Jasmine. "Does he also sound like that without the device?"

Jasmine pursed her lips. "It does a very good job of mimicking his tone and inflection, but since we're communicating mainly through earpieces, I'm mostly used to the sound as it is transmitted through them." She smiled at her mate. "Ell-rom says I sound much like what he hears through his earpieces. Isn't that right, darling?"

His expression changed, becoming softer, and he took Jasmine's hand. "Your voice is even more beautiful in reality than it is through the earpieces, but I love every sound you make." He shifted his gaze to Kyra. "Your daughter is a talented singer and actress. She has the most beautiful voice."

Kyra's heart expanded at the praise and ached at the same time for all the things she'd missed about Jasmine growing up, learning to sing, becoming an actress.

"I've missed so much," she murmured. "Motherhood was stolen from me, and you were deprived of a mother's love. Who was the monster who did that?"

"That part I'm not sure of," Jasmine said. "But we can speculate about it later. The good news is that we have eternity to compensate for time lost because we are both immortal, and I promised to explain how and why."

Kyra nodded. "You promised to tell me how I can have children despite not having periods."

Across from them, Fenella gasped. "Is that possible? I don't have periods either. I was sure it meant I was infertile."

"You can have children," Jasmine said. "But your fertility is extremely low. That's the price of immortality. Nature has to ensure that we don't overpopulate the planet, so it makes it difficult for us to conceive."

Kyra let out a breath. "That makes sense. What else should we know?"

Jasmine chuckled. "A lot, but before I launch into the grand story, let me set a few ground rules. There is no single 'aha' moment that explains everything in one sentence. It's a tapestry of events, going back millennia. Also, there are a lot of things I don't know yet because I'm a baby immortal and haven't had time to learn everything yet. I'll do my best to be clear, but if you can, try not to interrupt until I'm done, or we'll never get through the main arc."

Kyra nodded, though her heart thrummed with impatience.

Fenella took a shaky breath. "I'll do my best not to interrupt."

6

MAX

After Ell-rom settled into a seat across the aisle, Jasmine pulled five bottles of water out of the wall compartment and distributed them to her audience.

"I will try to do the story justice, but if I make mistakes, Max can correct me." She smiled at him. "Max has been an immortal for much longer than the three of us."

Fenella frowned at him. "How old are you?"

"Old." He cringed. "Five hundred and thirty-three in two months."

She gaped at him. "How old is Din?"

So, she remembered him. Good. He had thought she'd forgotten. "Older, but not by much."

Shaking her head, Fenella slumped in her seat. "What the hell were two ancient immortals doing in a pub in Invery?"

Max chuckled. "Hunting. What else?"

She uttered an incredulous snort. "Was I prey?"

He pinned her with a hard stare. "You were much more than that to Din."

"Please." Jasmine lifted a hand to stop their banter. "If you want me to tell the story of how it all started, you will have to discuss your past later."

Nodding, Fenella crossed her arms over her chest and cast Max one last glare before turning back to Jasmine. "I'm sorry for interrupting. Please continue."

Jasmine took a deep breath, glanced at Ell-rom, and then shifted her gaze to her mother. "Humans are not the only intelligent race of people on Earth. The gods of mythology are actually aliens who came to Earth from another planet. At first, they only came to mine for gold. They needed it for their technology, their space travel, and some other uses. I don't know the timeline, but I think they first arrived about half a million years ago and jump started intelligent life on Earth by combining their genetic material with some type of protohumans. An echo of that story can be found in the Bible, but that's not where our story begins."

Max was surprised that Jasmine had started with the least proven part of the gods' story, but perhaps that was the part she found most fascinating.

"Our story begins with a rebellion on the gods'

planet," Jasmine continued. "I won't go into the details of the rebellion because it's not really relevant to us at the moment, and it's a whole different rabbit hole, but the result was that the rebellion was quashed, and the rebel leadership was exiled to Earth. They formed a small community in Sumer and started teaching the population the lofty ideas they brought with them, making Sumer the first advanced civilization on Earth. That was the birthplace of all of Earth's major mythologies and later religions."

She scanned her small audience. "So far everyone good?"

Kyra nodded. "It sounds like a science fiction movie, but it also echoes the Biblical narrative, so I'm good with it."

Fenella seemed to approve as well. "So, the gods are living in Sumer and teaching the natives to be civilized. What's next?"

Max loved seeing them both intelligently engage in the conversation. It was a good sign that the drugs they'd been given hadn't fried their brains.

"The gods had a problem," Jasmine continued. "There were too few of them to provide genetic variety, and since all contact with the home planet was severed, they had to find a solution with what was available on Earth. They had to take human partners. The children born of those unions were the first immortals, or demigods, or giants as they were called in the Bible. Only the word giant was a bad translation from the original Hebrew." She chuckled. "Since the gods came in all sizes, some tall and some short, their immortal offspring were not particularly statuesque."

"What was the correct translation?" Fenella asked.

"The original word was Anakim, which was interpreted as giants. But Ankh represents the breath of life, or immortality, and therefore Anakim literally means immortals."

Fenella let out a slow breath. "Wow. I love this. So, Kyra and I were sired by gods? I'm pretty sure that my parents were ordinary humans. They are both gone now."

"You are the descendants of gods, but your parents were human. Your mothers carried the godly gene, but I'll get to that later. I didn't finish the story yet. When the immortal children of the gods took human partners, their children were born human, and the gods thought that their experiment was a failure. But then they discovered that the children of female immortals could be turned immortal. The children of the males could not, unless the mother was an immortal or a dormant carrier of the godly genes. The rest of the story is that the godly genes kept being passed on from mother to daughter throughout the generations, and there are many Dormants living among humans who can be activated but are unaware of the secret genes. They don't show up on any of the scans and are probably hidden among what is called junk DNA. Anyway, the two of you were dormant carriers, and both of you got activated by chance."

"How do those genes get activated?" Fenella asked.

Here it comes. Max shifted in his seat, considering ducking away to the bathroom to give the ladies privacy, but a wink from Jasmine communicated that he could stay.

"It's something that involves both biology and a bit of luck, or maybe fate." Jasmine reached for the water bottle, took a sip, and put it back down. "It is a sensitive matter that requires context, especially when one is told after the fact."

"After the fact?" Fenella asked. "What do you mean?"

Jasmine turned to Max. "Maybe you want to tell her? Since you were most likely the one who induced her transition?"

That was an underhanded trick, and Max cast Jasmine a glare that communicated his displeasure.

"We are all adults here, Max," Jasmine said. "You don't have to be bashful."

"Right." He turned to Fenella. "So, here's how it works. Immortal males have fangs and venom glands. They use those for two very different functions. In battle, the venom is used to incapacitate an opponent, and in sex, it provides females with incredible orgasms and euphoric trips. In order to induce an adult female Dormant, an immortal male needs to have unprotected sex with her and bite her. Sometimes once is enough, and other times several attempts have to be made before the transition is triggered. You were on the pill when we had sex, so we didn't use condoms, and I must have induced your transition. Do you remember being very sick for a few days after I left and noticing changes that didn't make sense?"

Fenella's eyes were as wide as saucers. "I was sick. I had the flu, and I grew an inch in height, and no one knew how it could be possible. Our doctor said it was just a rapid growth spurt. But that wasn't the only thing. I could hear things from far away, see much farther than before, and I got freakishly strong. I always thought that it was the virus that caused all those changes, and I was afraid that if people knew that about me, I would be turned into a lab rat. That was why I left home." She cast him an accusing look. "Do you think I wanted to leave? I didn't. I wanted to stay in Invery, meet a nice guy, and start a family. It's all your fault. You ruined my life!"

He glared back at her. "I gifted you with immortality."

"I don't want it!" She sounded almost hysterical. "It's brought me nothing but trouble. Why do you think that monster had me locked up and..." She shook her head. "I don't want to talk about it."

"I'm sorry," he muttered. What else could he say? He hadn't meant to induce her. "If I'd known, I would have taken care of you. I had no idea. That never just happens. We've spent many centuries looking for Dormants and found none."

"Well, you found me, fucked me over, and disappeared." Fenella crossed her arms over her chest. "Thanks a lot, Max."

7

KYRA

Kyra's face flamed, heat rushing from her cheeks to the tips of her ears because of what Fenella had just accused Max of, but then the heat was replaced by ice when she realized that the only one who could have induced her transition was the monster who called himself a doctor.

Refusing to go there, she focused on Max instead.

He'd tried to reason with Fenella, but she was hurling one insult after the other at him, and now he looked as if he wanted to sink through the floor.

Jasmine lifted a hand. "Max might have been your inducer, but you can't know that for sure. Were you with anyone else during that time? After he left maybe? That pub you worked at was frequented by immortals from the Scottish arm of the clan. There could have been someone else."

Fenella's hands trembled over the edge of her blanket. She seemed on the verge of tears or fury. "After Max left, I was with a couple of other guys. How do I know if they were immortal?"

"I can check," Max said. "Ask around. After all, there aren't many of us in the clan, and hopefully, those who shared your bed would remember you."

She shook her head. "Don't. This is embarrassing enough as it is."

He shrugged. "As you wish. I'm sure Din will be happy to hear you are an immortal now. He was in love with you back then. Maybe the two of you can rekindle your love."

"I didn't love him. I barely knew him."

"Then perhaps you should give him another chance," Max suggested.

Kyra tried to follow the conversation and understand the past that Max and Fenella shared. It seemed Max didn't have any feelings for Fenella, not now and not back when they were lovers. But there was another man named Din who'd loved her, but she hadn't returned his feelings.

Kyra hoped Fenella would find love with that other guy, and she was also delighted that Max was not in love with the woman and never had been. Then another tidbit of information registered.

Max had mentioned a clan and so had Jasmine before him.

She exhaled shakily. "What do you mean by a clan?"

"Oh, yes." Jasmine pushed a strand of her long hair behind her ear. "I didn't continue the story of the gods and what happened to them. You must be wondering about that."

Among the other revelations, Kyra had forgotten that, but Jasmine was right. If the gods were real, where were they?

"What happened to the gods?" Fenella asked, looking relieved to change the subject of who had been her inducer.

"As with any group of people, there were internal politics that I won't go into, but suffice to say that one god attacked the others with a type of weapon that was only available to the gods and that could kill them." She let out a breath. "I forgot to mention that gods and immortals are difficult to kill but it's possible. Anyway, he managed to kill most of them, and only a few escaped. One of them was a young goddess. Believing she was the only survivor, she set out to continue the gods' work. She took on human lovers and had several children with them. Her daughters continued her efforts, and one of them was very fruitful for an immortal. Her descendants and their descendants and so on form the clan. A community of immortals."

"Who activated the goddess's children?" Fenella asked.

"They were born immortal," Jasmine said. "The children who are born to a goddess or a god with a human partner are born immortal. It's only the second generation that needs activation."

"I see." Fenella pulled the blanket up to her chin. "I guess it will take time to sort this out. It's a bit confusing."

"It is." Jasmine smiled. "It took me a while to sort it out as well."

Just then a very tall and thin male passed by them on the way to the galley, and Fenella's eyes followed him with curiosity. "Is he also an immortal?"

A rueful half-smile tugged at Jasmine's lips. "He's a hybrid Kra-ell, half human and half another kind of alien from the same planet as the gods. How and why they got to Earth is an entire story of its own, and I don't want to overload you." She glanced at her mate. "Ell-rom is half Kra-ell and half god, and that's another story I will also save for later."

"I assume they are friends with the clan," Kyra said.

"They're our allies and helped us free you from the Doomers, our enemies."

"Is that also a story for another time?" Fenella asked, her tone laced with sarcasm.

"No. That part is relevant to you, so I'll give you the gist of it. The god who attacked the other gods perished with them, but his immortal son continued his hateful legacy, which was, and remains, the exact opposite of what the other gods wanted to do. They wanted humans to evolve and their society to reach enlightenment, while the clan's enemies want to keep humanity ignorant, savage, and divided. That ancient secret war has been raging since the dawn of human civilization and is still going on. The so-called doctor who was in charge of your torment was one from the group that seeks the clan's demise. We call them Doomers, which is the English acronym of what they call themselves. The Devout Order of Mortdh Brotherhood."

Kyra could see Max seething from the corner of her eye, and it warmed something in her chest to see him raging over the wrongs that had been done to her and the other females.

"What did he want with us?" Fenella asked.

"To find out what made us immortal," Kyra answered and then looked at Jasmine. "Am I right?"

Jasmine nodded. "That's what we suspect, but we will know more once we interrogate him."

Kyra's blood froze in her veins. "Is he here?"

"Don't worry about him," Max said. "I put him

in stasis. We are not going to revive him until we lock him up in the dungeon, and then it will be my pleasure to beat every last scrap of information out of him. You will get your answers."

Kyra inclined her head, letting the magnitude of the revelations settle. "Thank you. Can I be there to watch?"

Max grinned as if she had given him the greatest of compliments. "It would be my pleasure to give you a show. I hope you are not squeamish."

She snorted. "If I ever was, I got over it a long time ago."

8

MAX

Max had thought he was falling for Kyra before, but he knew that for sure.

Putting a hand over his chest, he sighed dramatically. "I have found my soulmate."

Kyra laughed, the first laugh he'd heard from her, and at that moment, he vowed to make her laugh as often as he could.

Jasmine regarded him with a small smile playing on her lips. "Soulmates is not something immortals joke about, Max."

"Who said I was joking?"

She didn't look amused. "I'm far from being an expert on post-traumatic issues, but I'm pretty sure that neither my mother nor Fenella are in the right state of mind to evaluate things of that nature."

He had to appreciate Jasmine's verbal gymnastics, trying to tell him to fuck off and not hit on traumatized women who were in a vulnerable state without actually saying that.

"It's okay, Jasmine." Kyra put her hand on her daughter's arm. "I know that Max is just teasing, and I like how it makes me feel. He doesn't treat me like a victim, and that makes me feel more like myself. Normal." She glanced at Fenella. "I can only speak for myself, though. I didn't spend as much time in captivity as you did, so your response might be different. If Max's banter rubs you the wrong way, say so."

Okay, so now he was falling even deeper in love with the woman. Where had she been all his life?

"I don't mind," Fenella murmured. "He's always been an asshole, so I shouldn't expect anything different now." She gave him a saccharine smile. "No offense, Max. I'm grateful for the rescue, and I fully appreciate you being one hell of a fighter to pull it off, but you were never boyfriend material. Not for me, anyway."

He could live with that. Fenella wasn't his favorite person either, but he was too much of a gentleman to return the favor and tell her so, especially after all she'd been through.

He could, however, make her feel guilty. "Don't forget that I made you immortal, so now you have forever to find your perfect match."

Kyra shifted in her seat. "I really need to use the restroom."

He rose to his feet. "I'll help you."

She shook her head. "Thank you, but despite your declaration of undying devotion, I prefer to have Jasmine help me."

Pouting, he put a hand over his chest again. "You wound me."

She laughed, which made his heart do a silly little flip. "You'll live."

Jasmine rose and headed to where Ell-rom had deposited the clothes he'd scavenged. "Let's see if we can use any of these."

"I'm good," Kyra said as she moved the blanket aside. "This sweater is like a dress." She smiled at Max. "Thank you for loaning it to me."

"You're welcome, and it's yours if you want it. A memento from the rescue."

She smoothed a hand over the front. "I would like that. I'll cherish this sweater forever."

Pretending to swoon, Max plopped down into the seat with a dramatic sigh, which had the effect he'd been hoping for, making Kyra laugh again.

"You're such a joker."

After Jasmine took Kyra to the bathroom in the back of the plane, Max was left alone with Fenella and Ell-rom. The awkward silence between them was deafening.

"I remembered you like this," Fenella finally

said. "You were always a clown." She closed her eyes. "But Kyra was right. Your stupid teasing made me feel normal for a few minutes. Made me forget what I went through."

Max swallowed hard, trying to come up with something teasing or funny to say, but Fenella's words had slayed him, and he had nothing. "I'm sorry. If I had known sooner, I would have come for you."

She nodded. "Even though you never loved me, I believe you would have come."

"Thank you." He let out a breath. "It means a lot to me that you believe I'm not a complete asshole."

"You're welcome. By the way, how did you know where to find Kyra?"

He debated what to tell her. "Would you believe it if I told you a seer saw her location and that she was in dire need of rescuing?"

Fenella snorted. "At this point, I'm willing to believe in anything and everything. I'm not the naive girl you met fifty years ago. I no longer believe that what they teach us in school or what they print in newspapers is true. Most of it is lies, manipulation, ways to keep the simple people in the dark so they will keep working, pay their taxes, and fight in wars that their leaders manufacture to make themselves rich. The world is a much darker place than most people imagine." She smiled at him with gratitude in her eyes. "I'm just thankful that there are still some people in this ugly world, people like you and your friends, who are willing to fight against the darkness. I thought no one would ever come for me, and that I would spend eternity in the hands of that monster."

9

KYRA

Kyra leaned on Jasmine's strength as her daughter led her down the aisle, past the handful of seats that had been reclined to make narrow beds. Some of the warriors were watching television, some were asleep on the reclined seats, and the other four rescued women were sleeping, cocooned in the same wonderful blankets as the one Kyra had left on her seat.

A few heads turned, followed by slight smiles and nods, which she took as encouragement.

At the back, Jasmine opened a small door that slid inward to reveal a compact lavatory that was nevertheless luxurious. A tiny shower stall was partitioned off by a frosted glass panel.

Jasmine stepped inside with Kyra, somehow fitting the two of them in the tiny space. "There's a new travel toothbrush in here." She pointed at a compartment side. "And this is the handle to switch from faucet to shower mode. The temperature knob is labeled." She demonstrated. "The tank isn't huge, so be mindful of the water usage. We want to conserve as much as we can, so at least all the rescued women can wash up if they want to. The rest of us made do with washing our hands. I'll give you some privacy, but I can wait outside if you need anything."

She wanted to be brave and tell Jasmine that she didn't need help and could return to her seat, but that would have been a lie, and Kyra had learned that pride was often detrimental to success.

"Thank you," she said. "I won't be long."

With a nod, Jasmine stepped back into the aisle and closed the door behind her.

Finally, some desperately needed privacy.

After taking care of the most pressing need first, Kyra brushed her teeth and then shrugged out of the enormous sweater, folding it carefully and putting it on top of the closed toilet lid.

Next, she peeled off the threadbare shift she'd been forced to wear.

It carried the stench of captivity, and as a wave of nausea rolled through her, she squeezed her eyes shut until it passed. The trash compartment was too small for the disgusting garment, but she stuffed it in there nonetheless. There was no way she was touching the thing ever again.

Standing completely naked, she glimpsed herself in the mirror over the sink. She looked thinner, pallid, but the bruises were gone and her eyes were bright. She was alive, she was on her way to freedom, and that was what mattered.

She still needed to let her friends know that she was alive, and after what she'd heard she no longer feared that these people could threaten the rebels. If anything, they could help, and once she was on a sure footing she would see what she could do to convince them to offer aid.

Stepping behind the partition, she flicked on the water and waited a few heartbeats until it turned warmer. Standing under the spray, she let the water cascade over her hair, shoulders, and back. Despite Jasmine's caution about being quick, she couldn't help but linger for a moment.

Scrubbing her scalp felt oddly cathartic, as if every clump of dried sweat or grime she sloughed off was one more layer of captivity washing down the drain. The fresh scent of the shampoo was clean and simple, but a luxury nonetheless.

She tried not to think about what she'd left behind and focused on all the incredible things she'd learned since being freed.

Gods, immortals, Dormants.

Her daughter.

Part of her was thrilled at the chance to reconnect, to compensate for time lost with her child, but another part of her grieved for Jasmine's childhood that she'd missed and could never recover.

After quickly scrubbing the grime from the rest of her body, she reluctantly twisted the knob, shutting off the water. Shivering in the cooler air, she grabbed the towel from a hook and dried off.

Hopefully, there were more clean towels for the other women.

She hung up the towel, and with a sigh, grabbed Max's sweater from where she'd folded it on the closed toilet lid. It was large, swallowing her frame, but it was clean enough—barely. It still hinted at that faint masculine scent she'd noticed earlier, layered with gunpowder and dust. But there was something comforting about wearing it, even if she barely knew the man.

Remembering his teasing about her being his soulmate, Kyra smiled and tugged the sweater on, letting it fall around mid-thigh.

She had no pants to wear yet, but at least the garment covered her decently. Well, as decent as having nothing underneath could feel.

She opened the door a crack. "Jasmine?"

"Right here," came the immediate reply. Jasmine's beautiful face appeared in the gap. "Feeling better?"

Kyra stepped into the aisle, hugging the sweater

around her hips. "Much better. Do you happen to have a comb?"

Her wet hair hung in messy clumps around her shoulders, and if she didn't comb it out, it would be a nightmare to do so when it dried.

"I do." Jasmine reached out, gently tucking a stray strand of wet hair behind Kyra's ear. "I also have some makeup, but I don't think you use any."

"I don't," Kyra admitted. "I don't need it."

"No, you don't." Jasmine wrapped an arm around her middle to prop her up. "You are beautiful without any help from cosmetics."

"So are you." Kyra lifted on tiptoes and kissed her daughter's cheek for the first time she could remember doing so. "You are so tall in addition to being beautiful."

Jasmine chuckled. "I grew more than an inch during my transition. I had to replace half of my shoe collection so I wouldn't tower over everyone whenever I wanted to wear heels."

10

JASMINE

Jasmine's acting skills helped her mask her shock at her mother's simple gesture of kissing her cheek.

Tears prickled her eyes, and a sob was lodged in her throat, but she refused to allow them out and distress Kyra. This was supposed to be a happy moment, the beginning of healing for both of them.

How many of her childhood nights had she lain awake, dreaming of what it would be like to have a mother who loved her? Not that she'd stopped dreaming about it as an adult, but she had done it less frequently, and then rarely since Ell-rom had entered her life.

Her sweet prince, who was still sitting across the aisle where she had left him.

She stopped next to him and leaned down to plant a quick kiss on his lips.

"Sorry." She smiled at her mother. "I just had to." She turned around and lifted the blanket so Kyra could return to her seat.

"Never apologize for showing your love." Kyra sat down and pulled the long sweater over her knees.

Jasmine draped the blanket over her and tucked it in. "Can I get you something warm to drink? Coffee? Tea?"

She desperately needed a few moments alone to collect herself, and preparing coffee was a great excuse.

Kyra's eyes brightened. "Coffee sounds heavenly." She sniffed the air. "But there is none brewed, and I don't want you to go to all that trouble."

"It's no trouble." Max rose to his feet. "They have a pod machine in the galley. How do you like your coffee?"

Damn. Why did the guy have to become so chivalrous all of the sudden? Perhaps he really was smitten with her mother.

"Usually, I drink it black with no sugar," Kyra said. "But I'm in the mood for something sweet. So, if they have cream and sugar, I'll take both."

When Max put a hand on his hip and struck a pose, Jasmine knew that another joke was coming, but since her mother seemed to enjoy them, she didn't mind.

"I'm offended," Max said. "Am I not sweet enough for you?"

Fenella rolled her eyes, but Kyra laughed again.

"You are too sweet," her mother said. "I need to pace myself with all that sweetness."

"Ouch." Max chuckled. "I'll dial it down a notch." He walked toward the galley.

Jasmine remained standing as she tried to find another excuse to get away for a few moments, and when Fenella shifted in her chair, it occurred to her that she might need to use the bathroom as well.

She leaned a hand on the back of her seat. "Since I'm already standing, would you like me to take you to the restroom?"

The woman looked down at herself then back at Jasmine. "I would love to take a shower, but I don't have anything to change into, and I don't want to wear only a blanket."

"Ell-rom found a few T-shirts and sweatshirts in men's sizes, but no pants. You can wear one of them as a top and tie a blanket around your hips like a sarong."

"Do you have a safety-pin to stop the blanket from falling off?"

"I don't," Jasmine admitted. "But I can check in the first-aid kit."

Jasmine helped Fenella to her feet and secured the blanket around her. "You can change in the bathroom," she said, grabbing a dark-green T-shirt from the small pile of clothing.

On the way, Fenella stopped next to each of the other rescued females. "I just need to make sure they are all breathing. Why are they still asleep?"

"Maybe because they finally feel safe and didn't sleep on the helicopter ride like you and Kyra did," Jasmine said. "Also, don't forget that they are human and need much more sleep than you do."

Fenella nodded. "I know. I feel so sorry for them."

"Do you know their names?"

Fenella shook her head. "I was kept in isolation. The only reason I knew they were there was because the bastard talked about the other women and how he had high hopes for them. Whatever that meant."

A shiver ran down Jasmine's spine. "He hoped that they were Dormants. I hope that he didn't know how Dormants are activated." She nudged Fenella toward the bathroom.

"It wouldn't have mattered," Fenella murmured. "The sick bastard would have done it anyway."

He couldn't have thralled Kyra and Fenella to forget his bite because they were immortal, but he could have sedated them, which was probably why they had been drugged more heavily than the others.

Why did he care if they remembered his bite, though?

In case they managed to run away or get rescued?

"I won't be long." Fenella removed the blanket, handed it to Jasmine, and took the T-shirt.

Jasmine repeated the instructions about the need to conserve water and then left Fenella alone in the bathroom.

Leaning against the door, she closed her eyes and pretended that no one was around and that she was alone with the storm of feelings raging inside her.

It was all good, she reminded herself. She had her mother back, and they needed to get to know each other, and this would take time. Those physical expressions of affection would eventually become the norm rather than the exception, and she hoped there would be many of them in her future.

She had a lot of catching up to do.

11

MAX

When Max returned with the coffee, Jasmine and Fenella were gone, and he was left alone with Kyra and Ellrom. The prince was sitting across the aisle and watching television or pretending to, so it was just him and Kyra.

"Thanks." She cradled the paper cup between her palms. "One of the things I love most about my immortal body is the speed of recovery. When I first woke up, I wouldn't have been able to hold this cup. My hands were shaking so badly that half of the coffee would have spilled out."

She sounded a little nervous, and he hoped that it was because of him, but in a good way. He wanted her to find him attractive, or at least likable, but Jasmine's words from before were still echoing in his head. Kyra was in no state to form an emotional attachment to any guy. If she did, it would be just in the pursuit of security.

For now, all he was aiming for was friendship.

"Take a sip," he encouraged. "Tell me if I made it to your liking."

"I'm sure you did." She blew air into the steaming cup and then took a tiny sip. "It's perfect."

For a short while, neither of them spoke. The low hum of the engines filled the silence, occasionally accompanied by a muffled sound of talking from elsewhere in the cabin.

Max leaned back in his seat but didn't recline it. "When did you discover that you weren't aging?"

She chuckled. "That wasn't how I found out that I was different. The first clue was breaking the chains that were holding me down and then breaking down doors and freeing all the other women in that place. I don't remember much because I was drugged back then too, but the others I freed took me with them, and when the drugs wore off, they told me that I had superhuman strength and that I killed some of the guards by clobbering them with a piece of broken furniture I must have collected somewhere. I thought that my friends were exaggerating, and that it was probably some odd mixture of drugs that gave me inhuman strength, but then I noticed the enhanced hearing, eyesight, and sense of smell, and I knew that I had been altered. I just didn't know how. I was convinced that they'd run experiments on me and had inadvertently changed me. I couldn't have imagined that I always had it in me and that it just needed to be activated."

Max hated to see the pain in Kyra's eyes that indicated she knew who was responsible for her induction, and he desperately wanted to change the subject.

Her bare foot peeking from under the blanket was the perfect thing. "I should have a spare pair of socks." He pushed to his feet. "I'll get them for you."

"No, please, sit down." She waved a hand. "I already feel bad about having your sweater."

"Don't. I'm not cold and it gives me pleasure knowing that you are wearing something of mine."

"Oh, that's just so sweet," she teased. "I feel bad about having more than the others. Not for taking your sweater."

Sitting back down, Max realized something important. Kyra used humor like he did—to mask awkwardness, to change the subject, to put others at ease.

He liked that about her. It was a sign of a leader, if he said so himself.

"I need a favor," Kyra said. "Not clothing related."

"Anything."

She chuckled. "Don't agree so fast before you know what it is that I need. My people are probably worried about me or think that I'm dead. I would like to let them know that I'm okay. Does anyone have a satellite phone, and is it safe to make such a call from here?"

"I have a satellite phone." He pulled it out of his pocket. "You can't tell your rebel friends who freed you. Tell them only that you are safe and will contact them later when you can."

She frowned. "How do you know that my friends are rebels?"

Kyra hadn't been there when he'd told Fenella about Syssi. "One of our people is a powerful seer, and she kept seeing you with the Kurdish rebels. How do you think we found you?"

"I was wondering about that. But a seer? Seriously?"

He chuckled. "I know how it sounds, but Syssi is incredible. The funny thing is that she wasn't looking for you when she asked the universe for a vision. She was looking for our Clan Mother's long-lost love, but when the visions showed her you time and again, she realized that you might hold the key to finding Annani's lost husband. Are you good at finding things?"

Kyra's hand flew to her chest, clutching the air where her amulet should have been. "I am very good at that, but not without my pendant." She shook her head. "I don't understand. I thought that you came for me because of Jasmine. That she knew something about me that I couldn't remember. Like the husband I supposedly had or still have."

Max glanced in the direction of the bathroom, where Jasmine was leaning against the door with her eyes closed. She was much more qualified to tell her mother about the whole convoluted vision mess than he was, but he could at least ease Kyra's mind regarding her husband.

"You sent your ex-husband divorce papers, and he remarried, but he never stopped loving you."

Her eyes filled with tears. "How do you know that?"

"Because I talked to him. He searched for you for a very long time, never giving up, and he blamed himself for your abduction. The poor guy was devastated. I think he remarried only because he needed a mother for Jasmine."

That got the tears flowing faster, and Max glanced at Jasmine again, desperately needing her to return.

"I'm sorry, Kyra. Jasmine should be the one to tell you all of this, preferably in private and not on a plane full of people with extraordinary hearing. I shouldn't have said anything."

12

KYRA

It hurt. Kyra didn't remember Jasmine's father, but the pain Max had described cut her nonetheless.

She had so many questions, but Max was reluctant to give her the answers, and she couldn't really blame him for wanting to stay out of the family drama.

Kyra shook her head. A family drama implied a family, and she was still shocked that she had one, but the man whom she'd loved enough to marry and have a child with was now married to someone else. There was no salvaging that past, and perhaps it was for the better. He was most likely not an immortal, and tying her life to a human made no sense.

She was no stranger to loss and grief, but that

didn't mean that she sought out pain when she could avoid it.

"I understand." She gave Max a reassuring smile, not wanting him to feel guilty. "Can I still use your phone?"

He hesitated. "Give me the phone number and I'll type a text message. It's not that I don't trust you, but I have safety protocols that I need to follow as well."

"Do you know Kurdish?"

He shook his head.

"Then we have a conundrum. My second-in-command understands English, but he will doubt a text that's not written in Kurdish."

"Then you will have to think of something to say that no one else would know. Can you think of anything like that?"

"Twelve," she said without pause. "My team knew about my obsession with the prisoner in cell twelve. I can tell them that she's safe."

"That's good. Also, the men we freed might have found their way to your rebels and told them about the rescue. Not that they would remember much."

Kyra tilted her head. "Why not?"

"We thralled them to forget what they witnessed. Yamanu back there, the tall guy with the long black hair, can blanket thrall people. I can do only one person at a time."

"What is thralling?" Kyra asked.

"It's like hypnotizing. I can enter a person's mind and see their most recent memories or whatever they were just thinking about immediately before. I can also replace those memories with something else or just push them down below the consciousness level so they will be forgotten like dreams."

"Fascinating." She rubbed her temple. "Is that a talent many immortals possess?"

"Most of us do. Those who transition as adults have a harder time with it. Their brain is already fully formed, and very few manage." He tapped his phone. "Tell me what you want to communicate to your friends."

Kyra finished the last of her coffee and put the cup down. "This is K. I'm using a friend's phone to let you know that I'm safe and I have Twelve with me. We are on our way to a secure location. I'll contact you as soon as it is safe for me to do so."

Max finished typing the message. "Now the phone number."

He typed the digits she recited, but didn't press send. "Do you want me to add that they can respond to this number?"

Kyra shook her head. "Even if your phone is untraceable, I'd rather not. The message goes to an app that my team checks. Not to someone's actual phone. We only use phones as the last resort.

That's also why my message is so vague. Even if anyone intercepts it, they won't know what it's about. Soran knows not to respond."

"That's smart." Max sent the text and lifted his eyes to Kyra. "So, Soran. Is he someone special to you?"

Was he jealous?

It sure looked like it, which was kind of funny. Was Max really falling for her?

The half-smile she gave him was knowing. "He's just my second, and now he is the leader of my team. I hope I taught him well enough over the years that we fought together."

"I'm impressed." Max crossed his arms over his chest. "You were a rebel commander."

"Didn't your seer see that?"

"Not as far as I know. She saw you with the Kurdish rebels, but she didn't tell us that you were commanding them, so I assume she didn't know."

Kyra swiped her tongue over her lips. "You speak fondly about your seer, so I guess she's not the scary conceited type."

"Not at all. Syssi is a sweetheart. She's mated to the head of the clan on the American continent, and she's the perfect counterbalance to him."

Kyra frowned. "Is he the scary type?"

"A little, but only to those who don't know him. Those who do also know that his bark is much worse than his bite."

Kyra laughed. "Does he know that you talk about him with such impudence?"

Instead of answering, Max looked at her in wonder as if he was trying to figure something out.

"Why are you looking at me like that?" she asked.

"Like what?"

"Like you are trying to solve a puzzle. Other than the immortality stuff, which you know more about than I do, I'm a very simple woman."

"I doubt that. I just wonder if you are always so quick to laugh."

The truth was that she rarely did that. There was just something about Max's easygoing attitude that made her feel lighthearted when she should feel anything but.

"Not at all," she admitted. "You just have a gift for presenting things in a funny way. A cheeky way."

A bright smile bloomed on his face as if she'd given him a great compliment. "I've been accused of worse. And as for Kian, he knows what we think of him, and he doesn't mind. He's not big on protocol, and we all call him by his given name, and we don't use titles when addressing him. His mother, on the other hand, is always referred to as the Clan Mother. She's the head of our clan, and although we all love her dearly, only a few are brave enough to call her by her first name."

"The goddess," Kyra said.

"Indeed."

"Does she punish those who dare to use her name?"

Max snorted. "The Clan Mother never punishes any of us unless we transgress greatly, and even then she's always merciful. It's just that the awe she inspires makes it nearly impossible to call her by her given name." He leaned closer to her. "Ell-rom is her half-brother, so Jasmine is one of the few with that privilege."

Kyra's head whipped over to Ell-rom, who didn't seem to have heard Max because he was watching a movie and didn't turn to look at them.

"My daughter is mated to the goddess's brother?" Kyra whispered.

"That's right. You are related to royalty, so to speak."

13

MAX

Max hadn't expected Kyra to react so strongly to the newsflash that her daughter was mated to Annani's brother. It wasn't Ell-rom being a half god that had impressed her so much. It was that he was related to the clan's royalty.

When she realized that he couldn't hear them, she turned to Max and whispered, "How is he as a partner, though? Does he treat Jasmine right?"

"He adores her, and he's a very gentle and mellow fellow until you threaten someone he loves."

She frowned. "What happens then?"

He couldn't tell her, and even if he could, it was better that she didn't know. "He turns into a beast." He chuckled. "Not literally. Just, you know, he becomes the protector. It's a good thing to have in a son-in-law, right?"

Kyra nodded and then sighed. "I haven't lived a normal life, so I don't have personal knowledge, but I've watched movies and heard people talk, so I'm not entirely clueless."

His heart clenched for her, but he knew instinctively that any show of pity would offend her, so he changed the subject. "What about books? Do rebels have time to read?"

She laughed. "Time is not as much of a problem as is space. I lived in tents most of the time, or in half-ruined buildings. I got to watch stuff on my phone."

"How did you pay for things? If you don't mind me asking."

Kyra tilted her head. "How do you think?"

He was about to hazard a guess when the bathroom door opened and Fenella stepped out, wearing a dark green T-shirt that covered her like a short dress.

Jasmine handed her the blanket, which she tied around her hips, and then the two walked over to their seats.

"That took a long time," Kyra said.

Fenella lifted her hands. "I didn't finish the water, if that's what you are implying. I just used the time for some self-care."

"I wasn't implying anything." Kyra glanced at

Ell-rom, who was still watching his movie, and then leaned toward Jasmine. "You didn't tell me that your guy was related to the Clan Mother."

"I didn't tell you many other things as well. There just wasn't enough time."

"True," Kyra conceded. "But that should have been part of the introductions. I should have been more deferential to Ell-rom."

Jasmine snorted. "He would have hated that, so don't even think about it. Just treat him like any other guy who's about to marry your daughter."

Kyra's eyes brightened. "Did you set a date? Is there a wedding on the horizon?"

"Relax." Jasmine put a hand on her mother's arm. "There are no plans and we don't need any. Ell-rom and I are truelove mates which means more than any human marriage tradition. Immortals who are lucky enough to find their one and only sometimes choose to celebrate their good fortune with the clan and sometimes they don't. Matrimony is optional."

Kyra pursed her lips. "I'm a modern woman and a fighter for women's rights, but I still believe in the importance of family. Marriage is a contract two people enter into not only to share their lives with each other but also to raise their children together."

Poor thing had no idea what her own family had done to her, but she would eventually find out.

Jasmine shook her head. "Unbelievable. I just found my lost mother, who I believed was dead, and she right away lectures me about marriage."

Kyra's face turned ashen. "You thought I was dead? Why?"

"Because that's what my father told me, and I had no reason to think he was lying since I never got a sign of life from you."

"I'm sorry." Kyra rubbed her temples. "I don't remember anything before the asylum. I don't know how I got there or what was done to me."

Jasmine's expression softened. "You came to the US to study, and you fell in love with my father. You knew that your family would never approve of you marrying a Christian, and you told him so. You changed the spelling of your name to Kira, assumed his last name, and you thought you were safe. But they found you, somehow got you back to Iran, and instead of killing you for dishonoring the family, they put you in an insane asylum, where I assume the so-called doctor was tasked with erasing your memories of the life you were forced to leave behind."

For a long moment, Kyra gaped like a fish out of water, and Max wanted to grab her and fold his arms around her to protect her from Jasmine.

What had she been thinking?

She could have waited with that information

for when Kyra was better or delivered it more gently.

"He drugged me and thralled me and did unspeakable things to me," Kyra said. "He was an immortal. Did my family know the kind of monster they hired?"

Jasmine's expression turned remorseful. "I don't know, and I'm sorry for dumping this on you like a bucket of ice water. I should have done that with more finesse. This is all speculation based on what we finally got my father to reveal. He believes that your family came for you, and the proof was the divorce papers he received from Iran. We also have what the seer saw in her visions. But that's all. The rest is guesswork."

"I see." Kyra deflated. "It was a shock to hear you say that, but I'd rather have it over and done with than get it delivered piecemeal."

"Perhaps you should rest a little," Jasmine suggested. "We don't have to cover everything at once."

Kyra sighed. "I'm getting a little tired. But there is one thing you promised to tell me that you haven't yet. You said that I can have children despite not having my monthly visitor, and I want to know how that is possible."

Max stifled a chuckle at the antiquated reference to a woman's monthly cycle.

"Immortal females don't get cycles," Jasmine

said. "After you transitioned, you stopped menstruating in order to preserve your eggs. It's an on-demand kind of system so we don't run out of them. The flip side is that it's very rare. Every birth is celebrated in the clan because there are so few."

"Well, that's good to know," Fenella said. "But what happens with us next?"

Jasmine looked at Max. "Maybe you should cover that part."

"When we land, we will be met by a doctor, a real one who is very nice, and he will check all of you for hidden trackers. You might not be aware of them being embedded under your skin."

Fenella looked at Jasmine. "Is that possible?"

Jasmine nodded. "It's not very likely with you because immortal bodies reject foreign objects, but the human girls might have them. Still, it's better to go ahead and check you as well than to lead the enemy to our home. Right?"

"Of course." Fenella released a breath. "So, the doctor checks us for trackers and then what?"

"Then you will be hosted in beautiful penthouses overlooking downtown Los Angeles. Mostly, because we don't know what the deal is with the other four ladies and what the Doomers wanted with them. If not for them, you would have been taken straight to our village, but we need your help with them. Also, our doctor needs to figure out what kind of sedative was used on you.

It's very difficult to keep an immortal sedated for as long as you have been. But that doesn't necessitate you staying in the penthouse. It's just a super fancy halfway house."

For a moment, a hush fell over their small group. The plane continued its soft rumble, and somewhere in the back, Max heard faint murmurs —probably the Kra-ell talking quietly among themselves.

"What did he want with us?" Fenella asked. "Were we just a plaything for a sadist?"

Max shuddered at the casual way she said that.

"We will find out when we interrogate him," he said. "We suspect that he was trying to find a way to identify Dormants. We haven't found a way to do that, and we've been researching the issue for a very long time, but perhaps he got lucky. If the other women are Dormants, that will prove it."

14

KYRA

Bile rose in Kyra's throat. She'd seen what the monster had done to Fenella, but she'd hoped the woman had been too drugged to realize what had been happening to her.

Apparently, Fenella had been aware, and seemed to be managing the horror much better than Kyra would have ever managed herself.

How had she gotten so resilient?

Was it just for show? Or was she an extraordinary woman?

She wanted to find out but was afraid to ask questions that might shatter Fenella's façade, in case she was just putting on a brave face, while actually bleeding inside.

"I have a question." She put her hand on Jasmine's arm. "Does the induction to immortality always happen the way you explained or is there another method that does not require such an intimate contact with an immortal?"

Jasmine cast a quick glance at Max, then cleared her throat. "I'm not an expert on the subject, but as far as I know, both venom and semen are needed. Venom cannot be harvested, so unless the Doomers found a way to do that, which is doubtful, the old-fashioned way is the only way."

The accusing glance Fenella cast Max sent a wave of pity crashing over Kyra.

Poor Fenella. She felt a sudden urge to reach out and comfort her, but she was pretty sure that the woman wouldn't welcome the gesture.

Jasmine leaned in. "We should pause the conversation here. You both have enough to digest. We'll have more time to talk after we land."

Kyra was tired, but she had so many questions she knew would keep her awake. "Do you happen to have a picture of your father?"

Jasmine shook her head. "I don't, but maybe he has one on his website. Would you like me to search for it?"

Kyra nodded. "Maybe seeing him would jog my memory."

"Don't forget that over two decades have passed since you last saw him." Jasmine pulled out her phone. "The picture on the website is old, but not that old."

Kyra wondered why Jasmine didn't have photos

of her father. Everyone had pictures of their families on their phones. "Do you have any brothers or sisters?"

A grimace twisted Jasmine's beautiful face. "I have two stepbrothers, but we are not close. They are nasty pieces of shit." She scrolled on her phone. "Here it is." She handed the device to Kyra. "Boris Orlov."

The man in the photo was in his mid-fifties or early sixties, with patchy blond hair that was gray in spots and a few extra pounds. He looked like someone who had been handsome back in the day, but his bitter expression detracted from his appeal. This was a man who had been dealt a nasty hand in life, and it showed in every line and groove on his face.

The worst part was that she felt nothing looking at him. There was no recognition, not even a sense of familiarity. She was looking at a complete stranger who was the father of her daughter, and someone she had once loved.

"Anything?" Jasmine asked.

Kyra shook her head. "Whatever they did to me, it was a thorough job."

Jasmine took the phone from her hands. "I wish I had a picture of him when he was younger. Maybe that would have stirred something. I have a photo album back home. There should be some pictures there."

"I would love to see it if you are okay with sharing it with me."

"Of course." Jasmine leaned over and kissed her cheek, making Kyra's heart swell with love and appreciation for this daughter she hadn't known she had.

"I feel so fortunate to have you." Kyra reached for Jasmine's hand. "I'm infinitely richer now than I was yesterday, and not just because I am free."

"Me too." Tears shone in Jasmine's eyes.

Kyra nodded, letting a moment of silence stand between them. She was exhausted, physically and emotionally, yet the adrenaline of learning these things about her past and her future kept her from fully succumbing to fatigue. She leaned back into her seat, letting her eyes drift over Fenella, who had settled deeper into the blanket, lost in her own thoughts.

Outside, through the airplane window, the sky stretched endless and open, the horizon a pale line of a pinkish dawn.

Some answers had come, but more mysteries remained—especially her own induction into immortality. She'd noticed how Max had flinched when that topic arose, so maybe she shouldn't discuss it in his presence.

She slanted a glance at him. He was such a handsome guy, tall and broad-shouldered. He wore a simple white T-shirt that was a little dirty now, and black cargo pants. His dark blond hair was mussed as if he'd run his fingers through it repeatedly, and it occurred to her that he resembled Boris a little. The blond hair and blue eyes, the square jaw, but Max was leagues above Boris, which made sense since he was the scion of gods.

Hey, so was she, and it was much better than being an experiment gone wrong or right, or the daughter of fanatics who had ruined their daughter's life because she had married outside their faith.

That was speculation, though. Jasmine didn't know that for a fact. Still, it made sense, given what Boris had told Jasmine. The divorce papers didn't make sense though. Why would anyone bother with that?

Oh well, unless there was a way to unlock her memories or the monster in the body bag knew what had actually happened to her, she would never know.

With a sigh, Kyra leaned back in her seat, letting her head rest against the cushion. At last, she closed her eyes, letting the faint hum of the airplane settle into her bones.

Soft chatter drifted from a few rows behind, and occasionally, someone stirred, but Kyra was enclosed in her own bubble of stillness. The events of the day—the rescue, the revelation that she had a daughter, and the story of gods and immortals—all blurred together in a surreal montage.

The gentle rocking of the plane lulled her. The sweater's fabric felt soft against her skin, and she kept thinking that this was the beginning of a new chapter in her life.

She drifted in that half-awake state, neither asleep nor fully alert, letting her mind parse what had been revealed to her since she was freed. She was immortal. She had a grown daughter. She had been locked away by enemies much more dangerous and formidable than she'd imagined, and she was wrapped in a man's sweater—a man who looked at her with longing in his eyes.

At least now, she was finally free to figure out her past and realize her future.

15

SYSSI

Syssi breathed in the crisp air and zipped up her jacket. Despite the overhead heaters near the hangar's large sliding doors, the winter chill still nipped at her cheeks.

"You don't have to stand outside," Mey said. "We can sit inside the warm hangar or with Okidu on the bus."

Syssi cast her a smile. "I like the cold. We don't get enough cold days out here."

It had snowed at the higher elevations surrounding the LA basin, but the hills around the clan's airstrip rarely got even a dusting of snow, which was a blessing, since Syssi did not want anything delaying or complicating the jet's landing. Kalugal's plane was as large as the clan's strip could handle, and if Kian ever decided to outdo his cousin and purchase a larger jet for the clan, he would have to invest in lengthening the strip and building a larger hangar.

Mey threaded her arm through Syssi's. "I'm not a fan of the cold, but I won't leave you alone out here." She chuckled. "We've done a lot of bonding over our shopping spree, you and I. However, I can't get over Amanda not jumping on the opportunity. She's supposed to be the queen of shopping."

"She is, but not this kind. Rodeo Drive is more her style."

"True." Mey sighed. "I'm not a fangirl of Walmart either, but there was no time to shop around or order online. Besides, we didn't have the women's sizes, so there was no point in buying quality stuff."

They'd even bought snow boots because those were the easiest to wear even if they were the wrong size.

"Walmart has some nice things, and you can find everything you need at great prices." Syssi pushed her other hand into her pocket to keep it warm. "Just don't tell Amanda I said that."

In fact, she'd been surprised to find all-cotton items, which was what she'd been looking for. Comfort clothing needed to be soft. They'd gotten leggings, T-shirts, sweatshirts, cozy socks, and undergarments, but given how cold it was up here, they should have gotten gloves and hats as well.

When Julian's van pulled up next to their minivan, it occurred to Syssi that the women could change in there instead of using the tiny bathroom in the hangar.

"Let's peek inside." She tugged on Mey's arm. "I'm curious about the equipment they have in there. I'm debating whether the women can change in there after Julian scans them or on the bus."

Mey shook her head. "Yamanu said that they are wearing threadbare shifts. I wouldn't let them off the plane like that. We should get all the men out and then let the women dress in what we brought before getting off the plane."

"Good thinking," Syssi agreed. "I've heard that Kalugal replaced the interior of his plane and I'm curious to see what he did."

Julian stepped out of the van and walked over to them. "They'll be here any minute." He spun around and eyed the hangar. "The pilot will taxi in and then when he leaves the plane, he'll shut the hangar doors behind the aircraft so no one is exposed to the cold for long."

"Mey suggested that we bring the clothing to the plane so the women can change in there. There are no zippers or buttons on any of the things we got, so they won't have to take anything off before the scan."

"Good." Julian let out a breath. "I'm dreading having to deal with traumatized women. You would think that I'd be an expert after running the halfway house for so long, but by the time they come to me, they have already completed most of the rehabilitation program. I wish Vanessa was here."

"We need more Vanessas," Mey said. "I wish William and his team could invent a device that can teach someone everything they need to know about mental health in weeks instead of years."

Syssi's hand closed over one of the small cases in her pocket containing four earpieces for the women who didn't speak English. "Perhaps it already exists. It's called artificial intelligence. Chatbots can offer psychological solace and even medical advice."

Julian winced. "My profession will soon become obsolete."

"Nonsense," said Gertrude as she joined them. "I will never trust those things enough to rely on their advice. No matter what they try to tell you, there is no substitute for a living brain."

Perhaps not yet, but one day, maybe soon, there would be. Everything in the universe was based on information, on data, but right now those large language models were based on written information, while living brains had been built to absorb so much more stimuli that was nonverbal information. Until machines were capable of doing that, they could never substitute for people.

"Here it is." Mey pointed at the sky.

Excitement built through Syssi's chest, mixed with anxiety over the women's state. She had even less experience than Julian in dealing with traumatized victims and feared saying or doing the wrong thing.

"We should clear the doorway," Julian said, leading them inside to the waiting area that consisted of a few chairs lined against the wall.

The looming shape of Kalugal's plane appeared in the sky, and once it touched down at the other side of the landing strip, Syssi let out a breath.

For some reason, landings always stressed her.

The jet taxied into the open maw of the hangar, then the pilot navigated it carefully inside and stopped it with a brief jolt before killing the engines.

When the cabin door finally swung open, Syssi's attention zeroed in on the first figure to emerge. Yamanu stood at the open door, his gaze sweeping the space until landing on Mey, and a huge grin spread over his face.

He jumped down the stairs, and in two long strides closed the distance, enveloping her in a fierce embrace as if they'd been separated for months, not just a couple of days.

Mey's hands flew up around his neck, and as she hid her face in his shoulder, a small laugh escaped her.

Syssi felt a rush of affection witnessing their reunion. In a world full of darkness, true love was a beacon. She was about to say something teasing—maybe about how Yamanu didn't even see anyone else in the hangar—but her own voice caught in her throat when her eyes snagged on Jasmine, who was standing inside the cabin door with a woman who could have been her sister.

Kyra was thinner and shorter, but not by much, and there was a regal tilt to her chin and determination in her eyes.

She didn't look like a victim.

She looked like a warrior.

16

KYRA

Kyra watched with a smile as Yamanu and his mate embraced like a couple of long-lost lovers finally reunited. The female was tall, as befitted someone of Yamanu's impressive stature, and she was absolutely gorgeous.

The beautiful blonde who stood next to the embracing couple had tears in her eyes, and Kyra had a feeling that she was the seer even though no one had physically described her. The kindness that Max had spoken of was written all over her expressive face.

She considered it a great honor that the clan leader's mate had come to greet them.

"Wait!" The blonde lifted her hand as Jasmine took a step down. "Let all the men deplane first so the ladies can change on board. We brought clothing and shoes for everyone."

Behind her, Kyra heard Fenella let out a breath. "That's a great idea. None of us have shoes, and we are wearing T-shirts for dresses."

"Will do!" Jasmine called back before turning around. "Did everyone hear Syssi?"

There were a few grumbles of acknowledgment, but most hadn't heard the seer, and Jasmine repeated the instructions.

The three of them returned to their seats, and in moments everyone else other than the four girls deplaned, including Max and Ell-rom who'd both seemed reluctant to leave them behind.

"It's okay," Kyra told the four frightened women in Kurdish. "We are getting clothes, and everyone else is leaving to give us privacy to change."

When they looked at her with puzzled expressions on their faces, she repeated what she'd said in Farsi.

"Who are these people?" one of the four asked. "Are they with the Kurdish resistance?"

Kyra had slept until the jet started its descent, so there had been no time to explain before. "They are friends, and we are safe. That's all I can tell you for now."

"Where are we?" another one asked.

"The United States of America," Kyra said proudly.

After all, she was a citizen even though she didn't have the passport to prove it.

The response was four wide-eyed expressions and then big smiles, followed by happy tears and hugs. The four seemed to know each other, but whether they had been abducted together or had gotten to know each other in prison was something she would have to find out later, because Syssi and Yamanu's mate appeared in the doorway with several shopping bags, and big smiles on both of their faces.

Syssi dropped the bags in the aisle, walked up to Kyra, and pulled her into a gentle embrace. "I'm so glad we were able to get you out. Your ordeal is over."

Tears pooled in Kyra's eyes. "Thank you. I was told that I owe my rescue to you. You are the seer who saw me getting captured."

"I didn't see that," Syssi admitted. "I saw you imprisoned, the first and the second time." She turned to look at Fenella. "Frankly, I'm not sure which one of you I saw. You look a lot alike, and visions are not always clear."

"I don't care who you saw," Fenella said. "I'm just glad to be out."

Syssi pulled her into a brief hug as well then turned back to Kyra. "I have translating earpieces for the other women who don't speak English. Can you explain to them what they are for?" She pulled a small white case out of her coat pocket and opened it. "I'll show you how to activate them so you can translate."

"Gladly."

After she explained what the earpieces were for, the girls eagerly snatched the translating devices out of Syssi's hands, and a few moments later, everyone knew how to use them.

"Say something," Syssi encouraged, pointing to her own ears to show them that she had a pair as well. "Mine will translate your language into English for me."

"Thank you for saving us," one of the girls said.

"You're welcome," Syssi replied.

Fenella shifted from foot to foot. "Do you have one for me as well? I know a little Farsi and a little Kurdish but not enough to converse."

"Of course." Syssi pulled another white case out of her pocket and handed it to her. "Do you need me to explain again how they work?"

"No, I got it." Fenella pulled the earpieces out of the case, put them in her ears, and activated them. "Say something in Kurdish," she told Kyra.

"I wonder how you got to be in that prison."

Fenella's face blanched. "That's a long story."

"It can wait," Syssi said. "Right now you need to get dressed. It's cold outside. We have a medical team waiting for you to check you for hidden trackers. If you have any medical concerns you would like to address, you can tell the doctor or the nurse. They are both wonderful people and you have nothing to fear from them. You are among friends, and you are safe."

Kyra appreciated Syssi for repeating that. Even though she already knew she was safe, hearing it reiterated peeled away another thin layer of fear.

She wondered how many of those were still coating her soul and how long it would take for all of them to slough off. Her eyes darted to the open door, searching for Max, but all she could see was the hangar wall.

17

MAX

Max waited until the last woman was scanned and had boarded the bus before motioning to Yamanu to follow him back into the jet.

He'd asked Okidu to keep the bus windows opaque so the women wouldn't see them transporting the Doomer to the van to get scanned. They had been through enough at the hands of this scum, and he might stress them even when in a body bag.

Yamanu lit a match to the trashcan containing what the women had been wearing when they'd found them, not because they feared any of those threadbare shifts could hide trackers but because it just felt good to burn those things.

Once the flames rose high, Yamanu turned around and strode toward the plane. "Let's get this over with. The faster we get rid of him the better."

They weren't getting rid of him. They were taking him to the dungeon, but Yamanu's job ended at the airstrip, and he would never have to see the vermin again.

Max, on the other hand, was looking forward to spending many satisfying hours with the monster, demonstrating how it felt to be helpless and abused by someone with no mercy.

"Payback is a bitch, motherfucker," he murmured under his breath as he followed Yamanu to the aircraft's cargo hold where they'd stashed the Doomer.

They worked quickly but carefully, maneuvering the dead weight down the cargo ramp.

Julian directed them to lay the bag on the foldable table he'd set up in the hangar. "I need him undressed before we load him into the scanner. You can leave the underwear on provided it doesn't have any zippers."

Yamanu chuckled. "I've never heard of men's undergarments having zippers."

Julian shrugged. "You never know. I don't want any surprises."

Max's lip curled as he unzipped the bag. The Doomer's face was slack in stasis, but Max could still see the arrogant sneer that had been there during the fight. He started unbuttoning the black jacket that was made from an exceptionally fine fabric.

"These aren't standard Revolutionary Guard uniforms," Yamanu commented, helping to work the jacket off the unconscious Doomer's shoulders. "Custom made, probably."

"Everything about him screams ego." Max yanked at the boots next, expensive leather, probably crafted by some Italian designer. "The monster was playing dress-up while torturing women."

As they stripped off the uniform pants, and Max started on the shirt, his hand brushed against a thin chain that was around the Doomer's neck. Frowning, he loosened the collar and pulled out an amber pendant.

His breath caught. "This is Kyra's. This is what she said was taken away from her. The bastard was wearing it like a trophy."

The amber stone was exactly as she'd described it, wrapped in an intricate setting that spoke of age and craftsmanship.

He removed the chain from around the Doomer's neck, careful not to break the links.

Yamanu peered at it. "Interesting piece. Not pretty, but somehow meaningful, right? Can you feel it?"

Max nodded. "Kyra was devastated when she thought she'd lost it. She said it guided her."

Tucking the pendant in his pocket, Max smiled as he imagined the joy on Kyra's face when he returned it to her.

Yamanu helped him maneuver the dead weight onto the scanning bed. "He probably doesn't have any trackers on him. Navuh tried that experiment once, but after their bodies rejected the implants, he gave up on the idea."

"If I learned anything about Navuh over the years, it's that he never gives up on ideas or anything else. He's a patient bastard, and he waits until the technology catches up. We need to check every Doomer before we bring him into the keep."

"Was there anything interesting in his wallet?" Yamanu asked. "You should give it to Julian to scan as well. Just in case."

Max had taken it when he'd initially gone through the Doomer's pockets after incapacitating him, but it hadn't contained any clues.

Grunting, he pulled the sleek leather wallet out of his pocket. "Lots of cash in various currencies, but no ID and no credit cards. There is nothing to indicate who this bastard is."

"Professional," Yamanu muttered. "Would have loved to get our hands on his phone, but it wasn't worth the risk. Who knows what kind of tracking or remote access the Brotherhood might have had on it."

"William's team could have probably cracked it,"

Max said, "but we never take phones unless we have the right equipment on hand to block signals, and we didn't have it." Max kicked the pile of expensive clothes aside. "Look at this shit—designer everything. Guy really thought highly of himself."

Julian looked at them from where he was sitting in the van. "You sure he's not one of Navuh's adopted sons?"

"I don't recognize him from any of the portraits that Dalhu drew of Navuh's top command." Max frowned. "Though it's been a while since I looked at them. My memory could be off."

"I took photos," Julian said, pulling out his phone. "Give me a second." He stepped out of the van and the two of them looked over his shoulder as he flicked through the images.

"I'm not seeing anyone looking anything like this guy," Yamanu said after they'd gone through the whole collection twice. "Not even close."

Max shook his head. "He could be a newly ascended commander, someone who has proven himself more useful than the others. Or maybe he's just an ambitious underling trying to move up the ranks while experimenting on the side."

When the dude was down to his fancy boxer shorts, Max and Yamanu lifted him into the van and put him inside the scanner.

The machine hummed, and while Julian did his

thing, Max put his hand in his pocket and rubbed his fingers over Kyra's pendant. It was cool, inert, and he wondered whether it reacted differently to her touch.

"He's clean," Julian announced after a few minutes. "I mean of the devices on his body. I'm not commenting on his personal hygiene, which is not on par with his clothing."

"That's not surprising," Yamanu said. "You could put an evening gown on a pig, but it would not turn it into a lady."

Max snorted. "In this case the analogy should be a tux on a crocodile that wouldn't turn him into a prince."

"That's an insult to crocodiles," Julian murmured. "They are just dumb reptiles. This creature is pure evil."

18

KYRA

The bus engine hummed, keeping the interior warm while they waited for Max and Yamanu to finish whatever task had required everyone else to clear out. Kyra had a good idea what that task was—the Doomer's body had to be scanned as well—but she pushed the thought aside.

She'd see him again when the time came for answers.

New clothes made a world of difference to how she felt. She'd kept Max's sweater, but now she was wearing a long-sleeved T-shirt underneath, soft cotton leggings, and a pair of thick socks inside snow boots that were a size and a half too big but kept her feet wonderfully warm.

The other women looked equally transformed

in their fresh attire, though their eyes were still haunted. The four humans looked incredibly young, and her heart ached even more, knowing that they had been robbed of their innocence. Fenella was holding up better than the rest, but that was no wonder given that she was much older, older even than Kyra, and immortal.

Syssi settled into the seat across the aisle, her kind face creased with concern. "Perhaps we can use this time to get introduced properly?" She motioned with her head at the four young humans sitting behind Kyra and Jasmine.

"Good idea." Kyra rose to her feet and Jasmine followed suit.

She stood next to the first two. "We haven't been properly introduced yet. I'm Kyra, and this is my...sister Jasmine. What are your names?"

The oldest, who couldn't have been more than eighteen or nineteen, straightened her shoulders. "I am Arezoo," she said, then gestured to the girl sitting beside her. "And this is my sister Donya. That's my sister Laleh and next to her is our cousin Azadeh."

Kyra's heart clenched at how young they all looked. Donya and Laleh had the same delicate features as their older sister, while Azadeh had slightly darker coloring.

"How old are you?" Kyra asked gently.

"I'm nineteen," Arezoo said. "Donya is seventeen, Laleh just turned sixteen, and Azadeh is eighteen."

Kyra exchanged a pained look with Syssi. Just children, really. Still, in Iran they were all considered old enough to marry, and they were all pretty girls. The fact that they weren't married indicated that they were from an urban area and members of an upper socioeconomic class. Those tended to marry their daughters off at an older age than those in rural areas.

"What happened to you?" Kyra asked. "How were you taken?"

Arezoo twisted her hands in her lap. "We were home, doing homework. Someone knocked on the door..." Her voice cracked. "Then we woke up at that horrible place. None of us remembers how we got there."

"One moment we were safe at home," Azadeh said softly. "The next..." She shuddered.

"We need to call our parents," Laleh burst out, her young face pinched. "They must be so worried about us."

Syssi leaned forward, her expression gentle but firm. "I know you want to contact your families, but it's not safe yet. The people who took you might be monitoring your family's phones, waiting for just such a call."

"It doesn't matter," Arezoo said, tears glistening in her expressive eyes. "We can never go home anyway. We would be killed for bringing shame to our family."

"Not true!" Donya grabbed her sister's hand. "Our parents love us. They wouldn't do that. Besides, we don't have to tell them what happened. We can say we were kidnapped but were rescued unharmed."

"They won't believe us." Arezoo's voice cracked.

"We can help you," Syssi said. "Don't despair. We will find a solution."

It was an empty promise, especially if the girls were Dormants, but right now they needed reassurance.

Kyra had so many questions she wanted to ask about what had been done to these girls, but the bus was too public. The Kra-ell warriors who had settled in the back of the bus all wore earpieces like the ones Syssi had brought for the girls, so they might understand what was being said, and it wasn't fair to the girls to discuss what had been done to them in front of these strangers, even if they had been their rescuers.

That reminded Kyra that she should thank each one of those fighters for coming for her. They didn't know her, and they had risked their lives to save her. That made them good people no matter how strange they looked. In her book, they were better people than a hell of a lot of humans.

She turned to Syssi. "Do all the earpieces translate Farsi and Kurdish?"

"I'm not sure," Syssi admitted. "Those languages were only recently added to the system, and mine were already updated with the latest version, but I don't know if all the devices were updated. I can check." She shifted her gaze to the back of the bus. "Jade? Can I bother you for a moment?"

One of the impossibly tall, thin females made her way forward. Up close, her alien features were striking. Her dark eyes looked disproportionately large in her delicate face, but she was still beautiful in a very alien way.

"Go ahead," Syssi motioned for Kyra. "Say something in Farsi."

Kyra offered the female her best friendly smile. "Thank you so much for coming to rescue me. I owe you a great debt of gratitude." She made a fist and thumped her chest. "Sisters."

The female returned her smile. "Sisters." She thumped her own chest. "Fellow warriors." She dipped her head, turned on her heel, and returned to her seat next to a younger version of herself.

A daughter?

Given the body language between the two, they were mother and daughter, but it was very subtle.

"Jade is a female of few words," Syssi whispered.

"But she's the deadliest warrior you will ever encounter. She saved my husband's life."

If Jade heard Syssi's whisper, she didn't acknowledge it in any way.

"And now she's saved mine," Kyra said. "Not on her own, but still. I'm in her debt."

19

MAX

After securing the Doomer in the cargo bay of the bus, Max bounded up the bus steps, his hand clutching the pendant in his pocket.

Regrettably, he couldn't sit next to Kyra because she was sitting next to Jasmine, so he had no choice but to deliver the good news standing next to her.

Yamanu, who got in behind him, passed by on his way to Mey, who was saving a seat for him.

"Look what I found." He pulled the pendant out and held it up. "The scumbag had it on him."

Kyra's eyes went wide, her hand flying to her mouth. "My pendant!" She reached for it, and as he let go of the chain, she clutched it to her chest. "I felt like a piece of me was missing." Tears welled in her eyes. "Thank you for bringing it back to me."

"I cleaned it thoroughly," Max assured her quickly. "That bastard was wearing it under his shirt, and I didn't want you touching anything that had been against his skin. I scrubbed it with a wet washcloth."

He hoped that was okay, and that she didn't have some crazy rules about the maintenance of that stone, like dunking it in salt to clean it instead of using soap.

"You have no idea what this means to me." Her voice was thick with emotion.

"Enjoy," he said, because he couldn't think of anything better to say.

Glancing around, he searched for a place to sit.

Across the aisle, Ell-rom sat with Syssi, while several rows back, Yamanu had already pulled Mey into an embrace. This left him with the choice of sitting alone or next to Fenella.

Sighing inwardly, he settled beside her. "How are you doing?" he asked.

"It feels nice to wear proper clothes," she said.

He nodded. "Have you been home in recent years?"

She cast him an incredulous look. "Are you kidding me? As who? My own daughter or granddaughter?"

"Right." He rubbed a hand over his jaw. "So, you haven't been in touch at all with your family?"

She shrugged. "At first, I sent letters, and I

called whenever I could, but making international calls was super expensive back then, and you had to find a place that offered the service. It wasn't easy." She chuckled. "Cell phones changed the world."

"They did."

A long moment of awkward silence stretched between them, and then Fenella shifted in her seat. "Have you been home recently?"

He shook his head. "I don't like going back and having to see Din. He still gives me the cold shoulder fifty years later."

Her eyes widened. "So, he's an immortal, like you. Who else?"

"I don't remember every immortal who ever visited your pub."

She shifted back and turned toward the window, which was no longer opaque. "You said that it might have been someone else who induced me."

He let out a breath. "That's not likely. I've been defensive." He chuckled. "I guess I deserved you calling me an asshole."

"You are." She looked at him from under lowered lashes. "So, what does it mean that you are my inducer? Are you responsible for me or anything?"

"I am," he admitted. "I want you to have a good life."

Her lips twisted in a sneer. "Right. Just not with you."

"We are not in love, Fenella, and we never were, but Din loved you."

Fenella scoffed. "Din was just a possessive asshole. He could have flirted with me, shown me that he was interested, but instead he just wanted to make sure that none of his friends got near me. That's the definition of an asshole."

She surely liked to throw that descriptor around. Perhaps it was her defense mechanism, and she used that word for every guy who had ever hurt her feelings.

Given what she'd been through, though, Max couldn't really blame her for being bitter and defensive.

"Din was just shy, and he was taking his time. If anyone deserves to be called an asshole, it's me. I earned the name fair and square."

"Is that what you think?" She snorted. "That he was just shy? I have news for you. After you left, he came to the pub and hurled insults at me. Called me all kinds of names that no one should call a woman. That's not what a guy in love does."

Max was aghast. "He insulted you right there in the pub in front of everyone?"

That was unforgivable, and Din didn't deserve to know that Max had found Fenella and that she was immortal now.

"Well, not exactly," Fenella said, her voice tight. "He asked me to step outside because he wanted to tell me something. I said fine, and then he proceeded to call me every name in the book for choosing you over him." She gave a harsh laugh. "Not that I knew there was even a choice to make. I'd seen him looking at me, and I knew he found me attractive, but he was always so quiet and standoffish, so I thought he was just one of those guys who liked to look."

"What did you do when he started calling you names?"

She crossed her arms over her chest and tilted her chin. "I slapped him and told him that I never wanted to see his face again." She narrowed her eyes at him. "Do you have a problem with that?"

"No. The asshole deserved it." Max slumped in his seat. "I guess there is no point in me calling him and letting him know that I found you."

She huffed out a breath. "You can tell him if you want. After all, the only ones who can know I exist are people in your clan, and I assume there aren't that many of you."

"No, there are not, but there are many who are desperately looking for dormant and immortal females who are not related to them, so you will have an abundance of suitors. If you are interested, that is. If you want, I can tell everyone to keep their distance."

She'd been hurt, and she might not want male company for the foreseeable future.

Fenella made a comical face. "Are you kidding me? I can finally find a nice guy who I don't need to hide my abilities from and who can live as long as I can, and you think I'll pass up the opportunity because some degenerate hurt me?"

He swallowed. "You are very brave. I don't know many women who could be as brave as you in similar circumstances."

She shrugged. "I've lived a tough life, and I've been through a lot."

"Would you consider ever forgiving Din?" he asked cautiously. "If he apologized profusely?"

"Once an asshole, always an asshole." Fenella's tone left no room for argument.

Max decided to let the subject drop for now. Time might soften her stance, but pushing would only make her dig in harder. Instead, he gestured toward the window.

"Wait until you see the place you will be staying at," he said. "The penthouse has floor-to-ceiling windows with an incredible view of the city, and there's even a lap pool on the terrace."

Her expression lightened. "Isn't it too cold for swimming now?"

"You can heat the pool up. Besides, Southern California doesn't get all that cold anyway, and spring is coming. Pretty soon it will be scorching hot on the terrace."

"That sounds nice." Some of the tension left her shoulders. "I haven't had a proper swim in I can't remember how long."

From the corner of his eye, Max caught Kyra still clutching her pendant, her thumb stroking the amber stone as if reconnecting with an old friend.

"Stop staring at her," Fenella murmured. "Women don't like guys who fall for them too fast."

"Shut up," he replied without heat. "That's not true."

"Which part? Staring at Kyra, or that women don't like guys who fall for them too easily?"

"Both."

She chuckled. "Some things never change. You are still a sucker for a pretty face."

"I'm not," he protested, but they both knew it was a lie.

20

KIAN

Kian paced the length of his old penthouse living room, each pass taking him from the wall to the floor-to-ceiling windows to the double front doors that led to the vestibule. Beyond the glass, Los Angeles sprawled in the afternoon light. The cityscape usually provided him with a sense of calm—a reminder that here, everyday life went on, even while wars and conflicts savaged people around the globe. Still, he was restless, partly because he wasn't a patient male and he hated waiting for anything, and in part because he was ill equipped to deal with a bunch of traumatized females.

Initially, he'd planned to wait in the dungeon for the Doomer's arrival. His fingers itched to get started on the interrogation, to extract every bit of information about what the Brotherhood was plotting, but then it occurred to him that celebrating the rescue and welcoming Kyra and the others should come first.

After all, they believed that Kyra would be instrumental to finding Khiann, and that made her a very important addition to the clan.

She should get the red-carpet welcome.

The aroma of fresh coffee and warm bread wafted from the kitchen where Ogidu was working his magic. Since Okidu was driving the bus, Kian had borrowed one of his mother's Odus to prepare the penthouses for their guests and to make a welcome lunch, or rather dinner, as it was after three o'clock in the afternoon and it would be another twenty minutes or so before they arrived.

"Is everything ready?" he called out in the direction of the kitchen.

"I am almost done, master," Ogidu replied.

He'd tasked the Odu with a lot, so even the cyborg's speed and efficiency might not be enough to have everything on time.

"Is there anything I can help with?" Kian offered, although he wasn't sure what he could actually do.

As someone who had enjoyed the services of Okidu since the day he was born, Kian hadn't had the need to develop any domestic skills. He knew how to make coffee, but given the aroma wafting from the kitchen, that had already been taken care of.

Ogidu appeared in the kitchen entrance, his expression mildly scandalized. "I assure Master that I have everything well in hand. The welcome luncheon is prepared, the rooms are ready, and fresh linens have been placed in all bathrooms."

"Of course." Kian smiled apologetically. "Thank you."

Ogidu bowed his head. "Master's offer of assistance is still appreciated, if unnecessary."

Kian had briefly considered leaving Ogidu here in the penthouse to care for their guests, but his mother would not have liked that and besides, Jasmine would want to stay close to her mother, making up for lost time, and naturally Ell-rom would want to stay with her. The two could help the women adjust.

There was a pleasing symmetry to it. Not long ago, Ell-rom had been the one being cared for in these very apartments, recuperating from a seven-thousand-year stasis. Now he could pay that kindness forward, helping others find their footing after their world had collapsed, plunging them into the pit of darkness.

Pulling out his phone, Kian checked his emails and messages, but nothing new had landed in either inbox since ten minutes ago when he had last checked. He returned the phone to his suit pocket and headed down the hallway to inspect the bedrooms, for no other reason than to settle his restlessness.

He had no doubt that Ogidu had followed his instructions to the letter and that he had made sure that each bedroom had clean linens and towels, and that the rest of the clothing Mey and Syssi had gotten for the women had been put in the closets.

His old office at the end of the hallway was still outfitted as such, but there was no computer or phone on the desk. In fact, there were no landlines in either one of the penthouses, and he hadn't asked William to provide any of the women with cell phones yet. Until they were sure the women could be trusted, they couldn't allow them to communicate with the outside world.

He was well aware that he was replacing their old prison with a new one, albeit much more luxurious and devoid of abuse, but one that still restricted their freedom.

Security concerns demanded that.

Yamanu had updated him after Julian had completed the scans that none of the women had trackers embedded in their bodies, and that they were doing relatively well considering what they'd been through. But the piece of information that had disturbed Kian most was how young the four other girls were, the youngest being sixteen and the oldest nineteen.

They were also all related. Three sisters and their cousin.

Bridget would arrive later in the afternoon to assess their health and begin whatever treatment they required.

His phone buzzed with a text from Syssi: *Entering parking garage now.*

Tucking the phone away, he made for the door, stepping out into the round vestibule with its high ceiling and colorful mural. A fresh bouquet of flowers had replaced the previous one on the round table, filling the small space with sweet smells.

Kian pressed the elevator button, and when the doors opened, he rode it down to the underground parking level. The hush of the elevator ride did little to calm the tension in his gut, and by the time he reached the bottom floor, his shoulders felt like coiled springs.

Perhaps he shouldn't have come.

Syssi and Mey had been enough of a welcoming party, and he could have postponed this until the six women were in a better state. That had been his intention when he'd driven to the keep, but it felt cowardly to wait in the dungeon for the arrival of the Doomer. It also didn't sit well with him that the brutal interrogation was his comfort zone, something he was looking forward to, but he felt completely out of his element welcoming six traumatized females.

He stepped off into the subterranean garage and waited for the bus.

Finally, the bright glare of oncoming headlights lit the wall, and the bus rumbled into view, stopping momentarily to wait for the gate to roll aside and then turning cautiously into the designated space.

21

KYRA

As the bus glided through the streets of Los Angeles, its large windows offered glimpses of towering skyscrapers and palm trees swaying in the gentle breeze. Kyra absorbed every detail, marking every turn and committing it to memory more out of habit than for any escape plans.

She was going home because home was with her daughter, so why would she want to escape it?

"Do you know if I ever visited Los Angeles?" she asked Jasmine.

"We didn't live in California," her daughter said. "I don't know if you ever visited here before I was born or when I was too young to remember. I moved here later for my acting career, after college."

Pride swelled in Kyra's chest. Her beautiful daughter was an actress and a singer. She hadn't heard her sing yet, and she couldn't wait for the right opportunity to do so.

"Do you act in films or television?"

Jasmine sighed. "Right now, in neither, and before, I mostly acted in commercials and a few tiny roles. It wasn't much of a career, and I paid the bills by working in a customer service center. In a way, it's good that I never got famous. It would have been more painful to leave a successful career behind."

"Why would you leave it?"

"It gets complicated for an immortal, for obvious reasons." Jasmine gestured toward her face. "Can't exactly keep appearing in films and never age. People would notice."

"That's a shame." Kyra took her daughter's hand. "Are there other avenues you could use your talent for? Perhaps as a recording artist?"

"That's a possibility, although I would be doing it more for fun than any hopes of earning a living from it. I've been exploring options with Perfect Match for gainful employment."

"Matchmaking? I've heard it's a profitable business, but does it align with your talents and what you enjoy doing?"

Jasmine chuckled. "It's not what you think.

Perfect Match is a virtual reality enterprise that allows participants to experience shared adventures. Some people use it for matchmaking or dating—hence the name—but it's evolved well beyond that. You can pilot a plane, skydive, and explore ancient ruins, all from the comfort and safety of a specially designed chair."

"That sounds fascinating." Kyra tried to imagine such technology. "What would be your position there?"

"I'm not sure yet." Jasmine shifted in her seat. "I haven't had much time to pursue it seriously. Other things kept coming up."

"Like me?" Kyra asked softly.

Jasmine wrapped an arm around her shoulders, pulling her close. "Finding you was one of the highlights of my life," she said fiercely. "Don't forget that for years I believed that you were dead. My father was convinced that your family had killed you for marrying outside your faith."

A shudder ran through Kyra. "I don't follow any religion, but I know what he was referring to. Most Iranians aren't so savage and primitive, but there are enough who are." She'd seen it firsthand in her years with the resistance—the particular brutality reserved for women who dared step outside the narrow confines of what was deemed acceptable.

Not for the first time, Kyra wondered what her family had been like. Were they the kind who would have killed their daughter for marrying a man from another faith? Or had they tried to brainwash her to forget him and marry someone else, someone of their choosing?

The only one who might hold the answers was the monster in the body bag, and she couldn't wait for Max to beat the truth out of him. She wasn't a bloodthirsty fiend, but she was looking forward to seeing him suffer.

The bus slowed, turning into a descending ramp. Concrete walls replaced the view of city streets as the bus entered an underground parking garage, and instantly Kyra's chest tightened. The walls seemed to close in, the ceiling hanging too low. Her breath came in quick, shallow gasps.

"What's wrong?" Jasmine's hand tightened on her arm.

"I don't like being underground," Kyra murmured, trying to focus on her breathing. "I don't know why. I know there is nothing dangerous down here." She concentrated on her breathing, trying to calm her racing heart.

"It's just the parking structure," Jasmine said. "We are not staying down here. We are going straight to the penthouse that has beautiful views of the city. You are going to love it."

Kyra closed her eyes, trying to visualize the

luxurious apartment, but she could still feel the walls bracketing the bus and realized that not seeing them wasn't helping.

Taking a deep breath, she opened her eyes, but instead of looking out the window next to her, she looked straight at the front window that didn't have a wall inches away from it.

Across the aisle, Max leaned forward. "It's a shame you have a problem with underground spaces. You'll miss the Doomer's interrogation, which is going to take place in the keep's dungeon."

Kyra lifted her chin and met his gaze. "I've overcome a lot of fears, and I'll get over this one too. I want to be there. I need answers."

Max gave her an appreciative nod, admiration flickering in his eyes.

As the bus continued its descent, spiraling deeper underground, Kyra focused on measuring her breaths.

In for four counts, hold for four, out for four.

Her fingers closed around her pendant, its familiar weight reassuring in her palm.

"Is that helping?" Jasmine asked quietly, nodding toward the pendant.

"Yes." Kyra managed a smile. "It has always guided me. I know that sounds strange, and I don't want you to think that your mother is a nut, but this stone is special."

"I don't think you are crazy." Jasmine smiled.

"The object itself might have no power on its own, but it might help you channel yours. I used a scrying stick that I made myself to find Ell-rom. Also, I still use the tarot cards you left me. I relied on them for guidance many times."

Kyra's heart leaped at that. "I left you tarot cards?"

"You did, and I put them to good use. I wish I'd had the foresight to bring them with me, but I left them in the village. If you'd like, I can bring them tomorrow, and we can do a reading together."

The tears Kyra had been holding back so valiantly and for so long finally spilled over. "I hate not remembering any of this."

Jasmine wrapped her arms around her shoulders. "Maybe the cards will jog your memory. Did you ever own another deck?"

Kyra shook her head.

"Awesome. I wonder if your hands retained the muscle memory of doing a spread."

Jasmine sounded light and upbeat, and Kyra knew that she was trying to cheer her up. It was working, and thinking about the tarot had managed to distract her from her sudden onset of claustrophobia.

Finally, the bus reached the lowest level, slowing to a stop before a large metal gate. As it began to slide open, Kyra caught sight of a solitary figure waiting on the other side—a tall, incredibly handsome man with an air of authority. He was impeccably dressed in a tailored charcoal suit.

"This is Kian," Syssi said, rising to her feet.

So, this was the clan leader. The man who had authorized the rescue mission, who had sent warriors halfway around the world based on his mate's visions.

The bus doors opened, and he climbed in, looking even more strikingly handsome up close, with an ageless beauty that marked him as a demigod.

"Welcome home," he said. "I would like to first thank the returning warriors who are heading to the village after this short stop. You've done an amazing job, and now that I know what you can do, be ready for more missions."

A rumble of voices sounded from the back of the bus where the Kra-ell sat.

Syssi moved to stand beside him, her hand slipping naturally into his. "Let me introduce you to our guests," she said as she walked him over to where Kyra was sitting with Jasmine. "Kian, this is Kyra. Kyra, this is Kian, my mate and the head of the local arm of the clan."

Kyra rose to her feet and extended her hand, meeting his steady gaze. "I owe you more than I can ever repay. Thank you for rescuing me and bringing me back to my daughter."

Kian's handshake was firm, his eyes measuring

as they assessed her. "You're welcome, and I'm sure you'll find a way to repay the favor. We are one big family here, and we take care of each other."

There was an underlying tension in him, something carefully controlled beneath the surface—the mark of someone who had a great responsibility resting on his shoulders. Lives depended on him.

She understood that.

"And this is Fenella," Syssi motioned to the woman. "Max's friend from Scotland."

Fenella stood and offered Kian her hand. "Thank you for the rescue and a place to stay."

"You're welcome." He shook her offered hand.

"These are Arezoo, Donya, Laleh, and Azadeh," Syssi said softly as if not to spook them. "They have the earpieces that William sent for them, so they can understand what is being said."

No one had told the four girls that they were surrounded by immortals, but they had seen the Kra-ell warriors, and it was difficult not to notice how alien they looked. Kyra had also forgotten that she'd introduced Jasmine as her sister and was now referring to her as her daughter. The girls must have picked up on that.

"Welcome," Kian said simply. "You don't need to worry about a thing. We will keep you safe."

The youngest girl, Laleh, actually smiled in response, while Arezoo, the eldest, gave a cautious nod and murmured her thanks.

"You'll have privacy, security, and whatever assistance you require. Our doctor will visit later today to assess your health and whether you need any treatment."

22

MAX

Max waited until the women were inside the elevator before heading to the cargo area of the bus. Part of him wanted to follow, to stay close to Kyra, but he had a job to do.

The Doomer wasn't going to process himself.

The cargo bay door opened with a hydraulic hiss, revealing the black body bag containing the self-proclaimed doctor. Max wrinkled his nose—the idea of what lay inside repulsed him.

"Want a hand with that?" Yamanu asked, peeking from the bus window.

He and Mey and the Kra-ell were returning to the village, and Syssi would go home with Kian. Max was staying, even though he didn't know what Onegus was planning for him yet. The chief might want him to resume his duties in the dungeon and relieve Alfie, who had taken over from him, or he might have something else in mind.

Max was planning on staying, and not just because he wasn't leaving the Doomer's interrogation to anyone else.

He wanted to stay close to Kyra.

Not that he had any plans of turning on the charm and seducing her right away. Even he wasn't that obtuse. For now, he would only offer her friendship while letting her know he was available for more if she was interested.

"I've got it," he told Yamanu. "Go back to your mate. I'm staying in the keep anyway."

Yamanu pursed his lips. "Did Onegus say anything about wanting you back in charge?"

Max shrugged. "Haven't heard anything yet. I'm going to request to stay here for now." He reached for the body bag. "I want to interrogate this scumbag personally."

"As you wish." Yamanu grinned before his head disappeared from the window.

Max reached for the bag, intending to sling the body over his shoulder, but the Doomer was stiff as a board and impossible to maneuver. Maybe he should have accepted Yamanu's help after all.

"Son of a bitch," he muttered.

"Let me give you a hand." A deep, heavily accented voice spoke from behind him.

Anton motioned at the bus. "Okidu will wait until I'm back. I'll help you carry this piece of shit to the dungeon."

"Thanks." Max gestured to the opposite end of the bag. "Grab that side."

Together, they lifted the awkward burden and carried it through the parking garage toward the elevator. The weight wasn't an issue, but the rigid body made maneuvering difficult.

"I didn't know that bodies in stasis got this stiff," Anton said.

"Me neither," Max admitted as they exited on the dungeon level. "Haven't dealt with many of them."

Anton arched a brow. "Really? How did all those Doomers get into your catacombs, then? Walk in by themselves?"

Max chuckled. "Good question. I just didn't get lucky enough to get a body in."

"First time for everything," Anton said. "Right?"

"I guess. And as firsts go, I want you to know that it was a pleasure fighting by your side."

The hybrid grinned. "Same here. I'll fight by your side anytime."

"Oh, wow." Alfie walked toward them. "All that bro love makes me emotional." He looked at the body bag. "Fresh meat?"

"One Doomer, not so fresh and in stasis," Max said. "Do you have a cell ready for him?"

Alfie nodded. "Follow me."

They trudged down the corridor lined with heavy metal doors. Each one concealed a prisoner—some human, some immortal, all dangerous in their own way. The keep had become the clan's de facto prison since they'd discovered the pedophilia ring run by the Brotherhood. Kian had insisted on keeping those monsters secure until they'd extracted every bit of useful intelligence out of them, and then they would be used for Ell-rom to test his powers on.

The sooner he killed all of them, the better. The Guardians manning the dungeon should be going on rescue missions instead of keeping an eye on these soulless creatures.

Alfie stopped at a cell near the end, aimed his phone at the scanner, and the door swung open. "This is the less secure interrogation cell. We still have the Doomer vermin in the other one."

"I know," Max said as he walked in with the body and Anton. "I ran this place. Remember?"

"Right." Alfie rubbed the back of his neck. "You can have the post back today if you want. I hate it down here. Not because I hate the dungeon but because of the occupants we have right now. This is the lowest of the low. The most evil of them all."

After Max and Anton had deposited their burden on the cot, the hybrid briskly rubbed his hands together as if trying to scrub away whatever contamination had clung to him from the body bag. "Good luck with the interrogation," he said, stepping back.

Alfie and Max followed Anton out of the cell, locking the door behind them.

"Got a name for me to input in the system?" Alfie asked.

Max shook his head. "This monster is known as 'the Doctor.' At least, that's what everyone at the compound called him. We found no ID on him."

"The Doctor it is, then." Alfie made a note on his tablet. "I heard that you brought back four potential Dormants?"

The excitement in Alfie's voice made Max uncomfortable. "Cool your jets," he said. "They're barely more than children. The oldest is nineteen."

Alfie shrugged. "Nineteen is old enough. Any of them pretty?"

Max stared at him, taken aback by the callousness of the question. The truth was, he honestly hadn't noticed. He'd been so fixated on Kyra and distracted by Fenella's presence that he'd barely paid attention to the girls.

"They're traumatized young women, not dating prospects," he said. "The poor things were cared for by Jade, Drova, and the other female warriors—not exactly the motherly or caring types. I didn't spend time assessing their appearance other than to scan for injuries."

Alfie raised his hands in surrender. "I was just curious. Don't be so touchy. We all deal with rescued trafficking victims, so you don't need to remind me that they are vulnerable right now. It's just that potential Dormants are a big deal."

"I know." Max let out a breath. "I'm just dirty, tired, and cranky."

Alfie nodded in understanding. "How did it go? I know that everyone came back in one piece, but I heard that Yamanu and Drova got hit."

"They did. Yamanu is as good as new, but Drova will take a while to heal. The Kra-ell are the best fighters I've ever seen, but they are more vulnerable to physical harm than we are."

Alfie leaned against the desk in the cell that had been turned into their command office. "How did the kid do other than get injured?"

"She was great. The girl's got a bright future on the force." He leaned against the wall, suddenly aware of how exhausted he was. "All the Kra-ell were incredible. They were like a well-oiled killing machine. You should have seen them tear through the Doomers. Unstoppable, and that includes the females. They are scary."

"Wish I could have been there," Alfie said. "Maybe next time."

"Yeah. They are good to have around when things get tough." Max pushed off from the wall.

"I'm dying for a shower and clean clothes. I'm heading upstairs to the apartment."

"Need anything else before you head up?"

Max shook his head. "I'm good. Thanks for the help."

As he walked back to the elevator, he suddenly felt all the exhaustion from the past few days settling over him. He hadn't gotten any sleep on the plane, and he could smell himself, which was gross.

When he got upstairs, the living room of the Guardians' apartment was thankfully empty, and his room was exactly as he'd left it. His bed was made, and everything was in its place.

Max liked his space clean and well organized.

Stripping off his filthy clothing, he dropped it into the hamper to wash later and turned on the water in the shower.

As the water heated, steam gradually filling the enclosure, Max's thoughts drifted to Kyra. The moment he'd placed the pendant in her hands, the pure joy that had transformed her face—he would fight a dozen more battles just to see that again.

He stepped under the spray, letting the scalding water wash away the reminders of the battle. If only emotional baggage could be so easily cleansed. Kyra would have her own demons to face and memories to process. He would need to be patient and resist his natural aggressiveness.

Max wasn't a patient guy, and women usually liked his no-nonsense, direct approach sweetened with a bit of charm. But Kyra wasn't like the women he usually went for. She needed time and space to heal, to reconnect with her daughter, and to find her footing in her new reality.

He would be there, offering friendship and support, making his interest clear but without pressure. And if—when—she was ready for more, he'd be there to fulfill her wishes.

Once there was nothing more to scrub, he turned the water off and rubbed a towel over his wet body. Dropping it in the laundry hamper, he returned naked to the bedroom and pulled fresh clothes from the dresser—simple jeans and a black T-shirt, comfortable but presentable enough for a visit to the penthouse.

23

KYRA

After Kian had escorted them to the penthouse and said a few more words of welcome, he excused himself and left them in the capable hands of his mate.

Kyra had a feeling he was going to check on the Doomer down in the dungeon, and she hoped he wouldn't start the interrogation without her. She'd meant it when she'd said she wanted to witness it.

She needed answers from that monster—she needed to understand what had been done to her and why. The memories of her first and second imprisonments were hazy, clouded by whatever drugs had been pumped into her system, but the emotions lingered—fear, helplessness, rage. She couldn't face those demons and put them to rest without having the full picture.

"Let me show you around," Syssi said, then

turned to Jasmine. "Maybe you want to do the honors? After all, you and Ell-rom were guests in here not too long ago."

Jasmine shook her head. "It's your place. You should do that."

What had she meant by that? That Syssi owned the gorgeous penthouse, or that it was where she lived when she was staying in the city?

"Is this your home?" Kyra asked.

"It used to be," Syssi said. "Kian lived here for many years, and then I joined him, and we lived here together for some time. When we moved the entire clan to the new village, Kian leased out this penthouse and the one across the vestibule that belonged to his sister, but then we realized that we needed these apartments for all kinds of guests, and after the last tenants left, we didn't lease them out again."

"Lucky us," Fenella said, turning in a circle. "I've never stayed in a place as fancy as this."

She was right.

The penthouse was spectacular. Floor-to-ceiling windows offered breathtaking views of the Los Angeles skyline. Everything spoke of luxury and comfort, from the plush sofas and armchairs to the state-of-the-art kitchen where a butler in uniform was working some culinary magic.

The smells were incredible, and Kyra's stomach

rumbled, reminding her that her last meal had been a while ago.

"This is the main living area," Syssi said as they moved through the space. "The two penthouses take up the entire top floor, and each one has its own terrace. There are three bedrooms in each, plus an office that has a convertible couch and can also be used as a bedroom if needed."

Kyra reached for her pendant, grounding herself with its familiar weight as she processed the opulence around her. How had she gone from living in a tent and using a communal bathroom in a half-ruined structure to a prison cell, and now to this?

The contrast was dizzying.

Syssi slid open a glass door, leading them out onto a terrace that wrapped around the corner of the building. "Each terrace has a lap pool and lush landscaping. Feel free to enjoy it anytime you want."

The pool was rectangular and long, its surface perfectly still in the windless afternoon. Potted trees provided shelter and seclusion, creating the illusion of a private oasis high above the city.

"It's like something from a movie," Arezoo breathed, voicing what Kyra had been thinking.

Once they were done exploring the terrace, they continued to the bedrooms.

"Each bedroom has its own bathroom." Syssi

opened a door to a room with twin beds. "The girls could share a room." She turned to Arezoo. "You and Donya in this one, and Laleh and Azadeh in the one over the hallway?"

Arezoo chewed on her lower lip for a moment. "I think Laleh should stay with me. Donya and Azadeh can take the other room."

"No problem." Syssi smiled. "All of the clothing in the closet is medium in size, and that should fit all of you. I'll write down your shoe sizes later and order some."

"Thank you," Arezoo said. "How will we ever pay you back for your kindness?"

"No payment will ever be required. We will help you in any way we can. That's what we do."

The doubt in Arezoo's eyes pierced Kyra's heart. The girl didn't have any reason to trust a stranger's promise, even after all that had been done for her and her younger siblings and cousin.

"I will not let anything happen to you," Kyra promised. "You have my word."

Arezoo nodded, but she still looked just as doubtful as before. "Thank you. But you are not in a better position than we are. We have nowhere to go, we are in a foreign country, and we don't have any money."

"She at least speaks the language," Donya murmured.

"That's true," Arezoo agreed. "It's a small advantage." She cast a suspicious glance at Jasmine and then back at Kyra. "You also have a relative who came to rescue you."

Kyra didn't miss the fact that Arezoo used the general term 'relative.' She'd obviously heard Kyra referring to Jasmine once as her sister and then as her daughter.

Sooner or later, they would have to explain to the girls what was going on, but it wasn't her decision. Her hosts had to decide when and how they wanted to enlighten the girls about the people surrounding them.

"So that's settled?" Syssi asked with mock cheerfulness. "The four of you will stay in these two adjacent bedrooms?"

Arezoo nodded. "We will. Thank you so much. The rooms are beautiful."

"Excellent." Syssi continued down the corridor. "This is the master suite." She opened the double doors and turned to Kyra. "I think you should stay in this one. The girls will feel more comfortable with you next door."

The room was so stunning that Kyra had a hard time formulating words. "Yes. Of course. I will be more than happy to stay in this gorgeous room." She walked in and spun around, taking in the four-poster bed on the elevated platform, the sitting area facing the fireplace, the bookcases overflowing with books. "I could live here for the rest of my life."

Syssi laughed. "I said the same thing the first time Kian brought me here."

"Sounds romantic," Fenella commented from behind them. "Where am I going to sleep? On the pullout couch in the office?"

"There are three more bedrooms in the other penthouse. Let's head over there."

"I don't want to be alone," Fenella muttered under her breath. "I'm very grateful and all that, and this is the fanciest place I've ever seen, but..."

"You won't be alone," Syssi said as she opened the double doors to the other penthouse. "Jasmine and Ell-rom will be staying here with you."

Jasmine arched a brow. "We will?"

"Well, yes. Someone who knows their way around the keep should stay here to take care of them until we figure out what's next, and I'm sure you want to spend as much time as you can with your...I mean with Kyra, now that you've found her."

"I do. But we don't have anything here. Ell-rom and I will need to go to the village and pack a bag. We can do that at night after everyone settles in."

Laleh looked suddenly stricken. "You're leaving us alone?"

Syssi's expression softened. "The building is

completely secure. There are Guardians stationed on the two floors below—"

"I'll stay," Ell-rom interrupted gently. "Jasmine can pack for both of us."

The relief on Laleh's face was immediate, and Kyra felt a surge of appreciation for her future son-in-law. There was something about him that radiated goodness and naturally put others at ease, a quiet strength that promised protection without demanding anything in return.

"Then it's settled," Syssi said. "Let's return to the other penthouse and eat lunch."

"Yes, let's." Kyra didn't need to be asked twice.

The delicious aromas wafting from the dining area had been teasing her senses since they arrived.

When they gathered around the table, she found an impressive spread of dishes—grilled chicken, roasted vegetables, fresh salads, and warm bread.

There was something odd about the butler. He didn't look young or pretty like the other immortals, but Kyra sensed that he wasn't human either. She wanted to ask Syssi about him, but with the girls listening, she had to wait.

Now that they all wore the translation earpieces, conversations that had once been private no longer were. The girls didn't yet know they were surrounded by immortals.

"This is incredible," Kyra said instead, savoring a bite of perfectly seasoned chicken.

"I am most gratified that you find the meal satisfactory," the butler responded with a perfect British accent and a dip bow that was almost comical.

Fenella, who was seated across from Kyra, raised an eyebrow but said nothing. She seemed to have noticed the same strangeness about the butler that Kyra had.

The conversation flowed naturally as they ate, carefully avoiding sensitive topics, with Jasmine telling stories about her acting career and Syssi talking about her baby daughter and showing everyone her pictures on her phone. No one mentioned captivity, torture, or the Doomer waiting in the dungeon below.

They were halfway through their meal when Kian returned. "I hope there is something left for me." He looked at the butler.

"Of course, master." He bowed again and rushed into the kitchen.

"Kian is vegan," Syssi explained. "He can't eat most of what's on the table."

"I can," he corrected as he took a seat next to his wife. "I just choose not to."

His presence at the table disturbed the relaxed ambiance they'd enjoyed before his arrival, but as the meal continued, hunger was satisfied, and exhaustion began to set in, relaxation followed.

The young girls looked ready to collapse, the combination of stress and relief taking its toll.

"Perhaps you should all rest after lunch," Syssi suggested. "It's been a long journey, and I'm sure all of you want to take a proper shower and get into a proper bed. As nice as the lie-flat seats on the jet are, they are not a substitute for a good mattress."

The butler bowed to Syssi. "Shall I serve coffee and tea, mistress?"

"Yes, please." She shifted her gaze to the girls. "You don't need to stay if you want to go to your rooms."

"Thank you." Arezoo looked grateful.

She rose to her feet and motioned for her sisters and cousin to get up.

They all murmured their thanks and goodnights, even though it was the middle of the day, before ducking out of the dining room.

The doorbell rang a few minutes later, and Kyra's heartbeat accelerated as she expected it to be Max.

He hadn't said he would be coming later, but she just knew he would, and she was proven right a moment later when the butler escorted him to the dining room.

He was freshly showered and changed—his blond hair still damp and combed back away from his handsome face. He wore simple jeans that hugged his muscular legs and a black T-shirt that emphasized the breadth of his shoulders.

A jolt of awareness shot through Kyra, sharp and sudden. She hadn't felt anything like it since—well, since forever, as far as she could remember.

Was she actually feeling attraction toward a man?

Max's eyes found hers immediately, his lips curving into a smile that seemed reserved just for her. "I hope there is still something left over for me."

"There is plenty," Syssi said. "Help yourself."

"Don't mind if I do." He sat down next to Kyra, where Arezoo had sat until a few moments ago.

As the butler rushed to put a clean plate and new utensils in front of him, Max leaned toward her. "Everything okay?"

"Perfect," she managed a smile, grateful that her voice sounded steadier than she felt. "This place is beyond anything I could have imagined."

What was happening to her? She'd never responded to a man this way—at least not since her memory began. In her years with the resistance, she'd been around plenty of men, some of them objectively handsome, but she'd felt nothing. No spark, no interest, no desire.

Yet here she was, practically vibrating with awareness of Max's presence.

Was this attraction a sign of healing? The first evidence that she was beginning to recover from her trauma? Or was there something specific about Max—some connection that transcended her usual barriers?

She was hyperaware of his presence beside her—the subtle scent of his soap, the warmth radiating from his body, and the occasional brush of his arm against hers when he reached for his water glass. Each small contact sent a current of electricity through her that was both thrilling and disturbing.

Across the table, Fenella watched their interaction with knowing eyes, a slight smirk playing at the corners of her mouth.

Syssi said something that Kyra hadn't paid attention to, and Max laughed, the sound of his voice sending a flutter through her chest.

What was it about this man that affected her so strongly? Was it just physical attraction or something deeper?

She thought of what Jasmine had told her about immortals—about mates and bonds that transcended ordinary connections. Was that what this was? Or was she simply grasping at magical explanations for a perfectly normal reaction to an attractive man?

Either way, she wasn't ready to explore it—not with so much uncertainty still clouding her past and future. Not with the Doomer downstairs, holding answers to questions she'd carried for decades. But neither was she willing to ignore the first spark of genuine desire she'd felt in her remembered lifetime.

24

MAX

Max felt the current crackling between him and Kyra—a tangible thing, like static electricity but warmer, more vital. He'd seen how Kyra's pupils had dilated when he'd entered the room and heard the almost imperceptible catch in her breathing when he sat beside her.

The awareness was mutual, and her reaction sent a surge of satisfaction through him.

Patience, he reminded himself. *Let her come to you.*

It was against his nature to wait, to play the passive role in any pursuit. But Kyra had been through hell and hadn't had any time to speak of to piece herself together yet. The last thing she needed was a guy, hyped up on centuries of confidence, coming after her.

As everyone moved to the living room, Max followed Kyra to the grouping of plush couches and armchairs, admiring the straight line of her spine and the confident set of her shoulders that were evident despite the baggy clothes she was wearing.

The trauma she'd endured hadn't broken her spirit—a fact he found impressive but also moving.

"What do we do about the girls?" Kyra asked in a hushed voice as they settled on a couch. She glanced toward the hallway leading to the bedrooms. "It's becoming difficult to hide what's going on from them. Arezoo is very perceptive. She doesn't miss much."

Syssi smiled. "You can speak normally. The penthouse has excellent soundproofing, and the doors to their bedrooms are closed. They can't hear us."

"Because they're human," Kyra clarified, still keeping her voice low.

"Even immortals can't hear through these closed doors unless someone is really loud." Syssi shot Kian a playful glance, a blush spreading across her cheeks.

Max stifled a chuckle at Syssi's unexpected innuendo. It was strangely endearing that she still blushed like a teenager.

He glanced at Kyra, wondering if she blushed as

well—wondering what it might take to make that happen.

Kian shifted in his armchair, looking uncomfortable, probably because of the amused looks he was getting. "We should wait to tell the girls about who we are until we have some answers. If we confirm that they are Dormants as we suspect, then we can tell them because they will be coming with us to the village."

"What if something slips out?" Kyra asked.

"Don't worry about it," Kian said. "We can thrall them to forget anything they shouldn't know yet, but it's much easier to thrall the memory of a little slip-up than the whole tale of gods and immortals. I always maintain that the less thralling, the better, especially for women as young as they are with still malleable minds."

Kyra didn't seem to agree, but she didn't voice her objections.

Fenella, on the other hand, seemed eager to do so. "What about us?" she asked, gesturing between herself and Kyra.

"You will join our community in the village." He turned to Fenella. "If you prefer to live in Scotland, you can choose to join the immortal community there instead. They will welcome you with open arms."

"Max mentioned I'd be in high demand." Fenella cast him a sidelong glance.

"Yes, you will," Kian confirmed. "We are always looking for Dormants and immortals to enrich our gene pool."

Fenella winced, sinking back into her chair. "I didn't picture my future living in a small village again," she admitted. "I enjoyed traveling the world, seeing new places, meeting new people." A shadow crossed her face. "But it's not safe out there, is it? Not even for an immortal with all the advantages that come with it."

Fenella had been on her own for five decades, surviving by her wits. No wonder she had grown rough around the edges. If Din decided to pursue her again, he would find a much harder woman than the barmaid he'd fallen in love with. Then again, she'd always been feisty and outspoken, but now she had decades of experience to back up her bravado.

"What did you do for money?" he asked.

A mischievous smile teased the corners of her mouth. "Poker."

Jasmine laughed. "What a wonderful coincidence. I'm an excellent poker player, and I was one even before I turned immortal. I never played for money, though. My father warned me that it would only bring me trouble, and in this one instance, I actually listened."

Fenella's smile wilted. "Your father is a smart

man. Not that I had a choice. How else was I going to survive?"

"How did you do that?" Syssi asked. "You turned immortal as an adult, so you couldn't thrall people to get into their minds."

"I didn't have to," Fenella said. "People don't realize how much they give away with their scents. Fear, excitement, disappointment—it all smells different. Between that and watching for the tiniest changes in their body language, I always knew what kind of hand my opponents had."

"You can smell those emotions because you are immortal," Kian said. "Humans can't smell that."

"Oh." She scrunched her nose. "I thought that I was just good at sniffing those out. I didn't know it came with immortality."

"How did you end up in that prison?" Max asked.

The question had been bothering him since they'd found her.

Fenella's expression shuttered, her eyes darkening. "That's why I said that Jasmine's father is a smart man. It was the poker that got me in trouble. I was unfortunate enough to meet the so-called doctor in a poker game. And even more unfortunate to lose to him, which I now know was because he could thrall me."

"He couldn't," Max corrected her misconception. "Immortals can thrall humans but not other immortals. But he could smell you."

"I see." Her voice grew flat, emotionless. "He beat me at my own game. He seemed to know exactly what cards I held each time." She paused, swallowing visibly. "When I couldn't pay, he demanded compensation of a certain kind." She let the statement hang in the air, allowing them to draw their own conclusions. "As I said, it's not safe for women out there. Not even immortals."

A heavy silence settled over the group. Max felt a cold fury building in his chest, his fangs elongating in response to the implied brutality Fenella had endured.

"I'm sorry," he said quietly. It seemed wholly inadequate, but what else could he offer?

Fenella gave a small smile. "I survived. I'm here. That's all that matters."

"When will Bridget arrive?" Syssi asked, addressing the question to Kian but glancing at Kyra.

"Tomorrow. I spoke to her and told her that everyone looked exhausted and that we should postpone the health check."

"What about the sedative?" Jasmine asked. "It will be completely gone from their bodies."

"It's already gone," Kyra said. "I'm back to myself. Will the doctor check the girls to determine if they are Dormants?"

"We don't have tests for that," Kian said. "We will have to get the answers out of that Doomer. He must have been working on something. It wasn't a coincidence that the six of you were under his so-called care."

An uncomfortable silence fell over the group.

"What if he just got lucky?" Fenella muttered. "He found me by chance."

Max considered this. "I think he knew what he was looking for."

"He was looking for me," Kyra said quietly. "He told me that he'd been searching for a long time. He knew what I turned into and how."

Kian let out a breath. "If the Brotherhood has found a way to identify Dormants, they will hunt for them to add to their breeders so they can grow their army of immortals even faster."

The implications sent a chill down Max's spine.

The Doomers always had an advantage over the clan because they didn't allow their breeders to transition. They only activated the boys so they could join Navuh's army but left the girls dormant so they could produce the maximum number of children. They didn't want them turning immortal and their fertility plummeting as a result.

He glanced at Kyra, expecting to see concern on her face. Instead, he found determined calculation—the look of a strategic mind assessing a threat and formulating countermeasures.

It was the expression of a commander, not a victim.

Fates, she was magnificent.

"When are we going to interrogate him?" she asked.

"Tomorrow," Kian said. "I know that you want to be there, but you need to rest. One night of recovery won't change much in the grand scheme of things."

"I've never been a patient woman," Kyra said. "My team often chided me for my impulsiveness." She clutched her pendant. "I always trusted my instincts."

"Oh, do tell." Fenella leaned back against the soft couch cushions. "Your life must have been so exciting."

"Not really," Kyra said. "I have a few good stories, though."

When she launched into the story of her latest prisoner rescue, Max's admiration for her grew with every twist of her tale.

When Kyra caught him looking, those golden-flecked eyes meeting his directly, Max didn't bother to hide his admiration.

The small smile she offered in return sent a jolt of warmth through him.

25

KYRA

"Here you go," Max handed Ell-rom a pair of loose gym pants and a T-shirt. "These should fit you."

"Thank you." Ell-rom tucked the small bundle under his arm. "I couldn't wait for Jasmine to return with our things to wash the filth off."

None of their saviors had showered on the plane, so the saved would have enough water to wash themselves, which Kyra appreciated greatly and had taken advantage of, but she craved a proper shower in the beautiful bathroom in the luxurious master suite.

More than that, though, she craved time alone with Max.

Syssi and Kian had departed a while ago, taking

Jasmine with them to the village, and now Ell-rom was leaving for the other penthouse, but Fenella didn't show any indications of wanting to retire for the evening.

The silence that settled over the living room after Ell-rom's departure was oppressive. He'd been the one doing most of the talking for the past hour, telling her and Fenella the incredible story of his seven-thousand-year journey from the planet of the gods to Earth and how Jasmine had found him and his twin sister mere days before they would have expired.

Max had explained about stasis and how it worked only for immortals and not the Kra-ell, and he'd also said something about the Fates guiding Jasmine's hand.

It hadn't been the first time the Fates had been mentioned, and Kyra wondered if the belief in them was part of the clan's lore or something more.

Perhaps she could ask him about that to fill the awkward silence.

She glanced at his profile, sharp and handsome without an iota of softness in him, but she'd witnessed his kindness, so she knew that the tough exterior didn't reflect the much gentler interior.

He evoked something in her that she hadn't felt before.

Not that she could remember, but she must have loved Jasmine's father for him to have loved her back so fiercely. Her heart still clenched at the thought of his suffering. It hadn't been her fault, but she still felt responsible for his pain.

With a sigh, she reached for a magazine that had been left on the table and started flipping pages, just to appear busy while examining these unfamiliar stirrings that were both exciting and peculiar.

She'd met her share of good men, kind, handsome, and smart, but none of them had evoked anything other than feelings of friendship or camaraderie. Her feminine awareness of Max felt like a revelation—a sign that perhaps she was healing, that her captors hadn't bludgeoned this part of her to death.

She needed to find out whether she could act on it.

Max had been giving all the signs that he was interested, so she knew her advances would be reciprocated, and she also knew that he would accept whatever she was comfortable with and wouldn't push for more.

She barely knew him, so that confidence wasn't based on anything tangible, but she trusted her instincts, especially when she had her pendant back to warn her when she needed to watch out.

Kyra lifted her hand to it, drawing comfort

from its familiar warmth. The amber stone seemed to hum with quiet energy against her skin, validating her instincts.

Fenella shifted on the couch, glancing between them with knowing eyes. After another moment of pointed silence, she yawned dramatically, stretching her arms overhead.

"I think I'm going to follow Ell-rom's example and get a proper shower," she announced. "Then it's off to bed with me. I've been thinking about that fluffy down blanket ever since I saw it."

Max stood up. "Do you need me to escort you to your room?"

Kyra tensed, suddenly unsure of her assessment. What if Max was more interested in Fenella? He'd spent most of the way back sitting next to the woman, and she'd heard them talking and laughing like the best of friends.

Fenella waved him off. "I'm sure it's safe for me to cross that magnificent foyer on my own and find my bedroom." She shot Kyra a quick smile. "Goodnight, Kyra. I'll see you tomorrow morning."

"Goodnight," Kyra said.

Once the door closed behind Fenella, the awkward silence returned. A new type of tension filled the space—anticipation mingled with uncertainty.

Kyra searched for something to say, some bit of small talk to fill the silence, but she'd never been good at coming up with trivial things to talk about, and speaking of the upcoming interrogation would kill the mood.

"So," Max said after several moments, leaning forward. "Tell me how you rose into the ranks of the Kurdish resistance forces. How did you become a leader?"

Kyra considered the question, debating whether to respond or simply cut to the heart of what was happening between them. She didn't have much time—Ell-rom might return from his shower at any moment.

"I don't think you're really interested in the Kurdish resistance," she said, deciding to be true to herself and shoot straight.

Max's lips curved into a half-smile. "I'm mildly interested in the resistance but very interested in you."

"Why?"

She knew she was a good-looking woman, but a man like Max must have had many who were more beautiful and not as damaged. Then again, there was a shortage of available immortal mates, so it might be less about who she was than what she was.

Instead of answering directly, Max tilted his head. "Do you feel it? The connection between us?"

The pendant seemed to warm against her skin, almost as if responding to his words, and Kyra let out a slow breath. "Yes," she admitted. "And it mystifies me because I have never felt anything like it—at least not that I can remember." She hesitated before adding, "I don't remember ever inviting a man to my bed."

The thought flickered through her mind that the fake doctor hadn't waited for an invitation, but he didn't count. She pushed the ugly memory aside, refusing to let it taint this moment.

Max's expression softened, and he rose from the armchair and came to sit next to her on the couch, but not so close that they were touching. He'd left a couple of inches between them.

When he extended his hand, palm up, the invitation was clear but undemanding.

Kyra placed her hand in his, and a jolt of awareness shot up her arm at the simple contact. It was as if a circuit had been completed, electricity flowing between them.

"Did you feel that?" she asked, her voice hushed with wonder.

"Yes." His fingers curled around hers.

The confirmation was both reassuring and bewildering. This wasn't just her imagination or some desperate need for connection. Something real was happening between them.

"Is it because we're both immortal?"

Max's thumb traced small circles on the back of her hand, each feather-light touch sending sparks through her nervous system. "It's the will of the Fates."

There it was again. "What do you mean by that? Is it some kind of myth about matchmaking Fates?"

26

MAX

Where to even begin?

Max rubbed the back of his neck. "The clan doesn't have any official belief system, but we loosely believe in the three Fates guiding people's destinies. One of the major tenets of that belief is that the Fates reward the most worthy of us with a truelove mate. Matching two people who are so perfect for each other that they immediately feel a strong pull, and the bond they form is so powerful it binds them for life."

Kyra smiled. "That sounds lovely, but it doesn't work like that in reality."

Max hoped that she would find out that, for a few lucky immortals, it was precisely how it worked.

"I used to think that it was a myth, something

our mothers told us to encourage us to be good people so one day the Fates would reward us with the most precious gift any immortal can hope for. But now I know it to be true. I've seen the Fates make the most unlikely pairs, people who meet under the most extraordinary circumstances and form an unbreakable bond. Syssi and Kian have that. Jasmine and Ell-rom have it. Mey and Yamanu. There are many more examples in the clan. And the thing is that it all started with Amanda finding Syssi about five years ago and getting her to meet Kian."

Kyra regarded him with a doubtful expression on her face, and he couldn't blame her. If someone had told him this story five years ago, he would have looked at them with the same half-smile that bordered on pity because he would have thought them naive romantics.

"What makes a person worthy?" Kyra asked.

Max hadn't expected that question. Frankly, he'd expected the brush-off.

"The belief is that they need to sacrifice a lot for others or suffer a lot themselves." He chuckled. "In our case, you qualify on both accounts, and I qualify on neither. I've had a pretty good life that didn't involve much suffering, and other than being a Guardian and fighting to rescue people the world has forgotten about, I haven't sacrificed much for others either."

Kyra's eyes softened. "You are doing God's work, Max, and you are doing it day in and day out. So don't belittle your worthiness. Besides, maybe I'm not such a great catch as you imagine me to be. I'm broken. I put on a brave face, and I plow forward, but on the inside, I'm damaged goods."

"We are all broken on some level. Everyone who has lived for a while and encountered the evils of this world either in person or as a witness has pieces of their soul missing. But when two souls that are meant for each other merge, they have the power to mend those missing pieces, to fill them up with the other's essence."

Max had never given much thought to these matters before, and the words pouring out of his mouth were not rehearsed or even thought through, but that didn't mean they weren't true. He believed in every word he'd said, even though he couldn't have said any of that before meeting Kyra.

She looked at him with a sheen of tears brightening her golden eyes. "That was a very romantic thing to say. I didn't take you for the sensitive type."

"I'm not." He smiled sheepishly. "I don't know where all of that came from. Well, that's not true. You are the inspiration for my poetic take on truelove mates. But I really believe in what I said."

She shook her head. "You are not in love with me, Max. You don't even know me."

"I don't claim to love you yet, but if you will allow me in, love will follow. And I swear that's not a come-on line."

She regarded him from under lowered lashes. "What do you usually say to the girls?"

He snorted. "Not much, really." He lifted his hand and smoothed it over his blond hair, which was shortly cropped at the sides and long in the front. "All I need to do is show up. They come to me."

He'd said that to lighten the mood and expected Kyra to berate him for being vain, but she didn't. Instead, she smiled and nodded. "I believe that. You are sinfully handsome." She sighed. "I seem to have a thing for blond men. Jasmine's father looks like he was blond as a young man."

Max had seen Boris up close, so he knew the man was no competition, but he still felt a surge of jealousy when Kyra bundled him with other light-haired men.

"Boris is fat and bald now, so don't entertain any thoughts about him."

Kyra laughed. "It's adorable how jealous you get at the mention of another man. It makes me think that you are sincere and really think I'm the one for you."

"I do."

"Wow." Kyra pushed a strand of hair behind her ear. "You are serious, and I'm clueless. I don't know how to respond to that."

He gently squeezed her hand. "Just be yourself and do whatever comes naturally. I have no expectations, and I will not be offended or hurt by anything you do or say." He smiled. "I have a pretty thick skin."

"I don't want to offend you, but there is something I need to do to prove to myself that I'm not as broken as I thought I was. That I can still heal."

"Whatever you need, I'm here for you."

She hesitated, chewing on her lower lip and making him want to free that puffy pillow from between her teeth and suck it into his mouth. When she lifted her hand and cupped his cheek, he leaned into her touch.

"Your skin is so smooth," she whispered.

"I shaved," he murmured.

27

KYRA

"Thank you," Kyra said quietly. "Did you do it for me?"

He didn't move, resting his cheek on her palm. "I just wanted to look good for you. I didn't expect you to touch me."

Max's pupils were dilated, and his grip on Kyra's hand was tight but not painful.

For a big man like him, Max was surprisingly gentle and very aware that he could easily become intimidating if he didn't keep his own desires under tight control.

He was putting himself at her service, allowing her complete control over the situation, and that not only touched her heart but also sent a new wave of desire through her, with unexpected heat pooling low in her belly.

God, she hadn't felt anything like that before, and it was intoxicating.

It made her feel alive.

"I wish..." she started and didn't continue because she wasn't sure what she wished for.

Looking less haggard and wearing something that actually fit her? Being less broken and more forward with her newly discovered affections?

"What do you wish for?" Max asked.

"I don't know. Maybe for us to meet under different circumstances—without the taint of my past. I wish I could be fresh and naive and excited like a young girl spending her first evening alone with a boy."

He lifted his head from her palm. "We can pretend that if you wish." There was mischief in his eyes but also longing and desire, which elicited a corresponding reaction from her.

She chuckled. "I don't even know what a young, inexperienced girl would act like."

He shrugged. "And I can hardly remember being a boy, but we can just make it be whatever we want. We can start with a little kiss."

"I'd like that," she said softly, leaning toward him before she'd consciously decided to move.

Max moved with deliberate slowness, telegraphing his intentions as he closed the distance between them. Placing a hand on her cheek, he kept his eyes on hers until her lids fluttered closed.

The first brush of his lips against hers was feather-light, almost tentative. Just the barest contact, yet it sent a cascade of sensations through her body. Her pendant pulsed against her skin, warm and happy, as if it was responding to the connection and liking it as much as she did.

Max drew back a little, his eyes searching hers. "Okay?"

In answer, Kyra leaned forward again, pressing her lips more firmly to his. This time, the kiss deepened naturally, his mouth moving against hers with gentle purpose. His hand slid from her cheek to cup the back of her neck, fingers threading into her hair.

The pendant's warmth spread through her chest, radiating outward until her entire body felt suffused with heat. Every nerve ending seemed to awaken, responding to his touch with an intensity that was almost overwhelming after so long of feeling nothing.

When they finally parted, Kyra was breathless, and her heart was pounding as if she'd run a great distance. "That was...nice."

"Yeah," Max agreed, his own breathing slightly uneven. "It was."

They stared at each other for a long moment, something unspoken passing between them. Then

Max smiled, the expression lighting up his entire face.

"What?" Kyra asked.

"You're blushing," he said, sounding inordinately pleased with the observation.

Kyra raised a hand to her cheeks, surprised to find them warm to the touch. "I am. I don't think I've ever blushed before."

"Of course not." He assumed a stern expression. "A rebel leader cannot blush. She needs to be fierce at all times."

"That's right," she picked up on his teasing tone. "What kind of leader would I be if I blushed whenever a handsome guy decided to kiss me?"

Max shook his head vigorously. "Not any handsome guy. Just me."

"Yes, Max. Just you."

She doubted anyone else would have made her feel so safe, so normal. He'd made her feel like a woman rather than a survivor or even a warrior. He'd helped her relearn how to feel desire and joy in a simple physical connection.

"Thank you." He dipped his head. "I'm not the sharing kind, and I want this beautiful blush to be mine and mine alone."

She sobered. "For how long?"

He seemed confused by her question. "What do you mean? It's forever."

The guy was sweet, but he was getting carried

away by the wings of romance. In real life, things didn't start with a little kiss and end up in eternal love.

"We are not truelove mates, Max. We might be, but we are not there yet. What I meant was that if you expect me to reserve my blush just for you, I expect the same in return, at least until we find out where this is going."

He seemed offended by her suggestion. "I'm yours, Kyra, for as long as you will have me, and I hope it's forever, but if it's not, then until you tell me to get lost."

She swallowed. Even thinking of such an eventuality was difficult, and that was absurd given that they weren't even a couple yet.

"Let's take it one day at a time," she murmured.

"I get it." He leaned over, stopping a fraction of an inch away from her mouth. "You want to take it slow. Want to try another kiss? That one was just the appetizer."

"Yes," she said. "I do."

As their mouths fused, Max snaked his arm under her bottom and lifted her onto his lap, but just as his tongue was about to breach the seal of her lips, the penthouse front door opened, and the two of them jumped apart like a couple of teenagers caught red-handed, doing something they were not supposed to.

"Sorry to interrupt." Fenella walked in and beelined for the kitchen. "I got hungry and came for the leftovers."

28

MAX

Max woke with a start, sheets tangled around his legs and the vivid remnants of his dream still burning behind his eyelids. Kyra's face, Kyra's lips, Kyra's body pressed against his—images that had tormented him through the night, leaving him aroused and frustrated.

He groaned, throwing an arm over his eyes. It had been a rough night, cycling between dreams of Kyra and periods of forced wakefulness as he tried not to disrespect her by taking matters into his own hands, so to speak. Though he wondered if she'd even find that offensive.

Some women might be flattered that a man fantasized about them.

But with Kyra, he wasn't willing to take any chances. Fates knew he'd screwed up enough relationships in his long life—not with women so much since meaningful relationships with humans had been impossible, but with friends and family.

He wasn't particularly smooth or naturally considerate, and despite his best efforts, someone always seemed to get hurt by an unintentional callous remark or something he was supposed to do but didn't, or vice versa.

Max wasn't going to screw it up with Kyra, though. She was too important to him.

Those two nearly chaste kisses they'd shared in the penthouse had blown his mind despite their simplicity. Just lips meeting lips, nothing more, yet they had been more profound than the best sex he'd had.

Maybe because she was the one, his one and only, his truelove mate, and nothing and no one could ever compare.

Was he jumping the gun on this?

Nah. He knew in his heart and gut that he was right. He just needed to prove it to Kyra.

After a quick cold shower, he dressed and made his way to the kitchen. The coffeemaker was already brewing, and its rich aroma was a welcome greeting. Alfie stood at the counter, staring blearily at his phone while waiting for the pot to finish.

"Morning," Max said, pulling two mugs from the cabinet.

Alfie grunted in response.

As the coffeemaker announced its completion with a beep, Max filled both mugs, sliding one toward Alfie before doctoring his own with cream and sugar.

"You're up early," Alfie observed, seeming to gain coherence with the first sip of coffee. "Are you on shift today?"

"I haven't gotten my assignment yet. I need to talk to the chief and see if I can stay here. I have a vested interest in that Doomer and an even greater one in Kyra."

There was no point in trying to hide his feelings for her. The more people knew that she was his, the better. He didn't want any competition.

Alfie cracked a smile. "Congrats. Does she return the interest?"

"It's too early to tell." Max didn't feel right to say that she did. It was better to leave things vague and let Alfie's imagination fill in the gaps. "I'm working on it," he added to make it clear that Kyra was off-limits.

"Good luck." Alfie finished his coffee, rinsed out the cup, and put it on the drying rack. "I'm heading out."

"Just a reminder," Max said. "I want to be the one interrogating the Doomer, so don't start without me. I'll be down after I talk to Onegus."

Alfie nodded. "Don't worry about it. We won't start anything until Kian gets here, and I don't expect him before ten. You know how the traffic is in the morning. He will want to avoid it."

"True. Do you know if he's bringing Toven?" Max asked.

The god's compulsion ability made interrogations easy—just ask a question, and the prisoner physically couldn't refuse to answer or lie—but where was the fun in that?

"I wasn't told, but probably." Alfie shrugged. "Things go much smoother with Toven doing the questioning."

"Yeah," Max agreed. "But I don't want easy. I want to beat that scumbag to a pulp and get him to sing the old-fashioned way."

A savage grin spread across Alfie's face. "I'm with you there." He clapped Max on the back. "Better get going."

After Alfie left, Max walked over to the couch, pulled out his phone, and sat down to call the chief.

"Good morning, Max," Onegus answered. "All rested and ready for your next assignment?"

Max had no doubt that the chief had already gotten detailed updates from Yamanu and Jade, so he didn't need to bother with a repeat unless Onegus had specific questions for him.

"I'd like to stay at the keep and resume my dungeon duty here if you don't mind."

"I don't. But it surprises me that you wish to

stay. You didn't like being cooped up with the vermin in the dungeon."

"I don't, but I want to interrogate the scumbag we brought back with us, and I want to stay close to Kyra. She might be the one for me."

Honesty was the best approach. Besides, with how fast rumors traveled through the clan, by tomorrow at the latest everyone would know that he and Kyra were an item.

For once, he was thankful for the rumor machine. He didn't want any of the single males getting ideas.

Kyra was taken.

"Congratulations, Max. I'm happy for you. You can resume your post and keep Alfie as your second so you can leave the dungeon whenever Kyra needs you."

That was unexpected and extremely generous of the chief, especially given how short they were on Guardians lately.

"I appreciate that," Max said. "I know how stretched thin we are these days."

"Kyra is the priority. She might hold the key to finding Khiann, and every member of the clan owes it to Annani to do their best to help that happen. Just try not to screw things up."

Max winced. "Thanks, chief."

"You are welcome. Good luck." Onegus ended the call.

Max pocketed his phone and headed for the elevator that would take him down to the dungeon level.

As the doors slid open, revealing the corridor that led to the secure cells, Max strode straight toward the cell he had left the so-called doctor at, his boots echoing against the polished concrete floor.

He'd put the monster in stasis, so unless there had been flooding in the cell, the guy was still in the same state he'd left him in. Max peeked through the small window at the top of the door anyway.

"You're going to tell us everything," he murmured, his breath fogging the reinforced glass. "Every last detail about what you did to those women, how you found them, and what you were looking for. And when I'm done with you, there won't be enough of you left to bury."

There was no response, of course, but saying the words aloud felt cathartic in a small way. Acting on them would feel so much better.

This wasn't just about revenge, though that was certainly a big part of it. It was about understanding what the Brotherhood was planning, how they were identifying Dormants, and what threat that posed to the clan.

And it was about justice for Kyra, for the years

stolen from her, for the trauma inflicted on her mind and body.

Max's phone buzzed in his pocket, and as he pulled it out, he saw a text from Alfie.

Kian's ETA 9:00 AM. Bringing Toven.

Max muttered a vile curse under his breath.

So, they were going the compulsion route after all.

29

KIAN

Kian rested his elbow against the SUV's tinted window and watched the city slide past. He felt a steady hum under his feet as the vehicle navigated a sparse stretch of highway on its way to the keep. Next to him, Toven sat with a notepad and a pencil, sketching what seemed to be a silhouette of a woman.

"What are you drawing?" he asked the god.

Toven shrugged. "I'm just relaxing before the interrogation. I don't enjoy dealing with filth, so I try to fill my mind with beauty before we get started."

Kian understood that perfectly, and he wished he had some artistic talent that could help take the edge off. Regrettably, he only knew how to do that with a smoke or a drink, and he had neither with him. He didn't have any smokes in the keep either, but at least he had a bottle of whiskey stashed in his old office.

Perhaps he could send Anandur to get him some cigarillos. Even cigarettes would do in a pinch.

Weariness settled in his chest, but he shoved it aside. The clan's work was never done, and there were always more monsters prowling in the night. This particular fiend played at being a doctor, and Kian had a feeling that he would be one of the worst he'd ever encountered.

He stifled a chuckle.

How many times had he thought that, and how many times had he discovered that there were worse demons out there and that there was no end to depravity.

"I need to know where you want me to begin," Toven said.

Kian shifted in his seat. "Start with the basics. We don't even know his name. We only know him as the Doctor, which is a lie. He's no physician, but he pretends to be. I also want to know his position in the Brotherhood and his relationship to Navuh. He's not one of the adopted sons, but Dalhu's information might be outdated, and I haven't checked with Lokan about new players."

Toven nodded. "I assume you also want to

know whether he was in Iran on the Brotherhood's orders or doing his thing on the side."

It hadn't even occurred to Kian that the Doomer might have been pursuing a private agenda. It was very difficult for Doomers to step out of line. They were always sent out in teams, and the team members kept rotating so no one gained a following or could do things behind Navuh's back. The Brotherhood's leader had learned his lesson after Kalugal, his own flesh and blood son, had assembled an entire platoon of warriors who had been loyal only to him and then given Navuh the slip during WWII.

"That's a good suggestion. I need to know his local ties and his connections to the regime." Kian let out a breath. "I suspect that he's found a method of identifying Dormants, and I hope he hasn't shared it with the rest of his brethren."

Toven put his small sketchpad in his pocket. "How likely is that?"

"Not very likely. The rank-and-file Doomers are clueless about Dormants. Navuh wants them to believe that only the Dormants on the island exist —the descendants of those he inherited from his father. They have no idea, or at least that was true until now, that there are Dormants in the general population."

Toven arched a brow. "How can they be so

blind? They know that they themselves start as Dormants and are induced into immortality. Don't they deduce that their sisters might be Dormants as well?"

Kian shrugged. "Perhaps the new generation of smart immortals Navuh is breeding will figure it out, but the older generations believed what they were told. Even if they knew, they believed that females are only good for breeding, and therefore inducing the girls' transition would be a waste of resources because their fertility would dramatically drop. They need the women to produce as many males as possible for Navuh's army."

"That ignorance is carefully cultivated," Toven murmured.

"It's possible that the Doctor is close enough to Navuh to have been told the truth, but the more likely scenario is that he encountered Kyra by chance. I need to know how he found her, though. What she was doing in that institute and what he did to her."

"You assume that he didn't know she was a Dormant when he encountered her."

Kian nodded. "He obviously took advantage of her and inadvertently induced her transition. Then, when she broke free and set other women loose, he must have realized where her super strength came from. They probably had camera surveillance in there. He could have seen a recording of her breaking chains and shattering doors."

"He could have thought that it was a psychotic episode," Toven said. "Maybe in combination with the drugs she was given. Humans can summon great strength in short bursts."

"He knew what he was giving her, so he wouldn't have had another explanation for it. She'd gone in a normal woman. Then the sedation wore off, and she had the strength and reflexes of an immortal. I want you to confirm all that."

Toven nodded slowly. "So, the theory is that the Doctor is dealing with personally discovered information, and we hope that he hasn't shared it with the Brotherhood and is operating on his own." The god lifted his smart eyes to Kian's. "Perhaps he figured he could have a little breeding program of his own on the side and start building his own army of immortals."

"That's possible. I think that's the main reason Navuh convinced the Brotherhood that the only Dormants in existence are on the island. He didn't want anyone to get any bright ideas."

"Did you ask the rescued women if the Doctor told them anything about his plans?"

Kian shook his head. "They just got here, and they are still shaken from their ordeal. I'd rather get the answers from the Doomer than torment the women with questions that will bring them pain."

Toven nodded. "I agree. Anything else you want me to ask him?"

"The team brought back four human girls," Kian said, leaning back and stretching his legs. "I want to know if they were taken because he thought they were Dormants."

Toven's forehead wrinkled in thought. "Did you ask them about paranormal abilities?"

"No," Kian admitted. "I didn't for the same reason I didn't ask them anything else. I'd rather get it all out of him."

The SUV slowed as Anandur steered off the main road onto the driveway leading to the keep's underground garage.

Kian ran a hand over his face. "It's borderline amazing, and not in a good way, how many atrocities we've learned about in the last few weeks alone. I half-wish I could close my eyes and pretend the world is normal. That no one else is hunting Dormants, or trafficking people, or preying on children." He gave Toven a tight smile. "But you and I both know that ignorance isn't bliss. It just allows the monsters to run free."

As the SUV descended the spiraling ramp into the keep's lower underground levels, Kian felt a slight shift in pressure, a reminder that they were going deeper than any standard basement or parking garage.

Finally, the SUV rolled to a stop, and Anandur cut the engine.

Brundar opened his door first, stepping out swiftly to scan the area. There wouldn't be a threat in the clan's secure parking level, but the Guardian was always vigilant.

Besides, Kian had been attacked in this very garage by Igor and held at fang point, so there was that. Brundar had taken his failure to protect Kian almost as hard as Kian had taken having his blood sucked by that fiend.

He took a slow breath, then pushed the SUV door open and stepped onto the smooth concrete. The air held a chill and a musty smell that always lingered underground. He patted his coat pocket, confirming that his compulsion-filtering earpieces were on hand. He would need them once Toven got started.

Toven emerged beside him. "We're heading straight to the interrogation room, right?"

"Not right away. He's in stasis, so Anandur is going to soak him in water first to revive him. Then he's going to be mildly sedated, and only then will we go in. Kyra wants to be part of the interrogation, but she's going to be disappointed that we are using compulsion instead of letting Max beat the shit out of the monster. She was looking forward to that."

Toven arched a brow. "That doesn't sound like the traumatized victim you described."

"She is a strange combination of victim and warrior. She's been hurt badly, but she's not ready to roll over and play dead. She's ready to fight."

30

KYRA

Kyra had lain awake for hours in the too-comfortable bed in the too-big room. Ironically, she missed her tent and her narrow cot, and she missed her friends. But she reminded herself to count her blessings and focus on what she had gained and not what she'd left behind.

Having both was not possible, and the choice was obvious.

She wasn't going back.

She finally knew who she was and where she belonged. She was with her daughter, and she'd found a male she was actually interested in.

But this new normal, which was anything but, still felt too foreign to her.

Eventually, she had fallen asleep when the sky outside the large windows started to lighten.

A few hours of sleep were enough for her though, and after getting dressed, she padded to the kitchen to get some coffee and found the girls already awake and watching television in the living room.

Cartoons.

They were watching a kid's show, as if to remind her that they were still children.

She needed to find them something to do other than veg in front of a screen. Heck, she needed to talk to them and see if she could help them, but the truth was that Kyra was better at fighting than she was at talking, and she'd rather go on a dangerous mission with a dagger in one hand and a handgun in the other than try to talk to these girls and offer them some solace.

She would probably do more harm than good, telling them that they needed to forget all the horrible things that were done to them and pick up a sword, so to speak. That was what she had done, and it had kept her mostly sane.

That was all she knew.

"Good morning," she said. "Did you have breakfast already?"

Arezoo turned to her and nodded. "We had cereal with milk. It was so good."

Kids.

Tomorrow, she would try to make them a healthier breakfast, not that she knew what that entailed. Hers usually was just a cup of coffee, and she didn't eat anything until lunch. Who had time to sit down for three meals a day?

Kyra had been lucky to get even one, and if she'd gotten hungry, she'd popped a can of beans open.

When the doorbell rang, Arezoo went to open the door, greeting Max with a bright smile.

Kyra's heart jumped at the sight of him. He was dressed in a sort of uniform, black cargo pants, and a black jacket over a black T-shirt, which made his blond hair stand out. He was so tall and broad, a man's man, and yet he had been so sweet last night.

He walked over to Kyra. "They are ready for us downstairs."

She swallowed, glancing at the girls. "Are you going to be okay by yourselves here? Jasmine and Ell-rom are next door, and so is Fenella. If you need anything, just go to the other penthouse across the foyer."

"We are okay," Arezoo said. "You can go."

"I'll be back in a couple of hours." Kyra assumed the interrogation wasn't going to take longer than that.

As she followed Max out of the penthouse and into the vestibule with its ornate mural on the ceiling and the huge flower arrangement on top of the round stone table in the middle, Kyra reflected on the different worlds contained in this one building, separated only by an elevator ride. Up here was the epitome of elegance and luxury, and down there was a dungeon.

She braced for what she was about to see.

Max pressed the button for the elevator and turned to her. "I'm afraid I have to disappoint you. The interrogation is going to be done with compulsion, not fists. Kian brought Toven with him, a god who is a very powerful compeller and can get immortals to talk. It's not as satisfying as doing it the old-fashioned way, but it's faster and more effective."

She smiled. "Can we beat him up after that just for fun?"

Max grinned. "Fates, woman. You saying things like that makes me fall in love with you deeper by the minute."

He was joking, of course, but the spark in his blue eyes and that sexy smile did things to her, proving that last night wasn't an aberration, some post-rescue gratitude response that had turned sexual.

She had been awakened, so to speak, and she was not going to fall asleep again.

The elevator doors slid open with a soft chime, and Kyra stepped inside, feeling a momentary tightness in her chest at the confined space. It wasn't quite claustrophobia—she'd slept in caves and dugouts during her time with the resistance—but she was heading underground, and it unsettled her.

Max leaned against the wall and crossed his arms over his chest. "Compulsion is fascinating to watch," he said, clearly trying to distract her. "They always try to fight it, and it's amusing to see their mouths open and close like fish out of water. Eventually, the bastards spill their guts as if they have been dying to confess their entire miserable lives."

"How does it work?" Her fingers closed around her amber pendant, drawing comfort from its familiar warmth.

"No one knows for sure. We know that it's a sound wave, but we haven't been able to isolate it." He tapped his earpieces. "These filter the compulsion. I have a pair for you as well." He dug into his pocket and handed her a small case.

"Are they the same as the ones the girls got?"

Max shook his head. "Theirs are not compulsion filtering. Just translating."

The elevator slowed to a stop, and as the doors opened, Kyra braced herself, half-expecting a medieval dungeon with stone walls and iron manacles. Instead, she was greeted by a surprisingly modern facility—polished concrete floors, gleaming metal doors, and bright LED lighting. It looked more like a high-security prison than the torture chamber that her imagination had conjured.

The hallway was wide, at least twelve feet across, and there were even reproductions of famous art pieces hanging on the walls. The panic she'd expected hadn't hit her yet, but that was because it was easy to imagine that there were rooms with windows behind the closed doors.

"Whose idea was the pictures?" She pointed at a reproduction of Van Gogh.

"Ingrid, the clan's interior designer. The dungeon is not always used to hold prisoners. At times, we've had people who needed to hide staying here, and we wanted to make the place look less like a dungeon and more like a secure hotel. Some of these cells are really nicely kitted out."

"I have to admit that it's much nicer than I expected." She released a breath. "I thought I would be walking past chains and cobwebs."

Max chuckled. "We save those for special occasions."

They passed by several metal doors that seemed more suitable for a bank safe than a holding facility, and there were security cameras mounted at regular intervals along the ceiling. "How many prisoners do you have down here?"

"Currently?" Max's expression darkened slightly. "Too many. A couple of Doomers and the rest are humans—members of trafficking rings, pedophiles, the worst kind of scum." He smiled. "I started to tell you about all the wonderful things that the clan does to save victims of trafficking and clean the world one dirtbag at a time, but I got distracted." He gave her a loaded look.

Thinking of the cameras that were no doubt also recording sound, Kyra felt a blush creeping up her cheeks. "Perhaps we shouldn't bring up things of this nature down here. Doesn't seem fitting."

Max nodded, but a sly smile danced on the corners of his lips. "You are right. My bad."

They reached an open door at the end of the corridor, and Max walked right in.

A handsome man with longish curly hair that didn't go well with the uniform he was wearing rose to his feet.

"This is Alfie," Max introduced him. "He took over for me when I was gone and is now my second-in-command." Max turned to her. "And this is Kyra."

Alfie offered her a warm smile and extended his hand. "It's a pleasure to meet you, Kyra."

Nodding, she shook his hand. "Same here."

"Is everyone there already?" Max asked.

Alfie nodded and then offered Kyra an apologetic smile. "Kian has decided to use the interrogation cell, which is connected to an observation room with a one-way mirror. He doesn't want the prisoner to see you during the interrogation."

Kyra suspected that Kian just wasn't comfortable with her being there, but he was the boss here, and he made the rules. She had no choice but to comply.

31

MAX

The split interrogation room hadn't been used in years, and Max wondered what had prompted Kian to change plans and move the prisoner there. Toven's compulsion was going to force him to talk no matter who else was present, and since they weren't going to beat up the vermin, there wouldn't be any blood and gore, so that wasn't a reason to keep Kyra out of the room.

The only thing he could think of was that Kian wanted to shield Kyra at least partially from what was about to be revealed, and there was some logic to that. She would still hear it, she would still see the monster who had abused her, but there would be a wall between them, which should give her a sense of security.

As Alfie aimed his phone at the scanner on the

door to the interrogation room proper, Max aimed his at the door to the observation room, and after a brief moment, both slid open with twin soft hydraulic hisses. Alfie entered the other room while Max motioned for Kyra to enter the observation room ahead of him.

Two chairs had been placed in front of the large mirror that looked like a window from their side and allowed a clear view of the interrogation room beyond.

Kyra froze in place, looking through the glass at her tormenter.

Strapped to a chair, his wrists and ankles secured with thick metal restraints, the Doomer sat blank-faced, his eyes half-lidded—partially sedated as per Kian's instructions.

"Please, take a seat," Max motioned toward one of the chairs.

Her head whipped toward him with a shocked expression as if she'd been startled by him being there with her.

He pulled the chair back a little, thinking that some distance from the glass would make her feel more comfortable.

"Can they hear us on the other side?" Kyra asked in a whisper.

"No. It's completely soundproof." He took a pair of headphones off a hook and handed them to her. "You can hear what's going on through these, and if you want to make a suggestion or ask a question, you can use the attached microphone. Keep it off until you want them to hear you."

She took the set from him but hesitated before placing it over her ears. "Do I put them over the compulsion-filtering earpieces or instead?"

"Over." He dipped his head to look into her eyes. "Are you okay? You don't have to be here."

"I need to." She waved a hand at the observation window. "Who are the three men with Kian?"

"The redhead and the blond are Anandur and Brundar, Kian's bodyguards. They are brothers. The dark-haired guy is Toven."

"The god," she murmured in awe. "How many gods are there on Earth?"

"Several," Max said. "But since you know now that they are just aliens with powerful mind-control abilities, you don't need to sound so worshipful. Besides, Toven is happily mated." He wasn't really jealous of her admiration of the god, well, maybe a little, but he hoped the teasing would lighten the mood.

Smiling, she rolled her eyes. "You're terrible."

"I know." He pulled out the other chair next to hers and sat down. "But you like me anyway."

She didn't pick up the banter like he'd hoped, her gaze focused on the monster who had stolen so much from her.

Max put his headphones on just as Kian turned to the god. "Toven, whenever you're ready."

"Open your eyes and look at me," Toven commanded the prisoner.

The effect was immediate. The Doomer's eyes snapped fully open, his back straightening as if pulled by invisible strings. His gaze fixed on Toven, and his expression shifted from confusion to alarm to resignation in rapid succession.

"Tell me your name," Toven commanded.

"Durhad," the Doomer answered without hesitation.

"What is your position within the Brotherhood?"

"I am a liaison to the Revolutionary Guard."

"Does that include thralling the Revolutionary Guard upper command to do whatever Navuh wants them to do?"

"Yes."

"Who do you report to?"

"Commander Hazok."

Hazok was one of Navuh's adopted sons, which meant that this Doomer was high up in the Brotherhood's chain of command if he reported directly to him, and Max wondered if Toven knew that.

"What were you doing in the facility we took you from?" Toven asked.

The Doomer tried to resist, holding his lips tightly pressed together, and for a moment, Max thought that he would be able to resist the compulsion, but then his mouth opened and he spat out, "Research."

"What kind of research?" Kyra whispered, but she hadn't activated the microphone, so Max was the only one who heard her.

"Let Toven do this his way, and in the end, if he didn't get all the answers you want, you can ask your questions."

She nodded.

"Was this research done for the Brotherhood?" Toven asked.

"No."

"Interesting." Toven turned to Kian and the two exchanged knowing looks.

"Were you conducting this research for your immediate commander?" Toven asked.

"No."

"Were you doing the research for yourself?"

"Yes."

Toven was asking questions that required just yes or no answers because it was impossible to answer them evasively or respond with partial answers that concealed more than they revealed.

It was a good way to prime the prisoner while getting the basics, so Toven would know what to ask when it was time to move to the type of questions that couldn't be answered with one or two words.

32

KYRA

The walls seemed to be closing in on Kyra, suffocating her, and it wasn't just her fear of underground spaces that was contributing to the sensation.

Even from beyond the glass the monster was affecting her, triggering her fight or flight response.

She forced herself to breathe normally and glanced at Max, whose body seemed to have swelled with aggression. For some reason, that provided her with a modicum of comfort, of safety, and she berated herself for her weakness.

She didn't need a strong male to protect her. She'd done an excellent job of keeping herself and others safe for over twenty years.

It had been bad judgment on her part that had gotten her captured. Everyone had warned her against walking into the lion's den each morning, but she had foolishly ignored them because she couldn't leave Fenella there to suffer as she had.

A smile curled the corners of her lips. If she'd known how contrary Twelve would turn out to be, perhaps she would have been more inclined to listen to her friends' warnings. She was joking of course. The woman was a little annoying and she definitely seemed to be still pining after Max, but she didn't deserve to be abused by the monster sitting on the other side of the glass.

"Tell me about your research," Toven commanded. "What were you hoping to find?"

Again, the so-called doctor tried to resist the compulsion, pressing his lips tightly together for a long moment. Then a harsh growl rushed out of his throat, and he emitted a curse in a language she didn't understand, but given the stiffening in Max's shoulders, he did.

"What did he say?" Kyra asked.

Max just shook his head, refusing to translate.

"Immortal and dormant females," Durhad said.

Toven waved a hand in frustration. "Tell me everything from start to finish, including what made you begin the research, the methods you used, your objectives, and your results. Don't skip over anything."

Kyra was glad of her compulsion-filtering earpieces because it looked like the god had used maximum power. The Doomer's eyes glazed over, and drool slithered down from the corner of his slackened mouth.

"Toven pushed too hard," Max murmured. "The scumbag looks fried."

A moment passed in silence as everyone waited to see if the Doomer would start talking or they would have to postpone the interrogation until he recuperated.

Kyra hoped the damage wasn't irreparable. She needed answers, and the dirtbag in the other room had them.

"It started with Kyra," he said, suddenly looking revived, even excited to share what he knew.

Kyra felt nauseous. All those women had suffered because of her?

"How did you find Kyra?" Toven asked.

"Her father was a commander in the Revolutionary Guard. He sent her to the United States to study in a university and join student organizations where she would promote whatever issues he told her to, but then she disappeared. Her father hired a detective, who found out that the little whore disgraced the family and married outside of her faith. If that stain on his honor was discovered, he would lose his position in the Guard. He sent local operatives to kidnap her and bring her back to Iran."

Kyra felt as if she'd been punched in the stomach. Jasmine had been right about suspecting her family. They'd stolen her from her husband, her child, and locked her away? Every word cut her like a knife, not only because of the unfairness and cruelty but because that ugliness was part of her genetic makeup.

One comforting thought was that perhaps her mother was a better person than her father, and Kyra wondered if she was still alive.

When Max reached out and took her hand, the warmth of that gesture melted some of the ice blocking up her veins.

"Why not just kill her?" Kian asked. "Isn't that what fanatics like him do?"

"Everyone knew that she was studying abroad. If she didn't come back, he would have had some explaining to do. Instead, he had her committed to a private institution under a fake name and asked me to make her forget everything from her life in America. Once she no longer remembered what she had done abroad, the plan was to marry her off expeditiously to someone who owed him a big favor and would keep her lack of honor a secret."

Kyra shuddered at the thought. In a way, the despicable Doomer had saved her from an even worse fate. If she'd remained human, she had no doubt that her reluctant husband would have beaten her up and violated her as well in retaliation for being saddled with damaged goods, but as a human, she wouldn't have been able to escape.

"Why did Kyra's father ask that of you?" Toven asked. "Does he know who you are?"

"He's dead, but, of course, he didn't know who I was. He thought I was a powerful hypnotist because I helped him out a few times when our interests intersected."

Kyra was relieved that her father was dead. If he were still alive, she would have felt compelled to face him, but he was gone, and she could forget about him once again.

"So, you thralled Kyra and decided to have a little fun while at it?" The god sounded slurred, and Kyra had a feeling that his fangs were out, but she couldn't see his face from where she was sitting. Just his profile.

The Doomer had the audacity to shrug. "She was already a whore, so what difference did it make? I was doing her a favor by keeping her alive, and as it turned out, I did her a greater favor than I could have imagined. I made her immortal."

33

MAX

Max held on to Kyra's sweaty hand, wishing he could do more for her. Her father was lucky to be dead, because if he were still alive, Max would have made it his mission to find him and make him pay for what he had done to his daughter.

The Doomer would also pay for what he had done and for insulting her on top of that, and Max didn't care if he was tried for insubordination after beating the scumbag to a pulp, but he wasn't planning on asking anyone's permission to do it.

"How did you know that she turned immortal because of you?" Toven asked.

The Doomer smiled for the first time since the interrogation had started.

"I put two and two together. Regrettably, Kyra escaped before I realized what had happened. I saw the footage from the surveillance cameras, and I knew that I hadn't given her any drugs that could have made her that strong. Naturally, drugs were the explanation I gave the bewildered doctors of the institution, and they had no choice but to accept it. I've been searching for her ever since, and then when I finally found her, you showed up out of nowhere. What were you looking for?"

"You are not the one asking the questions," Kian said. "We are. What about Fenella?"

Toven had to repeat the question since Kian's commanding voice wasn't enough to compel the Doomer to answer.

"That was another fortunate chance encounter. I took it as a sign from Mortdh that I should father immortal sons of my own, and then Kyra came right to me, after I'd looked for her for over two decades, to the facility I was using for my project, and I knew that I'd read the signs correctly. That was what Mortdh wanted me to do, and he sent two immortal females to me to become the mothers of my immortal sons."

Kyra's hand tightened around Max's. "What if I'm pregnant?"

"You're not."

"How can you be sure? Jasmine told me that immortal females ovulate on demand."

He turned to her and cupped her cheek. "Conception is rare, and it happens with the right partner. The monster on the other side of the glass is not that."

She let out a breath. "I hope you are right, and I hope that's true for Fenella as well. She doesn't deserve to carry the devil's spawn."

Max couldn't agree more.

"Why did you keep them sedated?" Kian asked.

This time Toven didn't need to repeat the question.

The Doomer shifted in his chair as much as the restraints allowed. "I injected them with every fertility drug I could get my hands on. I assumed that they were on some sort of contraceptives, so I found what could be given to counteract them, but neither conceived. I remembered Mortdh's teachings about the wickedness of women, and how they need to submit to breed, so I roughed them up a little. Nothing too excessive, just enough to show them who was in charge."

"I'm going to kill him," Max hissed. "I'm going to tear him apart with my fangs until there's nothing left of him to regenerate. Or maybe I will allow him to regenerate so I can do that all over again."

Tears glistened in Kyra's eyes as she turned to him. "That's what he did to Fenella and me. He beat us up and by morning we were as good as new. He thought it was great fun."

In the other room, silence stretched like hot tar

over the interrogators. Kian's eyes were glowing, and Max was sure his fangs were fully elongated by now, but the Doomer was too fried to realize that. He was still smiling like a fiend, happy with how smart he had been.

"What about the four human girls?" Toven asked in a surprisingly even tone. "Why did you capture them?"

"A stroke of genius." The Doomer straightened his shoulders as much as the chains allowed. "Regrettably, it only occurred to me recently that I knew where to find Kyra's relatives, and that if she turned immortal from my bite, perhaps some of them would too."

Kyra gasped. "The girls are my family?"

Max squeezed her hand, suddenly worried that one of them or more could be pregnant, even though the chances of that were negligible. Immortal males' fertility was as low as the fertility of immortal females, but the idiot didn't know that.

Bridget was arriving later in the afternoon, and she would conduct all the necessary testing. Hopefully, she'd confirm that none of the females were pregnant.

"Smart, right?" the Doomer continued. "The more the better. I could have started a breeding program of my own and created my own army of immortal warriors."

"How are the girls related to Kyra?" Toven asked.

"Three are the daughters of one sister and one is the daughter of another. Kyra doesn't have any brothers, but she has four younger sisters." An evil grin spread over his face. "I snatched them because they were all together, but there is more where they came from. I hope my men got their hands on the next crop, including the mothers and the children. The boys might be turned into soldiers and the girls can become my breeders. The mothers are old and not as pleasing to look at as the young ones, but they might still be fertile. I realized that the more of them I have, the faster I can grow my immortal army."

Had the idiot forgotten the situation he was in? He was never leaving this underground and never getting his hands on those women, but his buddies were another story.

The team had to go back and rescue the rest of Kyra's family.

34

KYRA

A chill made Kyra shiver while her blood boiled at the same time. "We need to save them before those monsters get to them."

Max pushed his chair closer to her and wrapped an arm around her shoulders. "We are probably too late to get them before they are taken, but we will get them out. I promise."

Kyra's entire body started shaking. It was just too much. She had four sisters, and the four girls upstairs were her nieces, and the demon in the other room had hurt all of them.

"Did you share your findings with anyone in the Brotherhood?" Toven asked.

The Doomer snorted. "Are you daft? I just told you that I want to create my own breeding program. You think Lord Navuh would approve of my plan?"

"No, I guess not," Toven said in a calm tone as if he was talking about the weather. "Those you sent to collect Kyra's family members, do they know what you intend to do with them?"

"They know I run experiments, but they think I just want to find out how to turn humans immortal. They are too dumb to connect the dots like I did."

"Those who were with you in the facility are dead," Toven said matter-of-factly, using the same calm tone. "And those who you sent to collect more victims will soon be dead as well."

Toven's words had no impact on the Doomer, and Kyra realized that he wasn't right in the head. Not that the cruel sadist ever could have been normal, but his behavior indicated a deeper problem than that. She would have suspected drugs, but she doubted he had been given anything other than sedatives. Then again, perhaps they needed him calm to tell them all he knew so they had given him something else.

She leaned over to Max. "What drugs did they give him?"

He shook his head. "Nothing that could explain his behavior. It's like he's not aware of what's going on with him. He still thinks that he's going to continue his breeding program."

"What did you do to Kyra during her captivity other than trying to get her pregnant?" Toven asked, changing direction.

Kyra tensed, her hand tightening around Max's.

"Blood work, tissue samples, hormonal analysis."

"You are not a real doctor," Toven said. "You didn't study medicine. How did you know what to do?"

"I found a fertility expert and got him to serve as my assistant," the Doomer said. "Did you kill him too?"

"Probably." Toven looked at Kian.

Kian shrugged. "I don't know, but I certainly hope so." He tapped his earpiece. "Max, did you kill the assistant?"

"Everyone who was around Durhad is dead. In fact, everyone who was inside the building and didn't run away when the attack started is most likely dead. We blew up the entire facility."

"Good." Kian tapped his earpiece again. "I would have hated to have to go back for the assistant and his laboratory." He turned to Toven. "We need details on Kyra's other nieces. We need to get them out."

Kyra tapped her microphone. "My sisters too,"

Kian nodded in her direction and then communicated her request to Toven.

The next several questions were aimed at

collecting information about her sisters' locations in Iran, and where Durhad's buddies would take the girls once they discovered that the compound was destroyed.

"I should contact my friends," Kyra said. "Ask them to be on the lookout for more strange guards arriving with women and girls."

Max shook his head. "They won't be able to deal with Doomers. Don't risk additional lives. We will get your family."

Once the information had been collected, or at least everything that the Doomer remembered, which was just the neighborhood her sisters lived in, Kian crossed his arms over his chest. "You took Kyra's pendant. Any particular reason other than to add insult to injury?"

Kyra's fingers instinctively went to the stone. Whatever the dark fiend had tried to do with her pendant would have failed because the stone reacted only to her.

The prisoner shifted, looking uncomfortable. "I wanted to study it."

That was what bothered him the most? He'd talked about torturing and violating women as if it was nothing, had not reacted to the reminder that his buddies were dead, but he was discomforted by her stone?

"What did you discover?" Toven asked.

"The inscriptions didn't make any sense, and I

compared it to every script known to humans that was posted on the internet. Other than that, I didn't have time to test it properly."

Relief washed over Kyra. She didn't want anyone to examine her pendant, neither friend nor foe.

"One final question," Toven said. "Is there anything else about your research, your methods, or the Brotherhood's plans that's notable?"

As the Doomer tried to resist the compulsion again, his eyes rolled back in his head and he slumped on the chair, remaining upright only because of the chains holding him up.

"It seems that we are done for now." Kian pushed to his feet. "Sedate him and put him back in his cell."

Alfie moved forward with a syringe, injecting a dose of something into Durhad's arm.

Kyra removed her headphones, feeling numb and excited at the same time, which shouldn't be possible, but here she was. She had more family than she'd ever imagined having, but the girls upstairs had suffered because of her and she needed to let them know that.

It was going to be a hard conversation.

Also, she had sisters, and more nieces and nephews who were in danger and needed to be rescued.

Her legs felt surprisingly steady despite the

emotional weight of everything she'd just heard. "I need to tell Jasmine," she said. "These girls are her cousins."

"And they are all Dormants." Max hung his headphones back on the hook and took hers to hang them up as well. "Which means that we get to tell them the entire story and that they get to move into the village."

35

KIAN

Kian waited for Alfie and Rupert to carry the unconscious prisoner out of the cell before rising to his feet and following them out.

Toven and the brothers joined him in the hallway, where Kyra and Max were waiting for them.

He didn't miss that Kyra's hand was clasped in Max's and that she'd pulled it out as soon as she saw him walking toward them. Did she think he had a problem with her having a relationship with the Guardian?

He should say something about Syssi having a hunch about the two of them, but this wasn't the time or place. Even he knew that.

"I suggest we go to my office to talk about what we just learned."

"The one in the penthouse?" Kyra asked hopefully.

"No, that one I haven't used since moving to the village. It's just a small home office that is not suitable for meetings. My old office in the keep is two floors up. Just a short elevator ride."

Kyra looked disappointed, but she nodded.

"Would you like us to get refreshments from the lobby café, boss?" Anandur asked.

"Good idea." Kian nodded. "Coffee for everyone?" At the collective murmurs of assent, he added, "And whatever pastries or sandwiches they have available."

People who experienced emotional upheaval tended to be comforted by food, and Kyra looked like she needed a boost.

As they reached the elevators, the brothers entered the first one, and Kian led the rest of the group to the other. After the doors slid closed with a soft chime, the tension radiating from Kyra intensified, though she maintained an admirable façade of composure.

When they emerged on the upper level, Kian strode down the familiar corridor toward his former office. The double glass doors were as spotless as always, and as he pushed them open, he was happy to note that the interior was just as clean.

He gestured for everyone to enter. "Please,

make yourselves comfortable," he said, gesturing toward the conference table that dominated the center of the room.

The exotic wood of the tabletop gleamed under the recessed lighting, its rich grain catching Kyra's attention as she settled into one of the leather chairs. Her fingers traced the intricate patterns, and Kian was glad that she was noticing that. The woman was holding up better than he'd expected, given what they'd just learned.

Max took the seat beside her, while Toven chose the seat on Kian's left.

"First things first," Kian said, pulling out his phone. "We have another rescue mission to coordinate, and we need Onegus on it." He activated the large screen mounted on the wall behind his desk before initiating a video call to Onegus.

The chief's face appeared on it moments later, his usual bright smile firmly in place. "How did it go? Did you learn anything significant?"

"And then some, but not what we were hoping for. The so-called Doctor, whose name is Durhad, didn't discover a new way to identify Dormants. He deduced it the same way we did." Kian continued to relay the situation succinctly—the revelation about Kyra's sisters, their children, and the immediate threat they faced from the Brotherhood's operatives.

"How many potential targets are we looking at?" the chief asked.

"There are four sisters and their families," Kian said. "We need to move quickly. The Doomers might have already taken them, but since the compound is destroyed and they can't contact Durhad, they might decide to do something else with them, like take them to the island, and then we won't be able to get them out."

Not that it made any sense for them to do that, but most Doomers were dumb, and their first instinct would be to take the prisoners to the island and wash their hands of them.

"I'll speak with Jade," Onegus said. "She might be amenable to joining another mission after getting a taste for blood." He chuckled at his own pun. "But I doubt she will be willing to take Drova. Bridget's patched her up, but it will take a couple of weeks until she's fully recovered."

It was a shame that the Kra-ell didn't heal as fast as immortals. According to the report from Yamanu, the two hybrids and four pureblooded females had performed above all expectations, and they'd enjoyed every moment of the carnage.

"Perhaps just Jade and the hybrid males this time. The search will start in Tehran, and those three can pass for humans more easily."

Onegus chuckled. "Not necessarily. We can

dress the females in burkas and sunglasses, and no one will be any the wiser."

"True." Kian waved a hand. "I leave the decision up to you. Kyra will find out the addresses of her sisters from her nieces and how many kids each of them has so we will know how many people we have to rescue."

"I want in." Max leaned forward in his chair. "The Kra-ell are awesome, but they are like a wrecking ball. They need someone to point them in the right direction or they will wreak a path of destruction and attract too much attention."

"I have to come too." Kyra's tone brooked no argument. "These are my sisters, my family. I have to be there."

Onegus's expression revealed his displeasure with her statement, but he must have realized that there was no changing her mind on that.

"If you feel that you are up to it, I won't stand in your way," Onegus said. "You're a warrior, so you know that the success of the mission comes first. You need to be sure that your participation will benefit the mission and not impede it."

"I don't have an ego when it comes to saving lives, but I'm sure my participation will be beneficial. I know the territory, the culture, and the language. I can blend in, ask questions, etc. The team needs me."

"I agree." Onegus nodded.

"Thank you." Kyra dipped her head before shifting her gaze to Kian. "What are we going to do with them once we get them out? After all, they are all Dormants, right? According to Jasmine, the gene is hereditary through the females. My sisters got the same genes I did from our mother, and so did their daughters. We need to bring them all here and allow them to transition."

Kian rubbed his jaw. "It's not as simple as with the girls upstairs. Your sisters are married. We can't just yank them out of their homes and their communities, although we might have to for their own protection. Still, we can arrange for the families to relocate somewhere safe instead of breaking them apart and bringing the Dormants to the village while leaving the fathers behind."

Kyra grimaced. "If my father arranged my sisters' marriages like he tried to arrange mine, they might welcome a way out." Kyra's expression hardened. "If they do, will the clan accept them?"

"Of course," Kian assured her. "Every Dormant is welcome. But you need to understand that their transitions aren't guaranteed. Adult transitions become more difficult with age, and we don't know your sisters' health status."

"First, we need to get them out," Kyra said. "Everything else can be decided later."

"There's another thing you should consider." Toven spoke up for the first time since entering the office. "Your sisters will recognize you, Kyra. But given your apparent age, they'll likely assume that you're your own daughter."

A smile brightened Kyra's face. "I can work with that. I can easily play the part of Jasmine. It might even make the extraction easier. A niece coming to visit with news of her long-lost mother will be welcomed and given a willing ear."

36

KYRA

The whoosh of the glass door opening preceded Anandur and Brundar's return, both holding cardboard trays stacked with coffee cups, pastries, and various sandwiches. The comforting scent of freshly brewed coffee drifted into the meeting room, and the pleasant aroma made her briefly close her eyes.

Kyra took a discreet deep breath.

She was good at projecting confidence, but the truth was that she could have used a few more days of quiet to recuperate in the comfortable bed in the beautiful penthouse.

Now that was not an option.

Her family was in danger, Max was going, and nothing could keep her from joining the team.

"Perfect timing," Kian said, accepting a coffee from Brundar. "Thanks," he murmured and then shifted his attention back to the large screen on the wall, where the clan's Chief Guardian was waiting patiently until the coffee was distributed. "We need to figure out fast transportation in and out of Iran. Kalugal took Jackie to visit an archaeological site in Egypt, so his plane is unavailable. The clan jet is big enough to take the team there, but we need backup in case we end up getting out more people than we have the space for."

"Eric can provide an additional charter plane," Onegus said.

Max grabbed a pastry from Anandur's tray and straightened. "What's our timeline? The Doomers have a head start, and we don't know exactly how close they are tracking Kyra's family and whether they've already gotten them or not."

"The sooner the better," Onegus said. "Tomorrow, if we can manage it."

Nodding, Kian set his coffee on the table. "That's good. Turner may also have contacts in Tehran who can do preliminary recon and gather local intel before the main team lands."

"It would certainly streamline things," Max said. "Better than going in blind."

On the screen, the chief lifted his gaze from what she assumed was a notepad. "I'll make arrangements with Eric about chartering his plane, and if his is not available, we can use one of the Alaskan sanctuary's planes, although I hope that won't be necessary. They only have one large enough for our purposes. As for the timeline, I think we can be ready by tomorrow. I hope the fake identities we prepared for you will be good enough to get you to Tehran. Iran's security is tricky these days."

Leaning back, Kyra sipped on her coffee and listened as Kian ironed out the mission details with the chief, with Max adding a comment here and there.

Hopefully, they wouldn't expect her to provide input because she was a native. It was true that she spoke the language and knew how to blend in without attracting attention to herself, but she didn't know Tehran at all, and she wasn't an expert on urban warfare.

"I'll talk to Turner." Kian put down his coffee cup. He turned to Kyra. "Given what we've learned about your father, your sisters are likely very traditional, which means that they might resist leaving. You need to be prepared for that possibility."

"They won't resist once they understand the danger their children are in," Kyra said. "No mother would."

"Provided that they believe you," Toven murmured.

Kyra was proud of being able to hold the god's gaze and not look away. "I will make them believe me." She wasn't sure how she was going to accomplish that, but she would find a way.

"We have all the fake paperwork ready from the rescue operation," Max said. "That will save us some time."

"True." The chief leaned forward, his handsome face filling the screen. "That's one of the reasons I suggested using the same team."

"I don't have any papers," Kyra murmured, hoping Kian wouldn't use that as an excuse to leave her behind.

"You do," Max said. "We prepared paperwork for you in case it was needed. We didn't know that we would be coming back with five extra women, so we didn't prepare anything for them, but there was no need to show anyone their papers." He shook his head. "I still can't believe I found Fenella in that shit hole."

Kyra was only mildly offended by Max referring to Tahav in such a derogatory way. He wasn't wrong, but it had been her home for many years, and her people still lived there.

"I need to contact my team," she said. "Max said I shouldn't because they can't deal with the Doomers, and I would just be risking their lives, but I can tell them to collect information in the Tahav area and not engage."

Kian nodded. "That's a good idea. Don't tell

them where you are or who took you. As far as they are concerned, you are on another mission."

"Of course." She chuckled softly. "They wouldn't believe me if I told them I was in America anyway."

Kian agreeing to her contacting her people lifted a weight off her chest. It hadn't felt right to just abandon them. Their paths had to diverge at this point, but she needed to say proper goodbyes and get closure. It wasn't easy to leave behind friends who had fought by her side for so long.

Kyra thought about her sisters, and how likely they were to leave their husbands behind. If they were anything like the man her father chose for her, they wouldn't be missed, but she couldn't just assume that. What if her sisters were happily married and loved their husbands?

The girls would know. Given how they were afraid to go home, Kyra imagined that their fathers were fanatical monsters, but even though some women were like that as well, she refused to believe that her sisters could embrace such psychotic, murderous customs.

"I don't even know my sisters' names or how old they are," she whispered.

Kian's eyes softened. "We will find out soon enough. Our hacker has limited access to Iranian information, but perhaps he will have more luck with this than he had tracking your family there."

"I doubt it," Max said. "I think Kyra's father made sure that information about his family was difficult or impossible to access given his position in the Revolutionary Guard. These guys are not very popular with the general Iranian public."

"True." Kian rubbed a hand over the back of his neck. "Perhaps your rebel friends can help us find out?"

Kyra shook her head. "We are a local group. They might contact other groups that operate in Tehran, but I wouldn't risk the contact for a personal matter."

Kian nodded. "I understand. Just let your people know to look out for another shipment of prisoners arriving at Tahav."

"I will." She turned to Max. "Can I use your phone again?"

"Are you going to call them?" he asked as he handed her the device.

"Of course not. I'll leave a message at a number they check from time to time. If they have any information for me, they will do that the same way."

She started typing the message, explaining in general terms what to look out for and to leave a message for her if they noticed anything, but not to engage.

37

MAX

Alone at last with Kyra in the elevator, Max was hyperaware of her presence. She was fidgeting with her pendant again, a sign that she was anxious about the conversation awaiting her in the penthouse.

Learning that the four young women they'd rescued were her nieces had been shocking enough, and now she had to explain to them not only their relationship but also the hidden world of immortals they'd unknowingly been thrust into.

"Are you okay?" he asked.

She gave a slight shake of her head. "Where do I even start? I'm so nervous."

Before he could overthink it, he cupped her face and kissed her. For a heartbeat, she remained frozen in surprise. Then her lips softened under his, and she melted into the kiss. Her hands found their way to his chest, fingers curling into his shirt.

Heat flared between them, but the kiss was about more than that. It was about comfort, reassurance, and the release of pent-up energy.

When she sighed against his mouth, he deepened the kiss, wanting to chase away her worries if only for a moment.

Time seemed to stretch and compress all at once. He could have stayed there forever, learning the taste of her, memorizing the small sounds she made in the back of her throat.

But the ping announcing the elevator arriving at its destination broke the magic, and they stepped apart.

Kyra's cheeks were flushed, her lips slightly swollen. "That was unexpected."

"Good unexpected?" He couldn't quite keep the hint of uncertainty from his voice.

She smiled, and his heart did that silly little flip. "Very good unexpected, but also reckless. What if someone called the elevator to one of the other floors?"

"When the destination is the penthouse, the elevator doesn't stop anywhere on the way." He led her out into the vestibule with a hand on the small of her back. "One of the perks of Kian owning the building."

"That's convenient," she murmured, still

looking a bit dazed from the kiss, but much more relaxed.

He desperately wanted to kiss her again but forced himself to refrain and to walk up to the double doors leading to the penthouse. "Should we ring the bell or just walk in?"

She looked up at him. "You tell me. I don't know what the protocol is."

"You live here now, so I guess you should just open the door."

Kyra put her hand on the handle. "Is this door ever locked?"

"There is no need." He motioned with his chin toward the camera above the door. "No one who doesn't belong here can get in. In fact, the elevator won't go up to the penthouse without at least one of the passengers appearing on the list of approved guests."

"Good." She let out a breath as she opened the door. "The more safety features the better."

The scene that greeted them in the living room looked deceptively domestic. The four girls were clustered on one of the sofas, while Jasmine and Ell-rom shared an oversized armchair. Fenella had claimed the other one, her legs tucked under her.

They all turned to look at Max and Kyra as they entered.

"Well?" Fenella asked, not bothering with pleasantries. "What did you learn from the bastard fake doctor?"

Max glanced at Kyra, noting how she'd tensed at the question. She needed a moment to collect herself, so he led her to the other couch and they both sat down.

"We learned quite a bit." He took Kyra's hand, noting how the girls caught the gesture and exchanged knowing looks. "Turns out that he didn't operate on behalf of the Brotherhood or the Revolutionary Guard. He was working independently on his own twisted side project."

Jasmine cast a quick glance at the girls, who were listening intently. Max wished they didn't have the translating earpieces so he could tell Jasmine what they had learned before telling the girls so they could figure out together the best way to do that, but perhaps it was better this way. They just had to get it out.

"We can tell the girls everything," he said. "Kian approved it."

Jasmine's eyebrows shot up. "So, they are Dormants? He found a way to identify them?"

"Yes to the first one and no to the second," Max said.

"What do you mean by Dormants?" Arezoo asked. "We are not hibernating animals."

The earpieces could only do literal translation, which left a lot to be desired, but he admired the girl for speaking up and asking, especially after all she'd been through. Now that he knew the familial connection, he could see the physical resemblance as well as the spunk that Arezoo shared with her aunt and cousin. The way she carried herself, the tilt of her chin, the intelligence in her eyes.

Max held up a hand. "I know that you have questions, and you will get answers, but I ask you to be patient so we can explain everything properly." He turned back to Jasmine. "The Doomer didn't discover anything new. He just suspected and teased out what we already knew. It's hereditary, so when you find one female who has transitioned, others in her family might too. The dude is evil but he's not stupid."

Understanding dawned in Jasmine's eyes as she looked at the four girls with new awareness. "That explains the connection I felt. We also look a little alike, but I thought it was because of our shared ancestry. But it's clearly more than that. We are family."

The girls exchanged confused looks. Laleh, the youngest, pressed closer to her oldest sister. "What does that all mean?"

Kyra squared her shoulders the way she did before facing a challenge, but before she could speak, Fenella lifted a hand.

"Hold on," she said, uncurling from her chair.

"Are you saying these girls can become like us? Like Kyra and me?"

Kyra nodded.

"What do you mean?" Donya asked, her voice barely above a whisper. "Become like what?"

"That's where the lengthy explanation comes in." Kyra motioned for Jasmine to come over and join her on the couch. "Jasmine can do a much better job of it than me because she's more knowledgeable, but Max knows the most out of all of us." She shifted her gaze to him. "Would you like to explain?"

He shook his head. "I'm a terrible storyteller. I'll jump in if you two get something wrong or need clarification."

She gave him a small nod and reached for Jasmine's hand, drawing support from her daughter or lending Jasmine hers.

The air in the room felt charged with anticipation, the four young women sitting on the edge of their seats, about to have their world turned upside down. But they came from warrior stock, even if they didn't know it yet. They would handle the truth with the same grit and courage as their aunt and cousin had.

38

KYRA

Kyra's fingers closed around her pendant as she watched her nieces.

Her nieces!

Sitting closer to each other on the plush sofa, looking uncertain and vulnerable, yet there was steel in their spines. They had survived horrors that would have broken adults, and here they sat, wary but undefeated.

She yearned to start with the biggest news that she was their aunt, but the damn Doomer hadn't provided her sisters' given names, just their married names and addresses. How could she prove to these girls that she was their aunt when she couldn't even tell them the names of their mothers?

Her own memories had been somehow erased

by that monster, either with thralling or drugs or both, so all she knew was what he had told Toven.

She had four younger sisters but couldn't picture their faces or recall a single moment shared with them. The loss ached like a physical wound.

"Perhaps we should start with the background," Kyra said to Jasmine. "You did a very good job explaining it to me."

Jasmine regarded her for a long moment, as if she was reading all the things Kyra wanted to say but couldn't, and then nodded and turned to the girls with a gentle smile. "Do any of you know the stories from the Bible?"

Since owning a Bible was illegal in Iran, Kyra doubted the girls knew anything about it.

As she'd expected, the question landed like a stone in still water. All four girls stiffened, their expressions closing off. Kyra understood their reaction all too well. In Iran, religion wasn't just faith—it was law, wielded like a weapon to control every aspect of women's lives. The modesty police enforced dress codes with brutal efficiency, and defiance could mean execution.

"The Christian Bible?" Arezoo finally asked.

"The creation story is almost the same in the Quran as it is in the Bible," Kyra said. "But they have demons instead of the sons of gods. These demons unite with women to create the giants of the Bible, and in return for the union the demons teach the women magical spells. That's the closest it comes to the story you are referring to."

"Oh, well." Jasmine waved a dismissive hand. "That will make things both more difficult and easier. I can just tell it like a fictional story, only everything I will tell you is true."

Arezoo, ever the protective eldest, lifted her chin. "You can spin any tale you want. That doesn't mean we have to believe you."

The girl's defiance made Kyra's heart swell with pride even as it broke for what they had endured.

Jasmine glanced at Max, a small smile playing at her lips. "Max will later demonstrate things that will convince you of the veracity of my claims."

Kyra didn't miss how all four girls tensed at the mention of Max. Their gazes darted to him, a mix of fear and suspicion in their eyes. Even lounging casually, Max's masculine presence filled the room. They felt safe with Ell-rom, who projected a very mellow character, but Max was so male that even when he smiled and tried to look nonintimidating, he was still imposing, and the girls had a bad history with immortal males.

They might not have realized that their tormentors hadn't been human, but they could have picked up on the different energy.

Jasmine caught the worried looks the girls directed at Max and turned to him again. "Would you be a sweetheart and make tea for everyone? Some cookies will sweeten the mood as well."

"Gladly." Max pushed to his feet with fluid grace, heading toward the kitchen.

It was a brilliant move on Jasmine's part. In a culture where women were expected to serve men, having this obviously powerful male prepare refreshments for them sent the right message.

"I'll help," Ell-rom said, following Max to the kitchen.

Jasmine leaned forward, lowering her voice conspiratorially. "Did you ever wonder how humans came to be?" Her tone invited confidence, creating an atmosphere of shared secrets between women. "I'm sure you don't believe that we were created from clay, right?"

The girls exchanged glances before shaking their heads in perfect unison. The movement was so synchronized that Kyra had to suppress a smile. They were just adorable.

"We evolved from apes," Arezoo said hesitantly, as if speaking such words was blasphemous and rebellious, which they were.

"That's true," Jasmine agreed easily. "We did, but not in the way most people think." She settled back, creating a storyteller's atmosphere. "A very long time ago, and I'm talking millions of years, the first humanoids branched out. There are all kinds of speculations about how they became bipedal and why their brains grew bigger than those of other apes, but I won't get into that. The short version of the story is that without outside intervention, we would still be just a little smarter than apes. Evolution works very slowly, and the rapid growth of our brains and what they can do can't be simply explained."

Kyra watched the girls' faces as they absorbed this. Arezoo maintained her skeptical expression, but Kyra could see curiosity flickering in her eyes. Donya and Laleh leaned forward, drawn into Jasmine's conspiratorial storytelling. Even Azadeh, who had been the quietest since their rescue, seemed engaged.

Jasmine was truly a gifted actress, and it was obvious that she loved performing for a crowd.

"What intervention?" Laleh asked.

Jasmine's eyes sparkled. "Ah. Now we get to the juicy part of the story."

39

MAX

As Max filled the electric tea kettle, his movements automatic while his attention remained fixed on Jasmine's voice drifting in from the living room, it suddenly struck him that Kyra hadn't told her daughter that the girls were her cousins. She'd only told her that they were family.

It mattered more for Jasmine than for the girls at the moment. The history she was going to tell them was much more interesting than how exactly they were related, and Jasmine was doing a masterful job of introducing them to their hidden world.

"...so gold is crucial for many things other than making pretty jewelry, and there was plenty of it on Earth, so these aliens who called themselves gods came to mine it." Jasmine's voice carried clearly into the kitchen, her tone perfectly modulated to create suspense. "They were neither angels nor demons, just powerful beings who had mastered the art of genetic manipulation."

Max exchanged glances with Ell-rom as they listened. Jasmine had added dramatic flourishes to parts that didn't strictly need embellishment, but her delivery was captivating. Even knowing every twist and turn of the story, Max found himself drawn in by her narrative style.

"She's good," he said to Ell-rom, searching for the tea service.

"I know." Ell-rom's eyes lit up with pride. "I wish she could continue performing. It's a shame to let such talent go to waste."

Max nodded as he examined the selection of teas. "True." He chose one that he'd had before and liked and added it to the tea kettle to brew. He then returned to search for a platter for the cookies and found a beautiful silver plate that didn't match anything else in the contemporary kitchen.

Perhaps the Saudi prince who had leased the penthouse a while ago forgot it there.

The Oreos looked almost comically ordinary on such an elegant serving piece, but it didn't matter. Oreos were the best, and the girls were going to like them no matter what they were served on.

As he arranged the cookies in concentric

circles, an idea began forming. "Maybe Jasmine can make productions only for clan consumption. She could put them up on our closed-circuit programming." The more he thought about it, the more excited he got by the idea. "It could be something as simple as story time with Jasmine. She could just sit there and read a book, doing all the voices and expressions and maybe even singing when songs were mentioned. I'd watch something like that, and I'm sure many others would."

Ell-rom's expression turned thoughtful as he helped Max gather teacups. "I'll suggest it to her. She doesn't even need to get anyone's approval for that. She can just do it and upload it to the clan's server."

The casual way Ell-rom referenced their technical infrastructure impressed Max. The prince had adapted remarkably well to modern technology considering he'd awakened from a seven-millennia stasis not too long ago and had to learn everything about Earth from scratch. "You've gained a lot of knowledge in a short time. I'm impressed."

Ell-rom shrugged. "It's easy to find answers on the internet if you know how to ask the right questions."

Max laughed. "Ain't that the truth." He opened another cabinet, guessing correctly he would find honey and sugar there. "Knowing what to ask requires wisdom that most lack." In the living room, Jasmine's voice continued painting pictures of ancient gods and their impression on early humans. "But back to Jasmine, I'm sure that Kian would gladly compensate her for producing content that clan members enjoy. Don't forget that our people in Scotland and Alaska are also potential content consumers."

Ell-rom lifted a hand in a calming gesture that reminded Max of Annani. "Let's not get ahead of ourselves. First, I need to suggest it to Jasmine, and then if she wants to do it, she can prepare one episode, and we'll see how well it is received."

"That's smart." Max began loading teacups onto a large round silver tray, positioning them carefully. "I get overexcited about my own ideas, which would explain why I failed at most of my independent endeavors. I never had the patience for proper market research."

Ell-rom looked aghast, and for a long moment he didn't respond, then he let out a breath and leaned against the counter. "I'm the opposite. I tend to overthink everything. Perhaps I'm too cautious."

From the living room, Max could hear Jasmine describing the first immortals, her voice painting vivid pictures of the society of ancient Sumer that were probably mostly fictional.

Ell-rom added the kettle of hot tea in the center

of the tray. "We could make good business partners, you and I. Except you are a Guardian and I'm an executioner."

Max cringed. It was easy to forget what the soft-spoken genteel prince was capable of, and it was also obvious how much he hated his ability.

"We are all many things, Ell-rom. You need to find something you love to do to counteract what you hate doing but have to."

The prince nodded. "Good advice. I just wish I knew what that thing was."

"You need to keep trying new things to find out." Max lifted the loaded tray, balancing it on his palm. "Show time."

"Is that how you found out that what you enjoyed most was being a Guardian?" Ell-rom asked.

Max stopped and turned toward the prince. "The things I enjoyed most were singing and hunting for pleasure, but after a while both got old. I needed something to nourish my soul. That's what being a Guardian and saving people does for me. But that's not to say that I enjoy it the most out of all the things I've ever tried."

"That's an interesting perspective." Ell-rom followed Max to the living room. "Not everything that we enjoy doing satisfies us, and the other way around. A balance is needed."

"Precisely."

The tray was steady in his hand as he entered the living room, ready to play his part in this delicate dance of revelation and healing. Sometimes the biggest battles were won not with fists or fangs, but with cookies and kindness.

He put the tray on the coffee table. "Come and get it, ladies."

40

KYRA

The transformation on the girls' faces as Jasmine spoke was remarkable. They had gone from wary and defensive to completely entranced, their expressions open with wonder as they drank in the tale of gods and immortals.

Kyra recognized that look.

It was probably the same expression she'd worn when she first learned the truth. That moment when the impossible suddenly seemed not just possible, but real.

Surprisingly, they hadn't asked for proof yet. They hadn't asked what would become of them either, but Kyra was sure they soon would. She expected nothing less from Arezoo. The girl was smart and inquisitive, and she didn't accept what she was told without questioning.

Kyra could see herself in the girl, and she wondered if she was like that in her youth. The seeds of rebellion must have started with asking questions and not accepting dogmatic answers as truth. Had she planned her escape before being sent to study in America? Had she played her father by pretending to be a dutiful daughter and loyal to the autocratic regime? Or had she simply met Boris, fallen in love, and decided to embrace a better life?

Perhaps it had been a combination of both. Once she rescued her sisters, provided that they wanted to be rescued, she might learn more about her past. Maybe they had known about her rebellious plans.

Or maybe her father had poisoned her sisters' minds about her, telling them terrible things about her, things they might have told their children.

She reached for her pendant again, its familiar weight offering solace as uncertainty bubbled beneath her composed exterior. Soon, she would have to tell them who she really was—who they were to each other—and hope they didn't turn on her.

The thought made her throat dry.

Jasmine was just reaching the part about Dormants when Max returned with the tea, Ellrom following with plates and napkins, and the spell was broken. The girls looked like they were emerging from a trance, their awestruck expressions turning back to wariness.

Max put the tray on the coffee table. "Come and get it, ladies."

"Perfect timing," Jasmine said, imbuing her tone with cheerfulness that was only slightly disingenuous. "I was just getting to the important part, but perhaps a short break for tea will ease your processing of what you've been told so far."

Arezoo fixed Jasmine with a direct gaze as Kyra poured tea into the small porcelain cups. "What does this story have to do with us?" She accepted a cup that Ell-rom handed her with a murmured thanks, but her attention never left Jasmine's face.

The time had arrived. Jasmine might not be done with the prelude, but by now, the girls had enough background to understand what she needed to tell them.

Glancing at Jasmine, Kyra caught her daughter's eye and gave a small nod, signaling that she would take over.

"I'll continue where Jasmine left off," Kyra said. "You ask what does it have to do with you, and my answer is everything because you are part of the exclusive club of the gods' descendants."

Four sets of eyes widened with incredulity.

"It's a great story, but we need proof." Arezoo looked at Max with defiance in her eyes that was mostly bravado. "Jasmine said that you will demonstrate something."

"With pleasure." He rubbed his hands together. "Immortals can project illusions, and I happen to be very good at that, which is why Jasmine asked me to demonstrate. But since I know you will think I'm tricking you in some way, I want each of you to get a piece of paper and a pen or pencil, and once I project the illusion, to write down what you see without telling your sisters or cousins what it is. Then you will all hand the piece of paper to Arezoo, who will read them out to confirm that all of you saw the same thing."

Arezoo narrowed her eyes at him. "Are you going to tell us what you are about to project?"

He shook his head. "I will give no clues, so you won't think that I influenced you subconsciously or in any other way."

"You've done it before," Azadeh said.

"No, but I have heard others talk about disbelieving Dormants and how difficult it was to convince them. It gave me food for thought, and I devised a foolproof method."

Donya rose to her feet. "I'll get paper and pens from the office."

Kyra realized that the girls must have snooped around to know that was where they could find writing supplies.

As everyone waited for Donya to return, Kyra

tried to prepare what she was going to tell them. The most difficult part would be to tell four very young women the method by which female Dormants turned immortal. In fact, she wondered how come none of the girls had transitioned given that Durhad had probably violated all four. Hopefully, given that immortal males had the same low fertility as immortal females, none of them had gotten pregnant, but it was also possible that Durhad had injected himself with fertility drugs in addition to injecting the women.

Were there even drugs for increasing male fertility?

Kyra's knowledge on the subject was nearly nonexistent.

The truth was that her knowledge on most subjects was superficial at best. She didn't remember what she'd studied at the university. And when she'd had time to read over the long years in the resistance, she'd read mostly fiction to relax. She hadn't worked on gaining knowledge in anything other than politics and warfare.

It was such a limited point of view.

Donya returned with a Post-it stack and four pens, and once each of the girls had what she needed in hand, Max rose to his feet and pointed at the front door.

"Look over there," he said.

Nothing happened as far as Kyra could see, but

the girls gasped and huddled together, and then Laleh got up and walked over to where the illusion was supposed to be and extended her hand.

Brave girl.

She turned to her sisters and cousin. "There is nothing here."

"Don't tell them what you see," Max warned. "If I want to, I can make the illusion tangible so you will be able to actually touch it. But for now, this is enough. Write down what you see and hand the notes to Arezoo."

Given the girls' reactions, they had all seen what Max had wanted them to see, but Kyra still didn't see anything. She waited to catch Max's eye to get an explanation, but when he finally looked at her, he only smiled. "Patience. I'll explain in a moment."

Perhaps he could control who saw his illusions.

Arezoo read over the notes and shook her head. "We all saw the same thing. A man-sized purple teddy bear jumping from foot to foot and waving a paw."

Max grinned. "Is that proof enough of my mental abilities or do you need more?"

Arezoo chewed on her lower lip, the same way Kyra did when she was thinking or unsure. "It proves that you can project illusions. It doesn't prove that you are immortal."

Max sighed dramatically. "I hoped I wouldn't

need to do this, but you are twisting my arm." He walked over to where the girls were sitting and crouched in front of them. "I'm going to make a small cut on my hand, so don't be alarmed when I pull out a knife. The cut will completely heal in minutes, so you will have a short time to get tangible proof, like dipping your fingers in my blood, so pay close attention."

Arezoo shook her head. "You could be projecting the image of your bleeding hand into our minds the same way you did with the teddy bear. You could even project the thought of us touching it and feeling that it was there when it wasn't. You said that you can make the illusions tangible."

Kyra was so proud of her niece. The girl was so smart, but that made convincing her that much harder.

Max rose to his feet. "Oh, well. At least that saves me from having to cut myself. But now I'm out of ideas. A show of fangs and glowing eyes is not going to convince this young lady either."

"Oh, for fuck's sake," Fenella huffed. "Just get on with the story, Kyra. I might be immortal but I'm getting old here."

"Please watch your language in front of my nieces."

Fenella snorted. "I doubt that translated well to Farsi."

"Nieces?" Donya asked in a near whisper. "Are you our aunt?"

Kyra nodded. "Your mothers are my younger sisters, but since my memory was basically erased twenty-three years ago, I don't know anything about them. I didn't even know I had sisters before the monster who calls himself a doctor told me why he took you and that he sent his minions to collect more of our family members."

The silence that followed felt thick enough to cut with a knife. Donya gaped, Laleh's eyes widened to an almost comical degree, and Azadeh simply stared, her face unreadable.

As usual, it was Arezoo who spoke. "You can't be our aunt. You are too young."

"I'm immortal, just like Max and Ell-rom and Jasmine. In fact, Jasmine is my daughter, but the monster who erased the memory of my family from my mind also erased the memory of the child I was forced to leave behind and her father. Since you have the same genes as I do, the so-called doctor had you kidnapped from your homes, and he probably tried to induce your transition, but something prevented it from happening."

Donya shook her head, her dark eyes skeptical. "Our mother never mentioned having another sister."

The words stung, though Kyra had expected

them. She'd been erased from her family's memory—whether by choice or by force.

"She told me," Arezoo said quietly. "Mother once told me in secret that she had an older sister who went to study abroad and never returned. She said she didn't know what happened to her and that she missed her. She also told me never to tell anyone because our grandfather forbade Mother and our aunts from even mentioning her name. It was as if the older sister had never existed."

The revelation hit Kyra hard. She had existed in whispers and secrets, a cautionary tale perhaps, or a painful memory too dangerous to acknowledge openly.

Had her sisters mourned her?

Had they wondered what became of her?

An awkward silence descended over the room as each of them tried to process their emotions. Kyra was unable to move, frozen by the weight of what had been lost—decades of sisterhood, of aunt-hood, of family.

Suddenly, Jasmine rose from her seat and crossed the space between herself and her cousins in two long steps.

"Come here," she said, and without hesitation wrapped her arms around Arezoo, hugging her tightly. "I always wanted to have a big loving family. Nothing could have made me happier than finding out I have four beautiful cousins."

The tension in Arezoo's body visibly melted as she returned the embrace. One by one, Jasmine moved to each girl, gathering them into hugs that acknowledged their newfound connection and a promise that there was much more love to come.

Kyra felt tears pricking at her eyes as she watched. The display of emotion and vulnerability was outside her comfort zone, but she enjoyed watching it.

"For the love of all that's holy," Fenella's exasperated voice cut through Kyra's paralysis. "Stop being such a pussy, Kyra. Get up and hug your nieces."

41

MAX

Max put a hand over his chest and rubbed it over the unexpected tightness there. Watching Kyra embrace her nieces made him surprisingly emotional. The fierce warrior, who'd fearlessly faced down the Revolutionary Guard and even Doomers, had tears in her eyes because she was hugging her family.

Hell, it even made him miss his mother.

Perhaps he should call her later and tell her about Kyra. She always complained that he didn't call often enough, but the truth was that he had nothing new to say.

His mother was always in the loop about the clan's latest gossip, so he had nothing new to share with her. He didn't want to discuss the rescue missions he was involved in because she didn't have the constitution for that. However, she would be thrilled to hear that he had finally found someone. It would give her a fresh, juicy piece of gossip to share with her friends.

He hadn't done a great job convincing the girls that he was immortal, but Fenella had been right. Learning they were related to Kyra and Jasmine had been the missing piece in the puzzle for them.

The supernatural element was secondary to that revelation.

Of course, they hadn't gotten to the more complicated parts yet. The girls still didn't fully understand why they'd been targeted, or rather the purpose for which they had been abducted, and that conversation would be difficult.

Max shifted his weight, wondering if it would be better for him and Ell-rom to excuse themselves when the time came. The girls might feel more comfortable speaking about their experience without men present.

He glanced at Ell-rom, who was watching the scene with a soft expression. The prince had that same otherworldly gentleness about him that Annani possessed, a radiating kindness that made people at ease around them. Max wondered who they had inherited that trait from.

According to everything he knew about their shared father, Ahn had been ruthless. Then again, his intentions had always been benevolent, so perhaps Annani and Ell-rom had inherited that side of him.

He glanced at Fenella, who was also watching the display with a small smile on her lips and a sheen in her eyes that looked suspiciously like tears. Despite her rough-around-the-edges attitude and snark toward Kyra, she appeared moved by the outpouring of emotions they were all witnessing.

Catching him looking at her, Fenella rose from her armchair and crossed the room to stand beside him behind the couch.

"It makes me wonder if I have any nephews or nieces," she said softly, her accent becoming more pronounced with emotion. "Are you still in touch with Din? Maybe he could find out for me?"

The question hit a sore spot. Max had been thinking about contacting his old friend and telling him about Fenella, but he was in no rush, especially since she wasn't interested in Din.

Instead, he offered, "I can ask one of my cousins to go to the pub and ask around for you."

Fenella's sharp eyes narrowed. "Why not Din?"

Max grimaced, knowing she wouldn't let it drop. "He won't answer my calls."

She studied him from under lowered lashes. "So, how did you plan to tell him you found me?"

He shrugged. "I planned on calling my mother

and asking her to talk to his mother to convince him to call me."

Fenella laughed, drawing a quick glance from Kyra before she returned her attention to her nieces. "Talk about being a mama's boy," she said, lowering her voice. "Just leave him a message using someone else's phone, or if you want, I'll do it. If he was so in love with me back in the day, he will respond to me, right?"

That was a complete change of heart on her part.

Earlier, she'd seemed uninterested in reconnecting with Din and called him an asshole.

"What happened that you suddenly want to connect with him? I thought you wanted to check out all the other available bachelors."

She pursed her lips, a thoughtful expression crossing her face. "Yeah, I did, and I meant it. He's a jerk." Then she shrugged, the casualness of the gesture undermined by the intensity in her eyes. "On the other hand, maybe I should give him a fair chance. If he doesn't work for me, I can move on to someone else, right?"

Din had been devastated when Fenella chose Max over him all those years ago. Would reconnecting with her now be a gift, or a cruel reopening of old wounds?

Did he even deserve a second chance after the way he'd acted?

The truth was that it wasn't Max's call.

It was up to Fenella and Din to sort out their issues and decide how to move forward.

Back then, she had been just another human girl, someone Din shouldn't have developed any deep feelings for, but now she was an immortal female, and there weren't many of those around. Din had an advantage, so to speak, and if he was enough of an idiot to give it up because he was still too sore to accept a truce and a second chance half a century later, then he didn't deserve her.

"I'll tell you what," Max said. "I'll send the bastard a message, and if he doesn't respond, you can do it using someone else's phone." A new thought occurred to him. "I think we should get you a phone of your own and Kyra should get one too."

"That would be much appreciated. Not that I have anyone I want to call, but having a phone these days is like having a window into the world." She lifted her hand and wiggled her fingers. "All the information you want at your fingertips. I find it exhilarating." She glanced toward the group of women still huddled together. "What about the girls? Shouldn't they get phones? What teenager these days can survive without one?"

It was a fair point, but it also raised a security concern. "You're right. We can give them phones with no outside communication capabilities. We can't have them calling their mothers and telling them where they are."

Fenella tilted her head. "Why? You said that the Doomer who caught me was acting on his own initiative, and now that you have him in your dungeon, the girls are no longer in danger. Well, except from their own families, but that's another story." She shook her head. "Most Iranians I've met are not like that, but I guess there are enough crazy fanatics out there that kiss the ground the Mullahs walk on. Literally."

He dipped his head and whispered in her ear. "The Doomers are still looking for more of Kyra's family members. We can't let them know where they are."

Understanding dawned in Fenella's eyes. "Right. That would be bad."

"Very bad," Max agreed. "We need to keep communication locked down until we can secure the rest of the family. Then they can talk all they want."

"How are you going to do that?"

"We are going back to Iran," Max said.

Across the room, the group hug was beginning to break apart. The women were wiping away tears and attempting watery smiles. Kyra looked both emotionally wrung out and somehow lighter, as if a burden she'd been carrying had been lifted.

Her eyes found Max's across the room, and

when she smiled at him, he felt the tension ease in his chest.

"You've got it so bad, Maxi boy," Fenella murmured, amusement in her voice.

Max didn't bother denying it. "Yeah, I do."

"Good for you." There was no bitterness in her tone, just a weary acceptance. "She seems like she could handle you."

"What's that supposed to mean? I'm not difficult."

She snorted. "Right. Whatever."

He still didn't understand what she meant by that. He was an easygoing guy. If anything, the question was whether he could handle this highly-strung rebel who struggled to rely on anyone but herself.

Fenella's expression softened. "That's actually kind of sweet, in a pathetic sort of way."

He hadn't realized that he'd spoken out loud. "Thanks. I think."

They shared a brief smile, and he realized that their awkwardness was mostly gone. They might become friends.

"About Din," he said, returning to their earlier conversation. "Give him a chance. Everyone is an asshole sometimes, including me. Or especially me."

"We were all young. Well, you two weren't actually young, but I was. I made choices based on limited information and even more limited experience." She shrugged. "Besides, if I'd ended up with him back then, I might have missed out on all the experiences I had. I'm not sorry for picking you." She gave him a coquettish smile. "You were much more fun than Din. I hope he's loosened up during the last fifty years."

Max stifled a wince. As far as he knew, Din still had a stick up his butt.

She chuckled. "Given your expression, the answer is no, but I'm curious anyway. I'll give him a tiny little chance."

"I'll talk to him tonight," Max promised.

"You do that." She nodded toward the group of women, who were now settling back into their seats. "But maybe we should focus on the current situation first."

She was right.

The difficult part was about to start, and he and Ell-rom should make themselves scarce.

He caught Ell-rom's eye and motioned with his chin toward the terrace. "I need some fresh air. Care to join me?"

"Yes. I enjoy being outdoors."

"Hell of a day," Max muttered as he closed the sliding doors behind them.

Ell-rom's lips quirked upward. "And it's not over yet."

"Not by a long shot." Max walked over to a

lounge chair that was not visible from the living room and sat down. "I don't envy Kyra and Jasmine the conversation they are about to have with the girls."

Ell-rom nodded as he sat on the other lounger. "I heard what you told Fenella about the Doomers going after Kyra's other family members. When are you heading out?"

"Tomorrow, if Onegus gets everything ready. Naturally, Kyra is coming, and probably the Kra-ell as well."

"What about me and Jasmine?" Ell-rom asked.

"You should stay here and watch over the girls. Jasmine can do fun things with them, maybe take them shopping. I'm sure they would love that."

Ell-rom nodded. "I'm happy to return the favor. Until not too long ago, I needed to be taken care of right here in this penthouse. Now I'm paying it forward."

42

KYRA

Kyra dabbed at her eyes with the back of her hand, unaccustomed to such an intense display of emotion. The girls seemed equally affected, but the ferocity of their reaction puzzled her.

These girls had clung to her as if she were a lifeline in a storm, yet they'd only just learned of her existence.

Was it simply a release of tension after the nightmare they'd endured? Or was it the profound relief of discovering they weren't alone in the world, especially when they believed returning home was impossible?

Max and Ell-rom slipped out onto the terrace through the sliding glass doors, which gave them privacy for the uncomfortable conversation to come. She appreciated their understanding that some things were easier to discuss in a women-only space, particularly given what these girls had been through.

She needed to learn more about her sisters and the rest of her nieces and nephews, but she didn't want to start by telling the girls that their families were in danger.

"Tell me about your families," Kyra said, settling back on the couch. "Do you have any other siblings? Are your mothers very religious? How do they get along with your fathers? Are they happily married?"

As she'd expected, Arezoo regarded her with that penetrating gaze that seemed too old for her nineteen years—a familiar wariness that Kyra recognized from her own reflection.

"Are you asking just because you are curious or for some pragmatic reason?" the girl asked.

Perhaps she shouldn't dance around the truth, especially given that she was leaving tomorrow, and they deserved to know why she was abandoning them so soon after finding them. "Both," she admitted. "I don't even know my sisters' names." The words tasted bitter on her tongue, a reminder of everything that had been stolen from her. "The other reason is that the fake doctor told us his minions are going to abduct more of our family members. Your other cousins. They might even take your mothers if they think they are attractive enough."

Arezoo paled, her olive complexion taking on an ashen hue. "Why does he want more of our family? Is it because he thinks all of them can turn immortal?"

Kyra nodded. "He thinks that he can have immortal children with you and with us. As Jasmine explained, immortal males can't have immortal children with human females. The only way he can have immortal children is with immortal or Dormant females." She waved a hand over the group. "That's me and Fenella because we are already immortal, and you because you are Dormants. Luckily immortals, males and female alike, have a very low fertility rate, so the chances that he got any of us pregnant are very low, but just to be sure, the clan's doctor is arriving this afternoon, and she will conduct some health tests to check that no permanent damage was done to us, and she will also check for pregnancies."

The girls exchanged glances, some silent communication passing between them, but they didn't panic as she'd expected.

Arezoo chewed on her lower lip. "He didn't do what you think he did to us. We are still intact."

That caught Kyra off guard, a wave of relief

washing over her so intensely that it left her momentarily speechless. But it was highly improbable, given what she knew of the Doomer's intentions, and she suspected that the girls were either in a state of denial or that they had been heavily drugged while the unspeakable had been done to them.

"Are you sure?" she asked, unable to keep the skepticism from her voice.

Arezoo looked to her sisters and cousin, who all nodded in confirmation. "Unless he did it when we were drugged, but we would have known, right? We would have been in pain and there would have been blood."

Kyra exchanged looks with Fenella, who had joined her on the couch and appeared equally perplexed.

"How is that possible?" Kyra asked.

Fenella shrugged, her expression contemplative. "Who knows what that crazy son of a bitch was thinking. Maybe he didn't want them to transition and thought about inseminating them just to get them pregnant." She turned to the girls, her voice softening. "You were probably injected with fertility drugs like me and Kyra."

"We were injected with all kinds of things," Donya said. "We felt sick most of the time."

"How long did he have you?" Fenella asked. "I

was so heavily sedated that I didn't notice anything going on around me. I didn't even know that you were there."

"I'm not sure," Donya said, twisting a strand of hair around her finger. "We were also heavily drugged, but I don't think it was more than a week. We were taken on Saturday afternoon."

"It's Friday now," Jasmine said. "That means that he had you only for a few days. He might have been just prepping you with the fertility drugs."

Arezoo nodded, her hands tightening into fists in her lap. "I didn't know what he was pumping us with, only that it was bad."

Something didn't add up in their story, and Kyra leveled her gaze at Arezoo. "If you are all still virgins, why did you say that your families will kill you for ruining their honor?"

The stark question silenced the room. Even Fenella, who rarely seemed fazed by anything, looked uncomfortable.

Arezoo sighed, her shoulders slumping. "It doesn't matter what really happened. The fact that we were taken and held by men is enough to put a stain on our honor. No one will believe us that we weren't violated." She swallowed audibly, her voice dropping to barely above a whisper. "Besides, he touched me. He just didn't...you know. I was drugged, but I still knew what he was doing." She swallowed. "I was sure that he wouldn't stop at that, but for some reason he did."

It occurred to Kyra that he could have thralled the memory from their minds and gotten rid of the evidence of blood, but there had been no logical reason for him to do so. He wasn't merciful, and the only reason to make the girls forget the violation would have been to spare them the pain, which he surely wouldn't have bothered with.

Donya nodded, wrapping her arms around herself as if suddenly cold. "He touched me too. I thought it was a nightmare, but it must have been real."

Laleh and Azadeh shook their heads as if to say that nothing like that had happened to them, but the haunted look in their eyes told Kyra they feared the worst.

The realization sent a surge of rage through her.

She took a deep breath, suppressing her anger. The girls needed her to remain cool and collected, to support them, and to maintain control.

"You don't have to go back if you fear for your lives. You can stay with us here. But you might be wrong about your families. Perhaps they will be more understanding than you give them credit for."

Arezoo shook her head. "I don't want to risk it.

I'd rather stay here with you." Uncertainty filled her expressive eyes. "If you want us, that is."

"Of course, I do."

She didn't know where she stood as far as the clan was concerned, but she felt Kian wouldn't say no to her hosting the girls.

"It's our father," Donya said quietly. "He's very traditional and he's a commander in the Revolutionary Guard. Our mother wouldn't…" A sob escaped her throat. "At least, I hope she wouldn't."

"We intend to save your mothers and aunts as well, but only if they are willing to come with us without their husbands," Kyra said. "We're mounting a rescue mission." She touched her pendant, drawing strength from its solidity. "I'll be leaving tomorrow with a team to find them."

"You're leaving?" Arezoo's voice sharpened with alarm. "But we just found you."

"I know," Kyra acknowledged. "I'd rather not leave you either, but I need to save my sisters if I can, and the team needs me. I know the territory, I speak the language, and most importantly, I'm family. Your mothers might trust me when they wouldn't trust strangers."

"How will they even know who you are?" Donya asked. "You look too young to be their sister."

Kyra hadn't fully worked that part out yet. "I'll tell them that I'm your cousin, Kyra's daughter, and that I'm searching for my mother." She shifted her gaze to Jasmine. "It will be easy to pretend to be you now that I know your history."

Jasmine nodded. "We need all the information we can get from the girls about your sisters and their families. That will help convince them as well."

Kyra turned to the girls. "The fake doctor didn't remember the names of my sisters or their addresses. He only provided us with the name of the neighborhood your family lives in. I need you to fill in the blanks for me."

Arezoo hesitated only for a moment. "Our mother's name is Soraya," she said. "She's the eldest. Well, eldest after you, and the three of us are her only children. She's married to Fareed."

"My mother is Rana," Azadeh offered quietly. "She's the next oldest. My father's name is Hamid. I'm their only child."

"And the other two?" Kyra prompted.

"Yasmin and Parisa," Arezoo said. "Aunt Yasmin has three daughters and two sons. Aunt Parisa has four sons."

Kyra absorbed the information, these names that should have been familiar but felt like those of strangers. Soraya, Rana, Yasmin, Parisa. Her sisters. Women who shared her blood but not her memories. Women who might not even want to see her, given what their father had done to erase her.

"You named me after your sister," Jasmine said, a tone of accusation in her voice. "You told my father that I looked like Jasmine from Aladdin and that's why you named me after her."

Kyra sighed. "I wish I remembered that. I also had a rebel friend named Parisa, but that had nothing to do with my sister. It's just a popular name."

"What if our mothers don't want to come with you without our fathers?" Laleh asked suddenly. "Our mother will miss us, but she will miss Father too."

Arezoo shook her head. "We can't bring Father here. He's a loyal Revolutionary Guard officer." She looked at Kyra. "He's gone a lot, and our mother is alone. She might not be as opposed to the idea as Laleh thinks."

It was a hint that things at home weren't as peachy as Laleh believed, but Arezoo wanted to protect her youngest sister from ugly truths.

"We will respect your mothers' choices," Kyra said. "We'll warn them of the danger, offer them protection, but ultimately it will be their decision. But your cousins deserve the same chance you're getting, the girls and the boys are Dormants. They could become immortal."

"How?" Arezoo looked at Jasmine. "You keep saying that the gods found a way to activate the dormant genes, but you didn't tell us how it is done."

Kyra wondered if they should tell the girls now or wait until later. They'd already absorbed too many revelations.

Fenella snorted. "That's a conversation for another day, girls. Trust me."

Kyra shot her a grateful look. "Fenella is right. This can wait. Tell me more about your mothers and your aunts. Are they happy? How do they get along with their husbands? How religious are their households?"

"Why does that matter?" Arezoo asked, that suspicion creeping back into her voice.

"Because it might tell me how receptive they'll be to what I have to tell them. And whether they'd consider leaving their homes or are they too deeply entrenched in their lives there."

The girl nodded. "My mother is not happy," she said bluntly. "My father is away a lot, which is good because when he comes home, he expects her to serve him." She cast a quick glance at her youngest sister. "She smiles when he's around, but it's fake." Her jaw tightened. "When he's gone, it's like she's a different person."

Kyra suspected that Arezoo was censoring the description for Laleh's benefit.

"My father isn't as strict as Uncle Fareed,"

Azadeh said. "But he doesn't love my mother. She cries a lot when she thinks I can't hear her. I think he blames her for not being able to have more kids and that the only one she gave him is a girl." She looked down at her hands. "I also think he has a mistress."

"Is that a thing in Iran?" Jasmine asked. "I thought that with the morality police and everything, people didn't fool around."

Fenella snorted. "You'd be surprised. It's do as I say but not as I do. There are different rules for those with power and those without."

Kyra's heart ached for these women she couldn't remember. Had her sisters been forced into these marriages as their father had planned to force her?

"What about Yasmin and Parisa?" she prompted. "Are their situations similar?"

"Aunt Yasmin got lucky," Donya said. "Uncle Javad is kind. They're always laughing together when they think no one is watching."

"Aunt Parisa is a widow," Arezoo said. "Uncle Hasan was in the Guard like our father and got killed. She hasn't remarried."

A widow with four sons; Kyra filed that information away. Of all her sisters, Parisa might be the most open to the truth because she wouldn't need to leave anyone behind. She could be the most willing to explore a different path.

"What about your cousins?" Kyra asked. "How old are they?"

As the girls began describing their cousins, ages eight to fifteen, with personalities as varied as the stars, Kyra felt a growing connection to this family she couldn't remember and an increasing sense of urgency.

Hopefully, they wouldn't be too late.

43

MAX

Max stretched his legs on one of the cushioned loungers and gazed at the city through the glass railing. From this height, Los Angeles was sprawled out before them, and the penthouse terrace, with its lush potted plants and elegant furniture, felt like an island floating above the bustling city.

"What else did you learn from the Doomer?" Ell-rom asked.

"The bastard was planning his own little breeding program, using Kyra and Fenella as the starting point, then going after every female in Kyra's family he could get his hands on. The boys are also possible targets as they can be turned immortal and trained to become soldiers."

"Did he go after Fenella's family as well?" Ell-rom asked.

Max shook his head. "We didn't ask, but we should." He frowned, trying to recall details from his history with her. "As far as I remember, Fenella had one younger brother, but I don't know whether her mother had sisters who could have daughters. We didn't spend enough time together for me to learn about her extended family." He ran a hand through his hair, considering the implications. "Still, Scotland isn't as easy to infiltrate and grab people from as Iran is, although these days, things are crazy all over Europe."

"What about your clan there?" Ell-rom asked, his expression turning concerned. "Are they safe?"

"For now they're okay." Max shielded his eyes from the glare of the sun with his hand. "That's where the Clan Mother started the clan, and it's been our stronghold ever since. We've weathered plenty of storms in that castle, which we built with our own hands."

"I would like to visit there one day," Ell-rom said. "Perhaps when things calm down here, Annani could take me and Jasmine to visit Sari."

"Good idea. If things continue on the same trajectory over there..." Max trailed off, not needing to finish the thought. Instability was spreading like wildfire across the globe. It was a vicious cycle that he'd witnessed too often to count, but the difference nowadays was how interconnected the world was. When the dominos fell, everything would collapse in rapid succession.

"They should leave," Ell-rom concluded quietly. "This country is safe."

"For now," Max said. "But convincing a bunch of obstinate Scottish immortals to relocate is a challenge that even Kian can't overcome. His sister stubbornly clings to that old castle, and I don't blame her. It's her home, and even though I chose to move away, I still love it. How are they supposed to just abandon it and move on?"

Ell-rom chuckled. "I'm not the one to ask. I'm a prince without a country, and maybe because of that my advice is to go where you are treated best and where your family is safe."

The sliding glass door opened behind them, and Max turned to see Kyra stepping onto the terrace. The sight of her still caused a little hitch in his breathing—something he hadn't experienced with anyone else.

There was just something about her that tugged at all his heart strings and lit up all of his soul. She checked all his boxes, including the ones he hadn't known he had.

Max had never imagined he would find a warrior female so attractive.

Ell-rom rose to his feet. "Is the talk over?" he asked.

"For now," Kyra said, offering a tired smile.

"We've got all the names and addresses, and Jasmine has forwarded them to Kian. She is ordering food delivery and showing the girls the options. She asks what you would like to order."

"I'll go inside and look at the menus," Ell-rom said, already heading for the door.

Max chuckled. "He probably can't even read the menus," he said as the prince disappeared inside. "I don't know how far along he is in his English studies."

"So, that's why he always wears the earpieces." Kyra settled onto the lounger Ell-rom had vacated. "I thought it was to converse with the girls."

"That too." Max turned on his side. "How did it go?"

She sighed, tilting her face toward the sun. "Better than I expected. I now know my sisters' names and how many kids each one has." A small smile played at the corners of her lips. "I have three more nieces and six more nephews, ages eight to fifteen."

"That's a lot of family to discover in one day."

Kyra nodded, her fingers hovering over her pendant. "I asked the girls to tell me about my sisters and the kind of relationships they have with their husbands. Three might want to join their kids here, but the fourth is happily married to a nice guy." Her brow furrowed with concern. "Then again, they have five kids together, and those kids need to be protected." She looked at him with rare uncertainty in her golden eyes. "I don't know what to do, Max. How can I take the children away from my sister? How can I leave my sister to her mortal life?"

The conflict in her voice plucked at his heart, but he had no answers for her.

"I don't know," he said frankly.

"And what if those who choose to leave everything behind and accompany their children to safety are too old to transition? What then?"

Max pushed himself up from his lounger, moved to sit beside her, and wrapped an arm around her shoulders. "Everything will work out," he said, hoping he sounded more confident than he felt. "The Fates will have your back." A thought occurred to him, and he couldn't help but smile. "Who knows? Maybe the nice husband is a Dormant?"

She gave him an incredulous look, one eyebrow arched skeptically. "What are the chances of that?"

Max chuckled. "Not great, but statistics are meaningless when the Fates are involved." He'd seen too many improbable coincidences to dismiss the thought as impossible. "Just look at me finding Fenella after all these years. What were the odds of that?"

"Fair point," Kyra conceded, though she still looked dubious.

She was quiet for a moment. "The girls think they're still virgins." Her voice had dropped to a whisper, as if concerned about being overheard despite the distance from the glass doors. "The Doomer touched them inappropriately, but he didn't do more than that, probably because he didn't want them to transition."

Max frowned, trying to reconcile that with what they'd learned during the interrogation. "Didn't he say that he wanted to create his own breeding program?"

"If he wanted to be the father, he could have done that with artificial insemination," Kyra pointed out. "As long as he didn't bite them, they wouldn't transition, and then their chances of getting pregnant would be higher. The guy is proof that insanity does not equal stupidity. They can coexist in one sick brain."

"How did he know that, though?" Max began, then shook his head. "No, that was a stupid question. The Doomers know how the male Dormants are activated, and that requires only biting." He thought through the implications. "The Doomer might have thought that the same was true for female Dormants. He might not have figured out that sex was part of it as well."

Kyra nodded. "That actually makes sense. If I hadn't been told, I would have assumed the same."

The knowledge that the girls had been spared the worst possible violation was a small mercy and a relief. Still, what they had endured was horrific enough. Max's jaw tightened at the thought of the Doomer's hands on those young women. The bastard was lucky he was locked up and they needed to keep him alive for further interrogation, or Max would have torn him apart with his fangs and claws.

He was still disappointed that Kian had brought Toven to get the Doomer to talk and deprived him of the pleasure of beating him up.

"Jasmine has collected everyone's sizes and sent them to Ell-rom's sister, who knows a personal shopper." Kyra changed the subject. "The shopper is going to deliver everything later tonight, so I'll have proper clothes to wear on the mission." She looked at the leggings and hoodie she had on. "I can't go dressed like this, although given that I can just throw a burka over whatever I'm wearing, this could have worked."

"What do you usually wear on missions?"

"Same as you. Cargo pants with lots of pockets for all my weapons, a tactical vest over a long-sleeved shirt. Boots. But I wore traditional clothing when I infiltrated the compound. I didn't even have any weapons on me because they checked everyone going in." She smiled. "I took the place of a domestic servant who looked a little like me. No one ever pays attention to the cleaning ladies."

"How did you get caught?"

Her shoulders tensed. "He recognized me. I don't know how, given that most of my face was hidden behind a scarf. Maybe he smelled me."

"It's possible." Max fought with his fangs, commanding them to stay dormant and not to elongate. "I should have thought about taking you shopping for clothes. I don't know how it didn't occur to me that you can't go on a mission in snow boots or slippers."

"It's fine." Kyra leaned over to plant a quick kiss on his lips.

It was just a brief peck, barely more than a momentary touch, but the fact that she'd initiated it sent a wave of warmth through Max's chest. This simple, casual gesture meant more to him than a passionate embrace could have because it spoke of comfort, of ease, of the beginning of something special between them.

Unable to resist, he slowly lifted her onto his lap, giving her plenty of time to object if she wanted to. But she came willingly, settling against him with a quiet sigh that sounded like contentment.

Then she leaned into him and kissed him properly, her lips soft but insistent against his. Max let her set the pace, marveling at how something so simple could feel so profound.

When they parted, her eyes were bright with emotion. "You have incredible lips," she said. "Can I admit something nasty?"

He grinned. "The nastier the better. I like nasty."

"Every time I look at Fenella I think of her touching you, kissing you, and I get jealous."

"I have no problem with that."

Kyra snorted. "I didn't think you would. She's been so helpful with the girls. She's much softer on the inside than she is on the outside, and she has been through a lot." She shuddered. "I kept coming back to the compound because of her. I saw what he did to her through the little window at the top of the door, and I figured out that she was like me because her bruises would disappear by the next day. I hoped she had the answers I was looking for, but I also needed to save her. I remembered what it was like to be chained and helpless. Only instead of saving her, I ended up in the same situation. If not for you, I would still be there and so would she."

"It wasn't just me." He rubbed soothing circles on her back. "It was a team effort, and I'm not saying that out of some fake modesty."

"I know. But you were the one who got me out. Thank you."

He leaned away, looking at her face. "I hope those sweet kisses weren't a thank you."

She laughed. "No. They weren't. They started as an experiment and then turned to something more."

"I like the sound of that." He returned to rubbing her back. "Are you nervous about tomorrow?" he asked, not knowing how to make romantic small talk.

"Not nervous the way you might think," she said. "I've led missions before." Her expression sobered. "I'm more worried about what happens after we find them. What if my sisters don't believe me? What if they reject me? What if they choose to stay behind?"

"Then we'll deal with it," he said, holding her gaze. "Whatever happens, Kyra, you're not alone in this. You have Jasmine. You have the girls. You have the clan." He hesitated, then added, "And you have me."

44

KYRA

The doorbell rang at precisely four o'clock, jolting Kyra from thinking about the kiss she'd shared with Max earlier on the terrace.

She didn't remember being a teenager, but given the household she'd been raised in, her first kiss must have been in college, and it had probably been with Boris who had later become her husband. That meant that she had only been with one man voluntarily.

"That must be Bridget." Jasmine pushed to her feet, leaving her newly discovered cousins huddled on the couch.

She opened the door to a tiny redhead in high heels and a curve-hugging dress. The only indicators of her profession were her determined stride and confident gaze.

Perhaps she was going out on a date once she completed her examinations, or maybe she had chosen not to exhibit any outer signs of her profession because she'd heard what the girls had been through at the hands of the fake doctor.

If so, it was a smart move, but the four-inch shoes were still a bit excessive.

Jasmine embraced her like an old friend, towering over the petite woman even though she was barefoot. "Thanks for coming."

"Of course." Bridget's gaze swept over the room, taking in its occupants with a healer's assessing eye. "Hello everyone. I'm Bridget." Her gaze landed on Kyra and she smiled. "You must be Kyra. You look so much like Jasmine that I would have known the two of you were related no matter where I met you."

Kyra stood up and took the doctor's outstretched hand. "Thank you for coming." She gave her a gentle shake, modulating her strength out of habit before remembering that the doctor was an immortal and not nearly as fragile as her tiny frame suggested. "I know that it usually would have been Julian's job to do the testing, but my nieces will be so much more comfortable with a female doctor."

"Of course." Bridget's gaze shifted to the girls.

Four pairs of wary eyes looked back at her,

their expressions ranging from Arezoo's carefully neutral mask to Laleh's barely concealed fear.

None of them spoke even though they had their translating earpieces on.

Kyra hoped the doctor had them too, but it was impossible to see her ears under the mass of her red hair. It was enviably gorgeous, and Kyra subconsciously smoothed a hand over her unruly waves which she never bothered to style.

Perhaps after she was done being a rebel, she could devote more time to her appearance. It would be nice to focus on such trivialities for a change instead of survival.

Bridget seemed unfazed by their silence. "I originally planned on conducting the tests here, but we will be so much more comfortable in the clinic in the underground complex. I brought Gertrude with me, and she's setting everything up." She smiled at the girls, who were sitting on the couch in sweatpants and hoodies, and socks on their feet. "No need to change, but I suggest you put shoes on."

"Why can't we do this here?" Arezoo's voice was sharp with sudden alarm, reflecting how the other three felt about leaving the penthouse.

Kyra should have anticipated this reaction. Of course, they wouldn't want to leave their newfound sanctuary, especially not to go to another medical facility, no matter how nice the doctor who ran it was.

"The clinic is much better equipped than what's available to me in a portable kit, which means we can be done faster."

Donya shook her head, shrinking back into the couch cushions. "I don't want to go anywhere."

Laleh nodded, clinging to her older sister.

Kyra approached them and crouched down to be at eye level with the seated girls. "I understand why you're hesitant, but this is important, and the clinic is only a short elevator ride away."

The girls exchanged glances, that silent communication that sisters seemed to master from an early age, but none of them indicated that they were ready to go. It was like they were bound to the couch by some magic spell.

It suddenly occurred to Kyra that it wasn't just the clinic they feared—it was leaving this safe space, this sanctuary, to go anywhere. After what they'd endured, the idea of venturing into unknown territory, even within the same building, triggered their survival instincts.

These girls needed psychological help that Kyra wasn't equipped to provide. She was a rebel fighter, not a counselor. She knew how to protect people from physical threats, but the invisible wounds of trauma were beyond her expertise.

Still, she had to convince them somehow that it

was okay. They were wasting Bridget's valuable time.

"I know you're scared," she said, steadying her voice. "But I promise you, there is nothing to fear in the underground levels of this building. They're even more secure than this penthouse. No one outside even knows the underground complex exists, let alone how to get there. Only the people who rescued you and want to help you have access to it."

"I'll come with you," Jasmine offered. "I will be the hand holder. If you want, I can stay with each of you while the doctor examines you."

"It needs to be done." Fenella rose from the armchair she'd commandeered. "Let's just get on with it."

"It needs to be done." Arezoo echoed Fenella's words and then turned to her sisters and cousin. "It's going to be okay, and we will all be together."

The journey to the elevator felt like preparing for a military operation. Jasmine and Bridget led the procession, while the girls moved in a tight cluster, flanked by Fenella and Kyra like protective sentries.

As the elevator doors closed, Kyra noted how Laleh pressed herself into the corner, as far from the doors as possible, while Donya's knuckles turned white from gripping the railing. Azadeh kept her eyes fixed on the floor numbers as they descended, as if counting down to an inevitable confrontation.

When the doors finally opened to the clinic level, Kyra stepped out first, silently signaling that it was safe. The corridor before them was surprisingly wide and well lit, with soft off-white walls adorned with small paintings of landscapes that looked incredibly vivid.

These weren't the reproductions she'd seen on the dungeon level.

"Except for the nice pictures, this looks like the hallway in my old high school building," Arezoo commented.

Kyra glanced at her, wondering if the girl was merely saying this to ease the other girls' fears. Whether it was true or not, the observation seemed to help, as the others focused on examining the beautiful pictures they were passing instead of on the examination waiting for them.

The clinic itself was not what Kyra had expected. Instead of cold sterility, it was small and smelled fresh, but not of disinfectant, which would have been triggering for her and everyone who had been imprisoned by the fake doctor.

The nurse who'd checked them for trackers when they had landed greeted them with a warm smile. "You all look so much better already." She motioned to a row of chairs. "Please, take a seat."

There were only six chairs, so Kyra remained standing because she'd volunteered to go first.

"Through here." Bridget opened one of the doors.

"Can we all come in?" Fenella asked.

"It's a bit small for everyone to crowd in, but I'll leave the door open to the waiting room. That way, you can all hear what I'm doing."

"I'll lock the door." Gertrude walked over to the entry door to the clinic. "In case one of the Guardians walks in, we don't want to be on full display, right, ladies?" She offered them a bright smile.

The girls nodded, smiling in return as if compelled by her cheerful attitude.

Gertrude was good at this, and as Kyra followed her into the exam room, she wondered if the nurse had children.

It was more of a patient room, with a proper hospital bed with railings that made her more comfortable for some reason. A padded table would have evoked unpleasant memories.

The nurse left the door partially open, as promised, which gave her some privacy but still allowed the girls to hear what was going on and even peek inside if they wanted to.

"Before you sit on the bed, I need a urine sample first," Gertrude said, handing Kyra a small plastic cup and a folded hospital gown. "You can change in the bathroom."

"Do I need to take everything off?" Kyra asked.

"You can leave your underwear on for now."

The process was simple and oddly familiar, even if Kyra couldn't remember the last time she'd had a proper medical examination. The rebel camps had medics, but their resources were limited to treating injuries and common illnesses. Comprehensive check-ups were a luxury of a different life, one she couldn't remember, and yet she went through the motions of providing the sample as if she had done it a hundred times before.

When she returned from the bathroom wearing the gown, socks, and panties, Gertrude motioned to the bed. "I need to draw some blood," she said while preparing a tray with several vials and a needle. "Do you prefer sitting up or lying down for it?"

"Sitting up."

"Awesome," Gertrude said.

"That's a lot of blood you are preparing to take," Kyra observed as the nurse lined up the vials.

"We're testing for a variety of things," Bridget said, entering the room. "Hormones, general health markers, genetic markers, and a few specific tests to determine what drugs might still be in your system."

Kyra nodded, rolling up her sleeve and extending her arm. Gertrude tied the tourniquet around her upper arm. "Just a small pinch," she warned before inserting the needle with practiced precision.

Kyra didn't even flinch, watching with clinical detachment as Gertrude filled vial after vial with her blood.

"All done," the nurse said once all the vials were filled, pressing a cotton ball to the puncture site.

Bridget pushed the door nearly closed, leaving just enough of a gap that the girls could hear their voices but not see inside. "Privacy is important, even in these circumstances."

The physical examination was efficient and thorough but still gentle and respectful, and Bridget narrated everything she was doing for the benefit of the listening girls.

"Everything looks good," Bridget said as she made notes on a tablet. "If the bloodwork is just as good, you have nothing to worry about. Your immortal body healed everything." She hesitated, which made Kyra tense. "I know that you are concerned about pregnancy, but I didn't feel or smell anything that might indicate that, and I'm pretty good at detecting pregnancy even in the very early stages. The blood test is the most definitive way to be certain, especially this soon after potential conception. But given what we know about immortal fertility, the chances are next to zero."

Relief flooded through Kyra, though she hadn't realized until that moment how much the possibility of pregnancy had been weighing down on her. "Thank you."

"You can get dressed now," Bridget said. "Let's see who wants to be next."

Together, they walked into the waiting area, where the girls were waiting with Jasmine and Fenella. They still looked nervous, but not as nervous as when they had entered the clinic.

"Everything is fine," Kyra announced.

Arezoo rose to her feet. "Did anything hurt?"

"The examination was quick and painless." Kyra sat down on the chair Arezoo had vacated, which was next to Laleh. "Dr. Bridget and Gertrude were very professional and explained everything they were doing. There's nothing to be afraid of."

"Who's next?" Bridget asked gently.

"I'll go," Arezoo said, her voice sounding steadier than her expression indicated.

She looked scared.

"Are you telling the truth about it?" Laleh asked once Arezoo was out of earshot. "I heard you and the nurse talking about lots of blood being taken."

Kyra took the girl's hand, noting how cold her fingers felt despite the comfortable temperature in the clinic. "The needle pinches a little when they take blood," she said honestly. "But it's over very quickly. Everything else is just like a regular checkup." She wrapped her arm around the girl's shoulders and kissed the top of her head.

This was what family felt like. Not just blood ties, but the fierce protectiveness she felt, the desire to shield and guide and heal. She had spent decades fighting for strangers, for principles, for freedom. But this—this bone-deep need to ensure these girls' safety and happiness—this was something altogether different.

She cast a glance at Jasmine, her daughter who was a grown woman and an immortal and did not need her protection anymore. But she needed her love, and Kyra vowed to shower her with buckets of it whether she liked it or not.

45

DROVA

Drova glared at the algebra problem as if it had personally insulted her lineage. The human in the YouTube video kept talking about isolating variables and moving numbers from one side of the equation to the other, but his words might as well have been in Chinese for all the sense they made to her, and Chinese wasn't one of the languages programmed into the translating earpieces.

"So, if we have $3x + 7 = 22$," the cheerful instructor said, "we first subtract seven from both sides to get $3x = 15$, and then divide both sides by 3 to get $x = 5$."

She paused the video and attempted the practice problem: $4x - 9 = 15$.

"Okay, so I need to add 9 to both sides?" she

muttered, scribbling on the notepad beside her. "No, that's not right. Subtract? No..."

With a frustrated sigh, she tossed her pencil onto the desk. Parker's textbook sat beside her tablet, its pages still crisp and barely touched. She'd tried to learn from it, but the dense paragraphs and neatly arranged formulas swam before her eyes after just a few minutes. At least with the videos, she could pause, rewind, and hear someone explain the concepts out loud over and over again.

Was she dumb, or were Kra-ell incapable of learning algebra?

Perhaps the gods had been right in restricting the Kra-ell access to their higher learning institutions. Perhaps the reason wasn't discrimination and the wish to keep the technological advancements to themselves, but that Kra-ell brains were not built for studying. They were warriors, hunters, and that was what they were supposed to do. They weren't meant to sit on their asses in classrooms.

Her wound throbbed dully beneath the bandage, a reminder of her failure during the mission. But that hadn't been the worst thing. Losing that loudspeaker had been by far her greatest failure. She'd let everyone down, but their team had persevered anyway.

She'd messed up, but thank the Mother, the rest

of the pureblooded Kra-ell females along with Dima and Anton had been awesome.

Still, Drova's confidence was crushed, and the damn algebra wasn't helping to boost it.

A sharp knock on her door pulled her from her self-pity fest, but before she could respond, the door swung open, and Jade's figure filled the entrance.

"What are you doing?" her mother asked, her eyes taking in the scene—the tablet, the scattered papers, the textbook.

Drova resisted the urge to close the video. "Studying," she murmured.

Jade arched a brow. "By watching a video?"

"It's a class. An instructional video." Drova gestured to the tablet. "Parker said I could find classes on YouTube if the book was too difficult. And trust me, algebra is just mind-numbing."

To her surprise, Jade nodded approvingly. "Adapting to overcome obstacles is a good strategy." She walked into the room, her gaze shifting to the algebra equation on the screen. "I applaud your initiative. This looks like a foreign language to me."

It was on the tip of Drova's tongue to ask her mother whether the Kra-ell had something equivalent to algebra and whether kids learned it at school, but she was afraid to ask in case her mother confirmed her suspicion that the Kra-ell were too dumb to learn things like this.

As long as it was just her, she could live with that, but she refused to believe that her entire race of people was either incapable of, or had difficulty with, learning what every human runt had no problem with.

"I'm going on another mission tomorrow," Jade said. "That's what I came in to tell you before I got distracted. We are going to Iran to rescue more likely Dormants."

Drova straightened, her wound momentarily forgotten. "Can I go with you?" It would be much more fun than what she was doing now.

"No." Jade's tone left no room for argument, but Drova had never been one to heed such warnings. "Your wound is still healing."

"I can help," she insisted. "My compulsion ability isn't affected by the injury."

Jade's expression remained impassive. "The mission parameters do not require your specific talents."

"That's ridiculous," Drova countered. "Compulsion is always useful."

"Not for this operation." Jade sat down on Drova's bed. "It's a simple extraction. The targets are more of Kyra's relatives. Her sisters and their offspring."

"Wait a minute." Drova lifted a hand. "Are the girls we rescued her relatives as well and she didn't know?"

"They are her nieces, daughters of her sisters, which makes them Dormants, and that's why the Doomer abducted them. The *diagara* wanted to create his own breeding program so he could amass his own army of immortal warriors."

"Wow," Drova mouthed. "That's even worse than what we imagined. But didn't we kill all of his underlings?"

"Apparently not. He told Kian and Toven that he sent people to get more of Kyra's relatives, who are also Dormants since Kyra has only sisters. Four of them."

Excitement flickered through Drova. "That's actually good. If the girls are Dormants, they will come to live in the village. I was worried about what would happen to them. I thought maybe Kian would send them to the sanctuary for Vanessa to take care of. They are no different than other trafficking victims."

Jade nodded. "You are right, but since they are Dormants, I have no doubt that they will come straight to the village. They will probably need a friend." She gave her a meaningful look.

Drova snorted. "And you think I'm the right person for that? Remember what happened the last time I befriended clan teenagers?"

She'd used them, compelled them to do things they would never have done on their own, and when she'd been caught and they had to determine her punishment, they had gone too easy on her, had been too forgiving. Perhaps that was why she was inflicting on herself the torment of algebra even though Kian pardoned her sentencing.

"That is in the past," Jade said. "These girls will be new here, and they have no preconceptions about you. On the contrary, you were part of the team that liberated them. They probably think of you as a hero."

"They have eyes, don't they?" Drova gestured to her face, with its pronounced Kra-ell features. "They'll be scared of me."

Something softened in Jade's expression, revealing a rare glimpse of the maternal concern she usually kept hidden beneath her warrior's exterior. "I think you're the one who's scared, Drova. We're born warriors, you and I, and fighting comes naturally and easily to us. It's the other things, the softer emotions, that challenge us. But if you want to become a leader one day, you need to confront obstacles and embrace challenges that lie outside your comfort zone." Jade rose to her feet and cast a glance at the video still playing in the background without sound. "I believe you already understand that."

Long after her mother had walked out, her words still echoed in Drova's mind.

She'd faced far more terrifying adversaries than four traumatized teenagers, but there was something about the prospect of friendship with them that felt more dangerous than any battlefield.

In combat, the rules were clear. Victory or defeat. Life or death. But friendship with humans who had never even heard of Kra-ell? There was no training manual for navigating those unfamiliar waters.

With a sigh, Drova returned to her abandoned algebra problem: 4x - 9 = 15. She stared at it, the numbers swimming before her eyes.

"Add 9 to both sides," she muttered, pencil hovering over the paper. "Then 4x = 24. Then divide..."

46

FENELLA

Fenella flipped through the pages of an old magazine she'd found on the table in the waiting room, not paying attention to the gossip articles that were old news or the Photoshopped pictures of celebrities that looked too good to be real and obviously weren't.

Not unless they were flawless immortals.

She'd been a pretty girl before her transition, but the subtle changes that followed smoothed out all the little imperfections, making her skin flawless, almost luminous, and her hair thick and glossy. Her figure was perfect no matter how much junk she stuffed down her throat or how much alcohol she consumed.

Makeup was no longer necessary.

Fenella had more trouble pushing men away than attracting them, and after five decades of that, she was pretty sick of that whole sexual dance. Men just weren't that great even though they thought they were, and she would have gladly done without, but another aspect of her changed physique was an almost insatiable libido. So, even though her mind and heart weren't into men and sex, her body was.

Next to her, the girls were talking with Jasmine and Kyra in hushed voices, but she tuned them all out. They were a family, and she was an outsider. The sooner she could carve out her own space, the better.

As the patient door opened and Laleh emerged, Fenella tensed.

She'd waited until all of them were done, and now that it was her turn she couldn't let them know she was nervous, not after all her tough talk about just getting it done and moving on. She'd offered to go last to buy herself time to steel her nerves.

Fifty years of solitary survival had taught her to project fearlessness even when she was terrified, and she was maintaining that façade with practiced precision right now.

"Fenella?" Dr. Bridget called from the doorway. "Ready when you are."

"Coming." She dropped the magazine on the table and rose with a casualness she didn't feel. She flashed the girls a reassuring grin. "No need to wait for me. I'll see you upstairs. Don't eat all the ice cream before I get there."

Laleh's eyes widened. "There is ice cream?"

"Three different flavors," Fenella said as she walked into the examination room. "Check the freezer."

Once the door closed behind her, Fenella felt her carefully constructed bravado begin to crack. Despite looking nothing like the cell she'd been kept in, it was small, and the sight of the tray with all the vials waiting for her blood triggered unwelcome memories.

The nurse handed her a container to pee in and a folded hospital gown. "The bathroom is through there." She pointed at the door. "You know what to do, right?"

"Pee in the cup and try not to pee on my hand." She winked at Gertrude before ducking into the bathroom and closing the door behind her.

There had been no bathroom in the cell, so this one should not have evoked bad memories, but it still looked like something that belonged in a hospital and Fenella hated it.

After taking off her clothes, she did her business in the cup, screwed the lid tight, and wrapped the thing in a paper towel in case a few drops had missed the container. She put the gown on without bothering to tie it in the back and walked into the room.

"You can put the cup next to the sink, then hop on the bed and give me your arm," the nurse said with too much cheerfulness in her voice. "It's just a standard blood draw. All you'll feel is a small pinch, and we'll be done before you know it."

Fenella nodded, sitting on the bed and extending her arm while focusing on a watercolor landscape on the opposite wall. The painting depicted a mountain stream winding through a meadow dotted with wildflowers, and she imagined herself walking through it, using it as an anchor against the memories threatening to pull her under.

"You're quiet," Bridget observed as she prepared her instruments. "How are you feeling?"

"Peachy," Fenella replied, her Scottish accent thickening as it always did when she was nervous. "Just eager to get this over with."

The doctor's smart eyes saw more than Fenella was comfortable with. "If there is anything that is bothering you or anything that you want to get off your chest, feel free to say it. This is a safe space."

A bitter laugh escaped before Fenella could stop it. "Yeah. Safe space." She hadn't intended to sound mocking. "Sorry," she added. "It's been a rough few... decades, really."

Bridget nodded, waiting for Gertrude to finish.

It took a while to fill all those blood collection tubes, but when it was finally done, Gertrude collected the tray and the pee sample and rushed off to the lab they had in the back of the clinic.

"I'm impressed that you can do everything in house," Fenella said as she lay down on the hospital bed.

"It's necessary." Bridget wrote something on her tablet. "We can't allow immortal blood to fall into the hands of humans."

"Is there anything that can give us away?"

Bridget gave her an incredulous look. "Not in a standard blood test, but someone might want to run more than the standard tests, and we can't have that, can we?"

The examination proceeded much as Kyra's and the girls' had, with Bridget explaining each step before taking action. Fenella responded to questions with minimal words, focusing on maintaining control as memories flickered at the edges of her consciousness.

"I need to do the internal exam now. Would you prefer me to walk you through it step by step, or would you rather I work quickly and quietly?"

The consideration in the question and the acknowledgment of her agency nearly undid her.

"Quickly," she managed, her throat tight. "Please."

Bridget nodded. "Deep breath. This will be over soon."

His hands had never been gentle. He'd called it

"examination" too, but his eyes had burned with something that had nothing to do with medical interest.

Fenella forced herself to focus on her breathing. In for four counts, hold for four, out for four. A technique she'd learned in a yoga class back home all those years ago, during that brief period when she'd tried to find peace in ashrams and meditation retreats. Before her restlessness had driven her back to the road, to poker tables and bars and the endless search for something she couldn't name.

"Almost done," Bridget assured her, true to her word about keeping the examination brief. "You're doing great."

The praise, simple as it was, lit a small flame of warmth in Fenella's chest. How long had it been since anyone had said something encouraging to her?

"There we go, all finished," Bridget said, stepping back. "You can get dressed now. I'll be in my office right off the waiting room. We can talk there."

"Yes. Thank you," Fenella murmured before escaping to the bathroom.

When she emerged into the waiting room, Kyra and the rest of the gang were gone, and the door to Bridget's office was open.

The room was tiny, with barely enough room

for the desk and chairs, but it looked much less threatening than the other spaces in the clinic.

The doctor sat behind the desk and motioned for Fenella to sit. "First things first, I didn't detect a pregnancy, and the urine test was negative. We still need to wait for the blood test to make sure, but I think you can relax. You are not pregnant."

Fenella let out a breath. "That's a relief. What about all the other stuff?"

"As we both expected, your body healed all injuries and probably all the chemical damage as well, but we still need to wait for the blood test results, and some of them take time."

Fenella nodded, having expected nothing less. One of the blessings of immortality was rapid healing.

"Thank you," she said. "What about the fertility drugs? Could they have worked?"

Bridget shook her head. "No. We tried using them to increase our females' fertility, but human fertility medications had no effect on us. Our bodies work differently."

"The fake doctor had no idea what he was doing," Fenella said dryly.

Bridget tucked a strand of flaming red hair behind her ear. "Would you like to talk to someone about the psychological impact of your captivity? We have a clan counselor with whom I can put you in touch."

Fenella stiffened. "I'm fine. I've dealt with worse."

"Have you?" Bridget asked, her tone neutral. "Fifty years of independence, suddenly stripped away. Imprisonment. Violation. Drugging and abuse. These are significant traumas, Fenella, even for someone as resilient as you clearly are."

She'd clawed, bitten, kicked—used every dirty trick she'd learned in back-alley bars across Europe and Asia.

He'd seemed almost impressed before the needle had slid home and darkness had claimed her. The second time, she'd still struggled. By the tenth time, she'd stopped counting, stopped fighting, stopped hoping...

"I survived," Fenella said flatly. "That's what matters."

"Survival is the first step," Bridget agreed. "But healing is the journey that follows. You don't have to do it alone."

Fenella looked away, uncomfortable with the direction of the conversation. She'd spent decades building walls around her vulnerabilities, learning to depend on no one but herself. The thought of dismantling those defenses, of examining the damage beneath, was terrifying.

"I'm fine, really," she insisted. "I'm not broken."

"I've never suggested you were," Bridget said. "But acknowledging your emotional scars isn't weakness, Fenella. It's the opposite—it's recognizing your own strength in enduring it."

Something about the simple statement caught Fenella off guard. All her life, or at least the last fifty years of it, she'd equated vulnerability with weakness. To admit pain was to invite exploitation. To show fear was to become prey.

"You might experience symptoms of post-traumatic stress," Bridget continued. "Flashbacks, nightmares, hypervigilance, emotional numbness. These are normal responses to abnormal situations."

Fenella frowned at the doctor. "I haven't heard you talking with any of the others about getting psychological help. Why me? Do I look weaker than the others?"

"Of course not. You are incredibly strong. The only reason I can talk to you is that I have you here alone and that I know you can handle it. The girls are not ready to talk, and Kyra is going on a mission tomorrow."

That was a relief. For a moment there Fenella had thought that Bridget could see through her tough façade.

"I've been having flashbacks," she admitted reluctantly.

The nightmares had started during her captivity—vivid dreams of freedom, of open skies and endless roads, only to wake to concrete walls and the smell of fear. Sometimes, even as she'd slipped in and out of drug-induced hazes, she'd no longer been sure which was the dream and which was reality.

Bridget nodded. "That's a common symptom of post-traumatic stress disorder. Your mind is processing what happened, trying to make sense of it."

"How do I make it stop?" Fenella asked.

"It doesn't stop overnight," Bridget said gently. "But there are techniques and therapies that can help manage the symptoms and, eventually, reduce their frequency and intensity. Vanessa will walk you through it."

Fenella scoffed. "Talking about my feelings is not really my style."

"There are many approaches," Bridget said, unfazed by her skepticism. "Cognitive-behavioral therapy, mindfulness practices. Vanessa is an expert. I don't know if you are aware of the fact that the clan rescues victims of trafficking and rehabilitates them. Vanessa runs the sanctuary."

"That's really nice, and kudos to you, but I don't want to be seen as a victim," Fenella finally admitted. "I can't stand pity."

"Healing isn't about victimhood," Bridget said. "It's about reclaiming your sense of self."

She didn't have a rebuttal for that, so she said nothing.

"The clan will support your recovery in whatever way you need," Bridget said. "If you don't want formal therapy, that's fine. Just living in the safety of our village and finally being among people like you might be enough."

"What if I want to return to Scotland or somewhere else entirely?"

Bridget hesitated. "We have a community in Scotland that you can join, but living alone is not recommended. There are many more Doomers than clan members, and as you've experienced, they are not good people. You are a highly coveted commodity to them, and it's much easier to identify an immortal female than it is a Dormant. That said, I don't want you to think you will be confined to either location. After you recover, you can travel as much as you want, but we will keep tabs on you to ensure you are okay."

"That sounds perfect. Thank you."

Bridget smiled. "You're welcome, Fenella. You have a home now, and you belong to a community of people like you. You are no longer alone."

47

MAX

Max's phone buzzed in his pocket just as he was about to head up to the penthouse.

Glancing at the caller ID, he saw Bridget's name and answered immediately. "Everything okay?"

"Yes," Bridget's calm voice came through. "Can you take Fenella back to the penthouse? The others are done and went ahead, and she doesn't have access to the elevator controls yet."

"I'm on my way." He ended the call.

Bridget had sounded a little off, and it got him worried. Jasmine had texted him earlier with a message from Kyra that everything was alright and that she'd tested negative for pregnancy, which had been a huge relief, but what if Fenella's news was not as good?

The clinic was only two levels up from the

dungeon, and as he exited the elevator, he had to force himself not to jog and limit himself to a fast walk.

When he opened the door, he found Fenella sitting in one of the waiting room chairs, a magazine open on her knees. She looked up at him and smiled.

"My knight has arrived." She rose to her feet and turned toward Bridget, who was in the office, sitting behind the desk. "Thanks again, Bridget. I guess I'll see you tomorrow when you come to talk to the girls?"

The doctor nodded. "Don't tell them that I'm coming. I want to do this casually."

"Got it." Fenella gave Bridget the thumbs up.

Fenella was fronting the tough-girl persona, but even though they weren't an item for long and it had been half a century ago, he knew her well enough to see the cracks in that façade. Her eyes were slightly too bright, her posture too rigid, and he got suddenly anxious. Despite everything she'd been through, Fenella had been unshakable so far. What had happened to tip her over the edge?

He prayed to the Fates it wasn't a pregnancy.

As soon as they were out the door, he turned toward her. "Everything alright?"

Fenella shrugged, the motion a bit too casual. "Fine. I'm not pregnant, and there's no lasting damage. No great surprise, since my body's really good at fixing whatever gets broken."

She spoke the words like something she'd prepared to say before he arrived, but he decided to let it go.

"Good to hear," Max said. "That's one less thing to worry about." He kept walking.

When they reached the elevator, she turned to him. "Did you call Din?"

The question caught him off guard. "Not yet. I had to put some work in or my boss would have been cross with me."

It was an exaggeration. He could have easily composed a text or called, but he needed a little more time to mentally prepare for the confrontation.

"I need Din to check on my family." She crossed her arms over her chest. "My parents are gone, but my brother's still around, and he has kids, who probably have their own kids by now."

"Your brother can't transfer the genes to his kids. Did your mother have sisters?"

"No. She had two brothers. One younger and one older. Why?"

"There is no reason for the Doomers to look for your family, if they know that. Did you tell him about them?"

Fenella laughed, a harsh sound that was devoid of humor. "I probably told him about every shit

I've taken in my seventy years of life." The bitterness in her voice was palpable. "He interrogated me endlessly, while drugged, semi-sober, or sober, and he never pulled his punches."

The casual way she referenced the abuse made something dark unfurl in Max's chest. He'd known intellectually what had likely happened during her captivity, but hearing her speak of it so matter-of-factly drove home the reality of what she'd endured.

With a soft ping the elevator announced its arrival, and the doors slid open, but Max remained motionless, a sudden rush of rage freezing him in place. He could feel his fangs pressing against his gums, demanding release.

"Max?" Fenella's voice seemed distant.

He tried to clear the red haze of rage, to force the primal response back down, but it was no use as horrific images kept bombarding his mind, and his fangs punched through, sharp and prominent, a physical manifestation of his fury.

Fenella took a sudden step back, her eyes widening with fear. "Your fangs..." she whispered, her Scottish accent thickening with alarm.

The fear in her voice snapped Max back to the present. He immediately raised a hand to cover his mouth, realizing what he'd triggered.

"I'm sorry," he managed, willing his fangs to

retract. "Don't be frightened. It's just a protective response. I swear."

"His fangs would elongate like that every time before he started beating me," Fenella said, her voice hollow. "Sometimes I wasn't sure if it was real or if I was hallucinating."

"It's not the same," he said carefully, ensuring his fangs were fully retracted before lowering his hand. "I'm not like him, Fenella. I would never hurt you."

She nodded, though wariness still lingered in her posture. "I know that. Logically, I know that."

The elevator doors had closed in the meantime, and Max called for it again.

"When immortal males feel protective, our fangs emerge," he explained, keeping his voice steady and calm. "It's a sign of aggression toward an enemy or someone who threatens us or anyone defenseless around us. It's an instinctual response. I was just so angry thinking about what he did to you."

"Protective," she repeated, as if testing the word. "But I wasn't a threat to him or anyone else and still his fangs came out."

Max met her gaze directly, wanting her to see the truth in his eyes. "There's a difference between fangs elongating in response to aggression or in response to sexual desire. The Doomer couldn't have been able to do both simultaneously."

"Why not?"

"The chemicals released in the venom glands differ depending on the trigger. Aggression produces a paralyzing toxin meant to incapacitate enemies, while sexual arousal produces something much milder, designed to enhance pleasure."

"But the Doomer…"

Max felt his jaw tighten. "An immortal male shouldn't be capable of doing both simultaneously. The systems are supposed to be separate, so I must assume that his was triggered by desire, but because he is a vile pile of shit, he hurt you."

The elevator arrived again with another soft ping. This time, Max held his hand against the door to keep it open.

Fenella stepped inside and leaned against the wall, crossing her arms over her chest.

He took the opposite side and mimicked her pose. "I'll call Din as soon as we get upstairs. It wouldn't hurt to check on your brother and his kids and grandkids."

She chuckled. "Grandkids. Can you imagine? I could be a great-aunt."

He was glad that she was back to her old self. "You get used to that when you're immortal. No one even speaks of ages in our community."

She nodded, and then let out a breath, the smile sliding off her face. "I wasn't scared of you. It was just a knee-jerk reaction."

"I know. I'm still sorry about it."

"Not your fault." She attempted a smile that didn't quite reach her eyes. "This whole post-traumatic thing is a bitch."

"Is that what Bridget said?"

"Among other things." Fenella shrugged. "Apparently, it's normal to be fucked up after being abducted, drugged, beaten up, and violated."

Despite her flippant tone, Max caught the vulnerability underneath. Fenella had survived fifty years on her own, relying on no one but herself. Acknowledging any kind of weakness, even to herself, had to be difficult.

"If you need someone to talk to, we have a great counselor."

"So I've been told." She glanced up at the floor indicator, watching the numbers climb. "Not sure I'm the therapy type, though. I don't have patience for someone asking me how I feel about this or that."

The elevator reached the penthouse and the two of them stepped out, but Max wasn't in a rush. "Immortals have unique challenges when it comes to trauma. We live so long that unprocessed experiences can compound over centuries."

"Are you talking from experience?" she asked, studying him.

"Some," he admitted. "Five hundred years gives

you plenty of time to accumulate baggage. And plenty of time to learn how to unpack it, too."

48

KYRA

After returning to the penthouse, Kyra had escaped to the luxurious bathroom of the master suite for a few moments of quiet. She could have just closed the door to her room and sat on the couch in the sitting area, but she'd pretended to need to use the restroom, so here she was, looking in the mirror and brushing her hair, trying to arrange it into something that had shape.

Everything about Bridget's appearance had been polished, including her hair and subtle makeup. Standing next to her, Kyra felt exactly like who she was—a rebel who had spent most of her nights in a tent, who was lucky to wash her hair once a week, and who had used a conditioner for the first time on the plane that brought her out of Iran.

Oh, well. Hopefully, there would be time to do all those feminine nonessentials when she returned with the rest of her family. With so many females, they could have giant makeover parties.

The thought made her chest feel lighter. Then she heard the doorbell ring in the living room, intensifying her buoyant feeling.

Was it Max?

Putting the brush aside, she raked her fingers through her hair, flipping it to one side the way she preferred, and headed toward the living room.

She heard Max and Fenella talking before she saw them, and even from more than twenty feet away she could detect something in Max's tone that sent a pang through her chest.

Their conversation sounded intimate, and her gut clenched when she saw them standing close together and looking into each other's eyes with some kind of shared understanding.

It wasn't just the intimacy of their conversation that made them look like a unit. More tellingly, they both seemed slightly unsettled, as if they'd shared an intense experience.

Max glanced up, catching her eye, and something in his expression shifted. Was it guilt? Regret?

"There you are," he said, his tone sounding deliberately casual. "I wondered where you'd gone."

Had he?

"I was in the washroom." She forced a smile and turned to Fenella. "How did it go?"

"I'm not pregnant, and pending the results of the blood tests, I'm a perfectly healthy immortal."

Kyra forced down the uncomfortable feeling squirming in her stomach.

What was wrong with her?

She had no claim on Max. They had shared a few kisses, nothing more.

It couldn't compare to the history he had with Fenella. The two had been lovers, even if it had been a brief affair, and as much as Kyra hated to admit it, Fenella's personality was much more compatible with Max's than hers.

They were both irreverent and snarky, and they didn't take anything too seriously, or at least pretended not to.

"That's good," she said, her voice sounding strained even to her ears.

The rational part of her brain tried to tell her that she was being ridiculous. Max was a free agent. Fenella was attractive, and they had a past. If they wanted to rekindle something, she had no right to interfere.

It wasn't her place to feel possessive over him.

Her pendant suddenly hummed against her skin, warming rapidly until it became uncomfortably hot. The sensation was so intense that she had to pull it out from beneath her shirt, letting it rest on top of the fabric where it couldn't burn her.

Mind your own business, she thought irritably toward the pendant. The amber stone seemed to pulse once in response, as if offended by her dismissal, before settling down.

She was losing her mind. That was the only explanation.

"Everything okay?" Max asked.

"Fine," Kyra said quickly. "It just gets warm sometimes."

He nodded and then checked his watch. "If you'll excuse me, I have something I need to attend to. I'm going to step out onto the terrace for a bit."

A look passed between him and Fenella, and she gave him a slight nod.

What the hell was that? Were they planning to meet outside to rekindle their romance?

As Max walked toward the sliding glass doors, Fenella stepped closer to Kyra. "Can I have a word with you for a moment?" she asked, her voice low enough that only Kyra could hear.

"Of course," she said.

Fenella led her toward the kitchen, glancing at the girls as if to check whether they were within earshot. "Bridget thinks we all need to talk to a therapist about what happened to us."

The statement was so unexpected that Kyra

momentarily forgot how upset she was. "A therapist?"

"A psychologist. You know, lie on a couch, answer questions that start with 'how do you feel about that?'" She mimicked a pretentious accent for the last part.

"I see," Kyra said, considering the concept. In the resistance, psychological support was given by your comrades in arms, and trauma was simply something you pushed through because you had no other choice. "Why does that bother you?"

Fenella crossed her arms over her chest. "I thought to warn you that it's coming not just for us, but for the girls as well. Bridget plans to talk to them tomorrow, and since you'll be gone and you are their aunt and all that, I thought you should know. You should say something if you are not okay with her talking to them while you are not here."

Therapy might help, and she didn't know why Fenella felt so strongly about it.

"I think it might be good for the girls," she said carefully. "They've been through so much, and I have no idea how to talk to them. I can't treat them like fellow rebels, and that's all I know."

Fenella's lips lifted in a small smile. "Hey, maybe that's exactly what they need. Tough love and all that."

An awkward silence fell between them, and

Kyra's mind wandered back to Max and what he was doing on the terrace. Was he really attending to some business or was he waiting for Fenella?

The pendant warmed against her shirt as if it was angry at her for having such thoughts.

She wanted to tell Fenella to keep her hands off Max, but what right did she have to do that? If Max and Fenella were reconnecting, who was she to stand in their way?

The doorbell ringing saved her from saying something she would have regretted later, although she wasn't sure what it would have been.

Stay away from my guy or good luck?

When Ell-rom opened the door, two big guys wearing the same uniform as Max entered, each balancing a towering stack of boxes.

"Delivery from the personal shopper," one announced, his voice muffled behind the packages. "Where would you like these?"

"By the door is fine." Ell-rom pointed.

The men deposited their burdens in the foyer, creating twin mountains of shopping bags and boxes, each neatly labeled with a name.

"This can't all be for us," Kyra said, eyeing the enormous piles with disbelief.

The taller of the two shrugged. "Whatever you don't like, put back in the bag or box it came in and leave it out in the vestibule. We will send it back to the shopper. Those were the instructions she left."

"Thank you."

The girls gravitated towards the piles like moths to a flame.

"Are those for us?" Donya asked hesitantly.

"They're for all of you," Jasmine said, appearing behind them. "Brandon's personal shopper is the best in the business. She'd outfitted Morelle, Ellrom's twin sister, with a wardrobe worthy of a queen. Go get it, girls."

They gave Jasmine one more tentative glance before going for the loot.

Watching them carefully examine the labels, looking for their names with growing excitement, Kyra got emotional and had to wipe her eyes with the sleeves of her hoodie.

Despite everything they'd endured, they could still find joy in something so basic.

"Thank you," she told Jasmine. "That was a stroke of genius. I just don't know how I will repay the person who financed all this."

"Don't worry about it." Jasmine regarded the girls collecting their packages with a smile. "If you find Khiann, all debts will be repaid."

"Find who?"

It had sounded as if Jasmine said Kian, but he wasn't lost.

"Never mind." Jasmine wrapped an arm around her shoulders. "That's something that will wait for after you return with the rest of our family."

The sliding door opened, and Max stepped back inside, clutching his phone. His expression was unreadable as he surveyed the scene.

"What's all that?" he asked.

"Brandon's personal shopper came through once again," Jasmine said.

Max walked over to Kyra. "I have something for you," he said, showing her his phone screen. "The message came through while I was outside." He handed it to her.

It was the prearranged signal from her rebel contacts to check the secure messaging app, and her heart rate quickened as she opened it.

The message from Soran was brief and couched in their standard code, but its meaning was clear: *suspicious activity in Tahav near the destroyed compound. Unknown men asking questions of the local residents. The rebels are moving to a new, more distant camp as a precaution.*

"Bad news?" Max asked, watching her face.

"Potentially," Kyra said, handing the phone back. "Some men are poking around Tahav, asking questions about the compound. My people are relocating as a precaution."

Max nodded thoughtfully. "Makes sense. Someone was bound to investigate what happened there."

"Do you think it's related to my family?" Kyra

asked, lowering her voice to prevent the girls from overhearing.

"It doesn't sound like it. Your sisters all live in Tehran, and your friends didn't mention any women accompanying these men, right?"

"They didn't, but maybe they had left the girls somewhere while they were snooping around the compound. Did your contacts in Iran find anything about my family yet?"

"I haven't heard anything from Kian, so I assume he hasn't heard anything from Turner."

Jasmine had sent over the information about her sisters and their families, but it was nighttime there, so Kyra shouldn't be surprised that there was no news.

"I still need to make that call," Max said, gesturing toward the terrace.

"Of course," Kyra said, stepping back.

As Max turned to leave, he caught Fenella's eye across the room, and once again, something unspoken passed between them—another of those significant looks that made Kyra's stomach tighten uncomfortably.

Fenella gave him a slight nod in response.

Whatever was happening between them, they were clearly in sync, operating on a wavelength Kyra couldn't access, and the realization hurt.

Her pendant warmed again against her shirt, almost in sympathy with her aching heart.

She watched Max slide the door closed behind him, his broad shoulders silhouetted against the late-setting sun. Tomorrow, they would leave for Iran together, and Fenella would stay behind. Perhaps by the time they returned, things between them would sort themselves out.

49

MAX

Max leaned against the glass railing with his phone clutched in his hand, gazing at the street below without really seeing it.

After fifty years of silence between him and Din, he wondered if Din had his number in his contacts, even though William and his team regularly updated everyone's phones. Knowing Din, the guy had erased Max's contact information out of spite after every update.

If he had, it would be an advantage because he wouldn't know who was calling him and would have to answer to find out. It was the middle of the night in Scotland, which would also work in Max's favor since Din would hopefully be confused.

The strategy was shock and awe—blast Din

with the incredible news before the guy could say a single word or hang up.

Max hit the call button and waited to deliver the opening he'd rehearsed in his mind. The phone rang a few times, then stopped, replaced by a groggy, "Hello?"

After all this time, Din's voice was unmistakable even when thick with sleep.

"I found Fenella and she's immortal." Max rushed the words out before Din could fully wake up and realize who was calling. "She was a Dormant, and I must have induced her unknowingly."

The silence that followed stretched so long that Max wondered if the connection had dropped. He checked his screen, and the call was still active.

"Din? You there?"

"Say that again." Din's voice had lost its sleepiness, replaced with a razor-sharp focus that Max remembered all too well.

"I found Fenella," he repeated, more slowly this time. "She transitioned after we were together fifty years ago, and now she is immortal."

Another pause, shorter this time. "Where did you find her?"

Max exhaled, relief flooding through him. Din was still on the line, which was more than he'd dared to hope for. His tactic had worked—

curiosity about Fenella had overridden five decades of stubborn silence.

"In Iran," Max said, leaning against the terrace railing. "We were on a rescue mission to extract Jasmine's mother, you know who I'm talking about, right?"

"I know who Jasmine is. I don't know anything about her mother."

Fair enough. The news about the rescue mission must not have reached Scotland yet.

"Jasmine's mother, Kyra, was being held in a compound in northern Iran. Syssi had visions about her, and we mounted a rescue operation. When we got there, I found Fenella imprisoned in the same facility."

Max deliberately kept his tone neutral, sticking to the bare facts. Din didn't need to hear the details of what they'd found—the state Fenella had been in, chained to a metal bed and heavily drugged. That was Fenella's story to tell, if she chose to.

"Is she okay?" Din asked.

"She's fine, physically," Max said carefully. "But she's been through a lot." He paused, uncertain how much to reveal. "She's worried about Doomers going after her family and she asked me to call you so you can check on them."

"She did? She remembered me?"

"Vividly." Max didn't add that she'd called Din

an asshole. It would have been counterproductive right now.

There was another long moment of silence. "Why would Doomers target her family?"

Max grimaced. There was no delicate way to explain this part. "The Doomer who held her captive was trying to create his own breeding program with the two immortal females he'd found, Kyra and Fenella, and he also abducted four of Kyra's nieces because he figured out they were Dormants. Toven got him to reveal that he sent his buddies to collect more of Kyra's family members, and even though he didn't mention doing the same in regard to Fenella's family, she's worried her brother's children might be in danger."

"Fates," Din muttered. "How did he know about her family?"

"She told him that she had only one brother and no sisters, and that her mother had no sisters either, but she was drugged during interrogations, and she's concerned she might have said other things. You know how it is in situations like this. People say what their captors want to hear just to stop the pain."

"She was tortured?"

Max winced. He'd said too much, but it was too late to take it back. "Yes."

"Where is she now?" Din's voice sounded

slurred, and Max imagined his friend's fangs punching over his lower lip.

"She and the other rescued women are at the keep in Kian's old penthouse but will be transferred to the village soon."

"I'll check on her brother and his family," Din said. "And then I'm booking a flight to California."

A big grin spread across Max's face. "Good. That's what I wanted to hear. It's about damn time you removed the stick from your ass and did the right thing. If you'd done this fifty years ago, we might have realized that she'd transitioned, and you could have been with her this whole time."

The unspoken hung between them—all the hardships Fenella might have been spared if they'd known about her transformation and brought her into the clan's protection.

There was another long moment of silence, and Max imagined Din's face hardening after hearing the uncomfortable truth.

"Are you sure you're not interested in her yourself?" Din surprised him with the question. "You always were a competitive bastard, and immortal females who aren't our relatives are too rare to give up so easily."

The question was fair, given their history. "I have absolutely no interest in Fenella other than friendship. I'm only interested in Kyra. In fact, I think I'm falling in love with her."

Din snorted. "You? Falling in love? I'll believe it when I see it."

"A word of warning. Fenella is just as snarky as she was fifty years ago, maybe snarkier, if that's possible."

"That was one of the things I loved about her," Din admitted. "It also made her intimidating as hell to approach."

"Look deeper than what she projects to the world," Max advised. "Fenella is hurting on the inside. She needs someone she can trust not to hurt her emotionally or in any other way."

"When did you get so insightful?" Din asked.

"Five hundred years of pissing people off and ruining relationships teaches you a thing or two. I'm still an asshole, but I'm trying harder not to be. Just don't tell anyone. I've got a reputation to maintain."

Din laughed. "Your secret's safe with me."

"Thank you. I'll tell Fenella that you are going to check on her brother and his family. Her parents passed away, naturally."

"Thank you for saving her. I owe you."

Max let out a breath, the gratitude in his old friend's voice making something in his chest loosen—a knot of tension he'd been carrying for fifty years. "You don't owe me. I just corrected a wrong and I hope that we can be friends again. I've missed you, bro."

"Can't say that I missed you, but maybe we can start over."

Ouch, that hurt. "I'd like that."

"I'll call you after checking on Fenella's brother."

"Thanks. See you in the village."

"Yeah." Din ended the call.

Max leaned his elbows on the railing and took a moment to process. The conversation had gone better than he could have hoped. Not only had Din not hung up on him, but they'd managed to navigate the complicated minefield of their shared past without reigniting old hostilities.

Best news was that Din was coming for Fenella. Hopefully, he wouldn't be disappointed.

Max headed back inside with a lighter heart than he'd had in years. The living room was a flurry of activity, with shopping bags and boxes strewn across every surface. The girls were nowhere to be seen, likely in their rooms trying on their new wardrobes, but Fenella and Jasmine and Ell-rom were there.

"Well?" she demanded as soon as he closed the sliding door behind him. "Did he hang up on you?"

Max couldn't suppress his triumphant grin. "Not only did he not hang up, but he's checking on your brother and his family, and then he's flying out here to see you."

For a moment, Fenella just stared at him, and

then, to his astonishment, her face lit up with genuine pleasure—not the sardonic smile he'd grown accustomed to, but something brighter and more vulnerable.

"Really? You're not shitting me?"

"I'm not," Max confirmed. "He sounded quite eager."

Fenella rose to her feet and before Max could react, she threw her arms around him in a fierce hug that nearly knocked him back a step.

"Thank you," she said, her voice was muffled against his chest.

Touched by her uncharacteristic display of emotion, Max returned the hug, awkwardly patting her back before she pulled away, looking almost embarrassed by her reaction.

50

KYRA

Kyra smoothed her hand over the soft fabric of the tactical pants she'd just folded into the closet drawer. The material was unlike anything she'd worn during her years with the resistance—lightweight yet durable, with reinforced knees and a multitude of cleverly designed pockets. No more makeshift gear cobbled together from whatever they could scavenge or buy on the black market. This was top-of-the-line stuff, far too fine to be military gear. Perhaps some Hollywood stars enjoyed the style, and an enterprising designer had created items that looked like they belonged on soldiers but felt like they belonged on royalty.

The personal shopper had thought of everything. High-performance base layers, a selection of tops in various weights, and boots that fit like they'd been custom-made for her feet.

After arranging the last of her new possessions, Kyra closed the drawer with a small sense of satisfaction. Having proper clothing felt like another step toward reclaiming her identity.

Heading out of her room, she intended to check on the girls and see how they were doing with their new wardrobes, but something—or rather someone—drew her toward the living room.

Was Max back inside, or was Fenella out on the terrace with him and were they sharing passionate kisses that should belong to Kyra?

When she cleared the hallway, the sight that greeted her was worse than anything she could have imagined, and she stopped short, her body freezing mid-step.

Max and Fenella were locked in an embrace, with Fenella's arms wrapped around Max's neck and her face pressed against his chest.

Something sharp and painful lanced through Kyra's chest at the sight, her earlier suspicions confirmed in vivid detail.

She should turn away and retreat down the hallway before they noticed her standing there like some pathetic voyeur, but she couldn't tear her eyes away from what was a horror show to her.

Then something grabbed her attention.

Max was awkwardly patting Fenella's back in a manner that didn't suggest anything even remotely passionate. He looked pleased, happy even, but his eyes didn't glow the way they had done when they'd kissed. They weren't hooded with desire either.

That didn't look like a lovers' embrace.

Kyra had confronted armed patrols, infiltrated military installations, and negotiated with tyrants who thirsted for her blood, so she could face whatever this was. She hadn't survived two decades as a resistance fighter by evading uncomfortable situations.

"What happened?" she asked, walking up to them, her voice steady and filled with just the right measure of concern.

Fenella had already stepped away from Max, and as she whirled around, she looked more animated than Kyra had ever seen her, her usual sardonic mask replaced by excitement.

"Max called Din," Fenella said. "Din is booking a flight to California to come see me."

"That's nice." Kyra glanced between Fenella and Max, reassessing the scene she'd witnessed. "But I thought you didn't want to see him. You gave me the impression you weren't interested in Din, and that you'd rather check out other guys in the immortal community."

Fenella shrugged. "I know I talked shit about

Din earlier, and he deserved it. But the guy is flying halfway around the world to see me. That has to count for something, right?" She struck a coquettish pose. "It makes me feel special. No one has ever invested that much effort into seeking me out and wanting to be with me before." Her expression turned reflective. "And the fact that he was mad at Max for half a century over supposedly stealing me? That's significant too. Not many men would hold a grudge that long over a woman they'd never even dated."

Kyra was relieved that her suspicions about Max and Fenella were proven wrong, and that all those secret looks were about Max calling Din for her.

On the other hand, though, she didn't like what she'd learned about Din so far. A guy who'd nursed resentment for decades and blamed others rather than take action himself was not the sort of man Kyra would have chosen for herself or anyone she cared about.

"I hope you won't be disappointed," she said, and immediately regretted the words.

Fenella was a grown woman, and she didn't need Kyra to question her judgment or offer unsolicited advice.

Fenella waved a dismissive hand. "I'm going in with low expectations. The guy supposedly fell in love with me when I was just a bartender in a village pub, and then spent fifty years being angry at Max for getting to me first. I'm curious to see what he's like now." Her eyes sparkled with mischief. "Besides, if he turns out to be a dud, there are plenty of other immortal males around, right? It's not like I'm committing to anything by agreeing to see him."

Despite herself, Kyra smiled. It was impossible not to like Fenella despite her snarky attitude and excessive use of profanities. She was beginning to understand why Max had a soft spot for the woman.

As long as it wasn't romantic, Kyra didn't mind. Well, she would need to work hard on accepting their friendship and not get jealous, but she'd overcome bigger challenges before.

"Dinner is on its way!" Jasmine called. "We should move to the dining room so there is space for everyone. I ordered from the Golden Dragon—one of my absolute favorites. You are in for a delightful feast." She glanced around the room. "Are the girls still trying on their new clothes?"

Kyra nodded. "I'll go let them know about dinner."

"I can do it," Fenella offered, already walking toward the hallway. "I want to see what they got anyway."

Max reached for Kyra's hand, his fingers warm as they closed around hers. "Did the shopper do okay with your things?" he asked. "Everything fit alright?"

The simple touch sent a current of awareness up Kyra's arm, and she was struck again by how physically drawn to him she was—something that was still new and exciting to her.

"Everything is incredible," she said, squeezing his hand. "Even the tactical pants and jacket are made from the finest fabrics—soft and comfortable, but durable too. They feel like a caress against my skin." The phrase sounded oddly intimate once it left her mouth, but Max's pleased expression encouraged her to continue. "And the boots! Such soft leather, yet so sturdy. They fit like they were made for me. Even the socks are amazing—cashmere! I've never had socks that felt so incredible."

Max's smile broadened at her enthusiasm. "I'm glad. I like you to have nice things. You deserve it."

The warmth in his gaze made her heart flutter.

This gorgeous, super-confident immortal, who could probably have his pick of women, looked at her like she was something precious, which was difficult to reconcile with what she'd seen in the mirror a few minutes ago.

She was no beauty, not in the conventional sense, and yet here he was holding her hand, looking at her with an intensity that turned her knees to jelly.

"Thank you," Kyra said. "I like having nice things, too. Who doesn't, right?"

He smiled and his fingers tightened briefly around hers before reluctantly letting go as voices approached from the hallway.

The girls tumbled into the living room, each wearing a selection from their new wardrobes. Their transformation was remarkable. They looked like ordinary teenagers. Even Arezoo, the most reserved of the four, had a glint in her eyes that hadn't been there before.

"You all look beautiful," Kyra told them.

"Is it too much?" Donya asked, smoothing her hands over the colorful tunic she'd paired with leggings. "I've never had anything this nice before."

"It's perfect," Kyra assured her. "Very fashionable."

Jasmine emerged from the dining room and beamed at her cousins. "Look at all of you! You are gorgeous."

When the doorbell rang, Ell-Rom and Max went to get the delivery, and minutes later, the dining table was laden with boxes of fragrant dishes: glistening stir-fries, steaming rice, dumplings that released aromatic steam when pierced.

Kyra couldn't remember ever having Chinese food before, but she recognized the dishes and could name each one. The smells were appetizing, and she eyed the various dishes Jasmine was transferring onto platters with curiosity.

Her nieces, however, seemed hesitant about trying the unfamiliar cuisine.

"We've never had anything like this." Laleh eyed a platter of orange chicken. "Is it very spicy?"

"Not at all," Jasmine said. "It's delicious. Try a little of everything. Whatever you don't like, you don't have to finish."

The meal unfolded in a surprisingly relaxed atmosphere, and after a few minutes of hesitation, the girls piled their plates.

Jasmine showed them how to use chopsticks, and after a few attempts they could all manage, albeit clumsily.

As chopsticks clicked and conversation flowed, the girls opened up and began sharing information about their mothers and aunts.

"My mother, Soraya, is about this tall," Arezoo said, holding her hand at shoulder height. "She has your eyes, but her hair is lighter. More brown than black, and she's heavier. She also knows a little English. She wanted to study in the USA, but after you disappeared, that wasn't an option for her anymore."

Kyra felt guilty. Because of her, her sisters had been denied a chance of a better life. She had to make it up to them.

"Aunt Rana, Aiden's mom, always wears blue," Laleh said. "She says it brings good fortune."

"She's also the most religious," Azadeh said quietly. "She prays five times every day, without fail."

Kyra absorbed these details hungrily, trying to construct mental images of her sisters. "What about Yasmin and Parisa?"

"Aunt Yasmin is the tallest," Arezoo said. "She walks very straight, like this." She demonstrated, sitting up ramrod straight with her chin lifted. "Uncle Javad jokes that she can balance books on her head."

"Aunt Parisa is the youngest," Donya murmured. "And the prettiest, everyone says so. She has a beauty mark right here." She touched a spot beside her left eye. "She likes to hum when she's cooking."

Each detail was another piece in the puzzle of Kyra's forgotten past. She leaned forward, hanging on every word.

As the girls moved to describing their cousins, thinking about the logistics of rescuing so many people seemed daunting.

As the meal drew to a close, a sudden hush fell over the table. The girls exchanged glances, a silent communication passing between them before Arezoo cleared her throat.

"We have something for you," she said, her

usual assertive tone turning soft. "We wrote messages for our mothers. It will make it easier for you to convince them to come with you." She chewed on her lower lip, something Kyra often did as well. "We didn't write about what was done to us. We said that we were kidnapped by people who wanted to ransom us for money, and the rebels saved us, and that you were their leader. I know it's not the truth, but we couldn't write about you being immortal and all that. We wrote that you are Kyra's daughter, Jasmine."

One by one, the girls handed their notes to her. She would read them later, making sure nothing in them could put her team or the immortals in danger, but for now, Kyra put the folded pages in her pocket.

"Tell her I'm safe," Arezoo said, her composure finally cracking. "If she can't come with you, tell her not to worry about us. Tell her..." She swallowed hard. "Tell her I remember what she taught me about being brave."

"Tell my mother that I've been looking after Laleh," Donya added, putting an arm around her younger sister. "That I haven't let her out of my sight."

Laleh wiped at her eyes. "Tell her I love her."

Azadeh's message was the briefest but perhaps the most poignant. "Tell my mother I understand now. About the blue. I understand."

The cryptic nature of the message raised questions in Kyra's mind, but the raw emotion in Azadeh's voice made it clear this was deeply meaningful to both mother and daughter.

"I'll tell them," Kyra promised, her own eyes misting. "And I'll make sure they know how brave you've all been."

The pendant at her throat warmed against her skin, not the uncomfortable heat from earlier but a soothing pulse, like a heartbeat, echoing the promise she'd made.

51

MAX

Max's phone buzzed just as he was helping Fenella and Ell-rom clear the last of the dinner dishes. He pulled it from his pocket, noting the late hour.

A text from Onegus. *Mission briefing in Kian's old office. Bring Kyra. Video conference in twenty minutes.*

He glanced across the room to Kyra, who was sitting with the girls. Her expression was soft as she listened to them share memories of their homes. The tenderness in her eyes touched him, making his chest expand with feelings for this incredible woman and her young charges.

"Hey," he called, hating to interrupt the moment but knowing they should be getting ready. "Onegus wants us downstairs. Mission briefing in twenty. Just enough time to grab a quick cup of coffee for a pick-me-up and head out."

As Kyra looked up, her expression transformed, and instead of the caring aunt of a moment ago, he was now looking at the rebel leader.

"Is the rest of the team on its way?" she asked.

"Video conference," Max clarified. "The others are meeting in Kian's office in the village."

She nodded, turning back to the girls with a gentle smile. "I need to go, and it will probably take a while. Go to sleep, okay? I'll see you in the morning before we leave."

"Is Jasmine going to stay with us?" Arezoo asked.

"Yes. She and Ell-rom will probably take you to the village, but I'm not sure how soon they will have a house ready for us, so it might happen after I return."

Arezoo nodded. "Is Jasmine going to tell us what's happening?"

Kyra shifted her gaze to Max. "I don't know the procedures."

"I will call her with updates," he said. "Don't worry, girls. We have a great team, and we will bring your mothers to you provided that they want to come. We are not going to force anyone."

There was so much hope in those four sets of eyes, and Max hoped he wasn't making promises he couldn't keep.

"Here are your coffees." Jasmine handed each of them a cup. "Take them with you. You don't want to keep the others waiting."

"Good point." Max took the cup from her. "Thank you."

"You're welcome."

"Ready?" he asked Kyra.

She nodded. "Let's go."

They rode the elevator down in companionable silence, Max keenly aware of her presence beside him. The determination radiating from her slender frame was almost palpable. She might look delicate, but there was steel in her spine that he admired. He considered pulling her in for a kiss and easing some of her tension, but he had a feeling she wouldn't appreciate that right now.

Maybe later.

Maybe she would like to do more than kissing.

There was nothing better for releasing stress before a mission than a good session in bed, but given what Kyra had been through, she probably wasn't ready for that.

Even an obtuse knucklehead like him knew that.

"How is the claustrophobia?" he asked instead.

"Strangely absent." She chuckled. "I guess the anxious energy before a complicated mission burns through irrational fears. Besides, it's not claustrophobia. It's being underground that bothers me. I don't like rooms without windows."

It probably had to do with her imprisonment, but he wasn't going to probe. Perhaps sometime in the future she would talk to him, after she'd had enough time to compartmentalize her experiences, so opening one can of worms didn't release them all.

The doors to Kian's office were never locked, and as they walked in, Max flicked on the lights and headed straight for the desk where a laptop had been left to be used for video conferences.

"This is such a nice office." Kyra took a seat next to the conference table. "It seems like such a waste that it's rarely used. Can't someone else use it as their office while Kian is in the village?"

He turned to look at her over his shoulder. "Would you like it to be yours?"

She laughed. "To do what? Manage my rebels from afar? Besides, if I ever have an office, I want it to have a window."

He turned on the screen, checked his phone's wireless connection to the laptop, and then joined Kyra at the conference table.

He glanced at the clock to check the time when the call came through, and the large screen over Kian's desk flickered to life, revealing Kian's office in the village.

Kian sat at the head of the other conference

table, which wasn't nearly as fancy and as big as this one. He was flanked by Onegus on one side and Turner on the other. Jade and her Kra-ell team took the other seats.

"Good evening," Kian greeted them. "Kyra, let me introduce Turner, the man I turn to whenever I need strategic advice or connections anywhere around the globe."

Turner smiled and lifted his hand. "Welcome to the clan, Kyra. I'm looking forward to seeing you in the village."

"Thank you." She smiled back. "I can't wait to see it."

"Let's get started," Onegus said. "Turner has intelligence from his contacts in Tehran." The chief waved a hand at the strategist. "Turner, go ahead."

"The good news is that so far, none of the other children have been taken."

"And the bad news?" Max asked.

"The families have arranged for additional security," Turner said. "Soldiers are now posted at all four residences. The missing girls' parents are trying to keep the disappearances quiet, but they're understandably distraught, and they have been making inquiries through various channels."

"What kind of inquiries?" Kyra asked.

"Official and unofficial," Turner said. "Fareed, Soraya's husband, is a commander in the Revolutionary Guard. He's the one who brought in the security personnel, and he also has powerful connections enabling him to pull a lot of strings. The fact that his own daughters have been taken might ruin his military career. He failed to protect them in his own home."

The dude couldn't have prevented Doomers from taking the girls even if he'd posted guards inside the house twenty-four seven.

"I assume they have surveillance cameras in the house," Max said.

Turner nodded. "Everyone has them these days, but the Doomers destroyed them. Fareed has no idea who took his daughters and their cousin. At first, they thought that the girls had escaped, but since they didn't take any belongings with them, that idea was dismissed. Fareed suspects either rebels or criminals, and he is waiting for a ransom demand."

Max exchanged a glance with Kyra. That complicated things. Her sisters and their children were being watched.

"My contact believes that the increased security is why no attempt has been made on the other children yet," Turner continued. "There are simply too many eyes on them at the moment."

"Is there anything your contact can do to protect them?" Kyra asked.

Turner shook his head. "They're human, and they can't protect against Doomers. Humans have no defense against immortals with even elementary mind control abilities."

"Which brings us to a tactical consideration," Onegus interjected. "The presence of these guards means that we need Yamanu. Max's shrouding and thralling abilities aren't strong enough to cover a large group, and neither is Jade's compulsion. Drova is still recovering from her bullet wound, so she can't join this time."

"You are right," Max agreed with the chief. "We can't do this without Yamanu."

"I'm calling him now," Kian said. "I hoped we would find another way, but it is what it is."

A moment later another window opened on the screen, revealing Yamanu.

"What's up, boss? Are we being invaded?" He then noticed who else was on the video conference in progress. "Ah. I see. You need me to go to Iran again."

"The extraction of Kyra's family is more complex than initially anticipated," the chief said.

Yamanu sighed. "I heard that the team is leaving tomorrow morning."

"That's right," Onegus confirmed. "If we are lucky, we will get the kids before the Doomers apprehend them, or we will dispose of the Doomers and leave the kids where they are."

Kyra frowned. "That wasn't part of the plan."

Kian shifted his gaze to her. "The kids are

young, Kyra. Eight to fifteen. It's better for them to stay with their families."

"I want to get my sisters out as well. Just one of the husbands is decent enough to consider leaving them be, but they are the couple with the two daughters, who are most in danger. We need to get them out."

Kian raked his fingers through his hair. "We'll leave the decision up to them if that's possible. But if we can't eliminate Durhad's cronies, we will have to take Yasmin and her family whether they want to come or not."

"Okay," Onegus said. "Now, let's talk strategy." He looked at Kyra. "Which sister should we approach first?"

Kyra didn't hesitate. "Soraya and Rana—the mothers of the girls we rescued. They'll be desperate for news, and with their daughters already gone, they'll be more receptive to what I have to tell them."

"Their husbands will be complications," Turner noted. "Especially Fareed with his Revolutionary Guard connections."

"There's also the issue of surveillance," Max added. "With that level of security, their homes are being monitored, possibly bugged."

"It would be easy for me to make contact with them by myself," Kyra said. "Dressed in traditional garb, a chador or burka, I'd blend in, just another female relative coming to offer support."

"You can use the bathroom with water running to talk to them inside the house, or you can take them outside for a walk," Max suggested. "Something casual that wouldn't arouse suspicion."

"I need to think about a good excuse," Kyra said. "I'll have something ready by the time we get there. I'll just need to stop in a store to get what I need for camouflage."

"You've obviously done this type of work before," Turner commented.

The ghost of a smile crossed Kyra's face. "Many times."

On screen, Jade shifted impatiently. "What is our extraction plan once we make contact? Even with Yamanu's shrouding, their absence will be noticed."

"Not necessarily," Yamanu said. "I can plant all kinds of things in the guards' heads. Like one sister visiting the other, and vice versa. By the time they untangle the web, we will be gone."

Max took the idea and ran with it. "There are also doctor's appointments, shopping trips, and other seemingly legitimate reasons. You can shroud each group as they move to the extraction point."

"Where do we come in?" Jade asked. "From what I've heard so far, you don't need us."

"If the Doomers show up, your job will be to dispatch them," the chief said. "And since we don't know how many of them you'll encounter, I'd rather you had enough on your team to take on as many as might show up."

Jade leaned back in her chair. "We are not attacking an entire stronghold like we did in Tahav. I think I can make do with just Dima and Anton." She turned to the female warriors. "Unless you are eager to come."

"I liked it," Rishba said. "The village is so boring."

"I also want to come," Asuka said.

The other two shrugged, indicating that they didn't mind either way.

"Okay then," Jade said. "Rishba, Asuka, Dima, and Anton. That's more than enough."

Max wasn't sure she was right, but since Onegus and Kian seemed to agree, he didn't comment.

"Speed is crucial," Onegus said. "We go in, make contact, and extract as quickly as possible. Ideally within a forty-eight-hour window or less."

"That's ambitious," Max said, mentally running through the logistics. Coordinating the movement of multiple families across Tehran without detection would be challenging, to say the least.

"It has to be quick," Kyra said softly. "The longer

we wait, the more time the Doomers have to make their move."

She was right, of course.

"What about transport on the ground?" Max asked. "We'll need multiple vehicles, safe houses, a secure route to the extraction point."

"Already arranged." Turner tapped his yellow pad with his pen. "We have a large safe house for you and several vehicles."

They continued hashing out details for another thirty minutes or so—contingency plans, communication protocols, equipment needs. Max contributed where appropriate, and so did Kyra.

She was definitely in her element—strategic planning, identifying vulnerabilities, anticipating obstacles.

His warrior queen.

It struck him again how perfectly matched they were. Both fighters, both willing to risk everything for those they considered family or helpless. The thought sent a warm current through his chest that had nothing to do with physical attraction.

Well, there was always that, but this was different. It had an additional dimension to it. A sense of his very soul expanding. This was a new sensation for him and now that he owned it, he vowed to do all he could to preserve and nourish it.

Finally, Onegus glanced at his watch. "We

should wrap this up. You all need rest before tomorrow. Ten hundred hours at the airstrip."

52

KYRA

The penthouse was quiet when Kyra and Max returned from the briefing. The living room was empty, and for a moment, Kyra wondered if everyone had gone to bed, but then she heard soft voices drifting from the girls' rooms.

"They're still up," she murmured, relieved she would have a chance to see them once more before going to sleep. She needed to hug each and every one of them.

Max squeezed her hand gently before releasing it. "Go, do some bonding with your nieces. I'll be in the home office, going over the mission specs again."

Kyra nodded. "Thank you," she said, suddenly feeling the inadequacy of words.

How did you properly thank someone who had

not only risked his life to save yours, but was willing to risk it again for people he'd never met, simply because they mattered to you?

"No thanks needed," Max replied with that crooked smile that never failed to stir something inside her. "Get some rest, my warrior queen. Tomorrow we fight."

As he disappeared down the hallway to the office, Kyra watched him walk with that confident swagger of a man who knew his own worth. Only when he was out of sight did she head toward the sound of voices.

She found Jasmine and the girls in Arezoo and Laleh's room, Jasmine sitting cross-legged on the floor between the two beds. The girls were wearing new pajamas, looking impossibly young and sweet with their damp hair and fresh faces.

"Everything okay?" Kyra asked from the doorway.

Five heads turned toward her. Jasmine's face lit up with a smile that was quickly followed by a more complicated expression—relief mingled with worry.

"We were just talking about the village," Jasmine said.

"Did you hear anything about our family?" Arezoo asked.

"They're all safe for now. Extra security has been posted at each sister's home."

"They can't stop the bad people," Laleh said softly. "They have magic," she added in a whisper.

"It's not magic," Arezoo said. "They have mind control like what Max showed us. But you are right. The regular guards can't stop them."

Kyra crossed the room and sat on the edge of Laleh's bed. "You're right," she said, not sugarcoating the reality. These girls had endured too much to be patronized now. "But we're going to get them out."

"All of them?" Donya, who was hugging a pillow while resting her back against Laleh's knees, asked, "including our father?"

"No, not him," Kyra admitted. "I'm still not sure what to do about him."

"Leave him," Donya said. "He doesn't love us."

"I'm sure that's not true." Jasmine turned toward the girl. "He might not show his emotions, but I'm sure he loves you."

"He doesn't." Donya joined Jasmine on the floor. "He calls us useless girls and berates our mother for not giving him a son. The idiot doesn't even know that he is the one who determines the baby's gender. Didn't he go to school?"

The other girls looked at her with stunned expressions, probably because none of them would have dared to say a thing like that before, but Donya's eyes blazed with defiance. "You are all thinking it, and it's time someone said it."

The other girls did not protest, so Kyra took this to mean that they agreed with Donya.

"Okay. That's good. I mean it's bad because you deserve a father who loves you. But it's good that no one would care if he's left behind." She cast a quick glance at Laleh, who had previously voiced a different opinion.

She'd said that her mother would miss their father, but perhaps her sisters had convinced her that wasn't true.

"You'll be doing him a favor," Arezoo murmured. "You have no idea how many times he threatened our mother that he will take another wife. The only reason he hasn't is because it is frowned upon even though it is allowed."

A long moment of silence followed, and then Jasmine rose to her feet. "Time for sleep, ladies. It's a big day tomorrow for all of us." She bent to kiss Laleh's forehead, then Arezoo's. "I'll be right next door if you need anything, okay? And tomorrow Ell-rom and I will move into Kyra's room so we can be close to you."

That seemed to ease some of the tension, and after several rounds of hugs and kisses, final good-nights, and promises to wake them up before Kyra left in the morning, Kyra and Jasmine retreated to the living room.

Jasmine's posture changed as soon as they were alone, a subtle slumping of her shoulders that revealed the strain she'd been hiding from the girls.

"Finally," she said, sinking onto the sofa with unusual weariness. "I don't know how you maintain that steady confidence all the time. I'm exhausted just from an evening of trying to pretend everything is hunky-dory, and I'm an actress, which means pretending is my thing."

Kyra joined her, tucking one leg beneath her as she turned to face her daughter. "You've had a full life with many experiences. My life was one-dimensional. I was a rebel and then a rebel leader, and I always had to keep up the brave face because I could never let the team see me wobble." She smiled when a sudden thought occurred to her. "Perhaps you got your knack for acting from me. During the many infiltrations and reconnaissance missions, I've played different characters. Frankly, those were the moments I was most terrified because I was on my own without any backup."

"You were?"

"Well, maybe terrified is too strong of a word. Anxious. Determined. A little angry."

"Angry?"

"At those who took my memories away." Kyra's hand went to her pendant, finding comfort in its familiar weight. "I'm still angry about all the time that was stolen from us."

Jasmine's eyes started to glisten. "And now that

we've finally found each other, you have to leave." She shook her head, frustration evident in the tight line of her mouth. "I know you have to go, but I don't have to like it."

The raw emotion in her daughter's voice pierced Kyra's heart. She reached across and took Jasmine's hand. "I don't like it either," she said softly. "If there were any other way..."

"There isn't." Jasmine squeezed her fingers. "I know that. Those are my aunts, my cousins. They deserve the same chance we've been given." She attempted a smile that didn't quite reach her eyes. "Doesn't mean I won't be counting the minutes until you're back."

"I'll be careful," Kyra promised. "I've survived worse odds with far less support."

"You'd better." Jasmine's voice took on an imperious tone. "I have plans for us when you get back, you know."

"Like what?"

Jasmine's expression softened. "Mother-daughter things. Shopping trips. Movie nights." She pursed her lips. "We can sing together."

Kyra had no idea if she had a good singing voice. She occasionally hummed a tune, but she didn't remember ever singing.

"I don't know if I can measure up."

"I remember you singing to me when I was little. In my mind, it sounded beautiful."

"I don't remember that," Kyra admitted. "I don't know any children's songs or lullabies. In fact, I don't remember the lyrics to any songs. The best I can do is hum a tune." She sighed. "Even my short-term memory leaves a lot to be desired. The monster in the dungeon might have given me immortality, but he did irreparable damage to my mind."

"You can train yourself to remember lyrics," Jasmine said. "It's a skill, and like everything else you want to get good at, it needs to be practiced." She smiled. "By the way, Max is an amazing singer. You should ask him to sing for you. If you have a good voice, we can have fun singing together."

She hadn't known that. What else didn't she know about the man who had captured her heart?

"Oh!" Jasmine straightened suddenly. "I almost forgot. I've got something for you. I'll be right back."

She hurried from the room, returning moments later with an object clutched carefully in her hands. As she settled back onto the sofa, Kyra saw that it was a jewelry box.

"I brought this from the village and forgot about it." Jasmine shook her head. "Perhaps the memory thing is hereditary." She opened the box and handed it to Kyra. "I thought these might help you remember."

Two delicate rings, a gold chain, and a photograph, worn at the edges and slightly faded with age.

Kyra took the photo, holding it gently with just the tips of her fingers, and her heart accelerated as she absorbed the image. Three people smiled back at her from another lifetime—a handsome blond man, his arm wrapped proudly around her shoulders. She hadn't changed much except becoming harder. Between them sat a small dark-haired girl, her tiny hands reaching up to cup both parents' cheeks, her smile radiant with uncomplicated joy.

They looked happy. All three of them. The man —Boris—was younger than in the photo Jasmine had shown her before, his face unlined, his eyes bright with contentment. And Kyra looked soft and carefree, with a wide smile and rosy cheeks.

"That's the three of us," Jasmine said softly. "Before you were taken."

Emotion surged in Kyra's chest, a complicated mixture of loss and longing so intense it threatened to overwhelm her. Her fingertips traced the faces in the photograph, lingering on her sweet child.

"You were so beautiful," she whispered. "Are beautiful."

"I have your eyes," Jasmine said, leaning closer. "And your hair. But I have Boris's build. He's a big guy, and I'm a big girl. I mean tall. Well, I also have the hips and ass to match, but I'm not complaining. I like my curvy body."

"You are perfect," Kyra managed through a tight throat.

This was evidence of a life she couldn't remember—proof that she had once been someone else, someone who had loved and been loved in return.

"I'm sorry," Jasmine said, misreading her silence. "I thought it might help you remember. I didn't mean to make you sad."

"No," Kyra managed, finally finding her voice. "It's precious. Thank you for showing me." She reluctantly put the photo back in the box. "You should keep it safe."

"The box is yours, and so are the rings and the chain, but I'll make a copy of the photo for you," Jasmine promised. "In fact, I'll make two blown-up copies so we can both have one to frame and hang on the wall in our houses."

"I'd like that," Kyra said, wiping at her eyes. "Very much."

"I also want to keep the tarot cards if you don't mind." Jasmine opened a secret compartment in the box and pulled out a velvet pouch. "I'm attached to this deck. I can get you a new one."

Kyra shook her head. "Keep everything. I just want a copy of the photo."

"Would you at least take the rings?" Jasmine

asked. "I've never worn them. I've just kept them in the box, cherishing everything inside because that was all I had left of you. But now I have all of you, and it would make me happy if you put the rings on."

Kyra couldn't say no to that. Pulling the two rings from the box, she slid them over her fingers. "If I brought these with me from home, my sisters might recognize them "

"It didn't even cross my mind, but you are right." Jasmine pulled out the thin gold chain and handed it to Kyra. "Put this on as well. You can keep it under your shirt."

The rings still fit perfectly, and the chain rested against her chest without interfering with her pendant.

For a long moment, the two of them sat in comfortable silence, both lost in thoughts of what might have been.

"I've been thinking about what happens when you bring everyone back," she said. "Practical matters, I mean. Housing. Integration."

Kyra welcomed the shift to more pragmatic issues. "Is there enough room in the village for everyone?"

"More than enough," Jasmine assured her. "Right now, Ell-rom and I share a house with his twin sister Morelle and her mate Brandon—he's the one who arranged for the personal shopper—

for reasons that I don't want to bother you with, but we've been talking about getting our own place." A smile curved her lips. "I would love us to live next to each other."

"That would be amazing. How many available houses are there?" Kyra asked, already trying to envision what life might look like with all her sisters and their children in one place.

"Enough," Jasmine said. "Kian wanted his sister Sari to move her part of the clan into the village, and he built it to be big enough for every clan member to have a house of their own, but she decided against it. Then the Kra-ell joined the clan, which is another story that I will tell you when you come back. Then there is Kalugal and his former Doomers, who have a dedicated section of the village as well."

Kyra frowned. "Former Doomers live in the village? I thought they were the enemy. The devil's spawn."

Jasmine laughed. "Most of them are, but there are exceptions. I'll tell you about that too." She squeezed Kyra's hand. "We have so much to talk about, so many things to tell each other."

"I'm looking forward to it. And I'm also looking forward to reconnecting with my sisters and hearing all of their stories."

Jasmine's face lit up. "There's a cul-de-sac near the old center of the village with four houses around it, and by old I mean nearly brand new, but I digress. Anyway, they're all empty right now because the Guardians who lived there moved to Kian's part of the village." Her eyes sparkled with enthusiasm. "It would be perfect for us. You, me, Ell-rom, and all your sisters with their families. Everyone together but with their own private spaces."

The image was so vivid, so tantalizing, that Kyra clung to it. A safe haven for all of them, a place where they could heal and reconnect, where the children could grow up surrounded by family.

"It sounds magical," she admitted.

A shadow crossed Jasmine's face. "I wish I could come with you," she said, the words bursting out as if she'd been holding them back. "I hate the thought of you going into danger without me there. But I also know the girls need me here."

Kyra reached out to brush a strand of hair from Jasmine's face. "You're their anchor, Jasmine. Their link to this new world. And you are so strong. They know that they can count on you."

"Yes, and they are not wrong, but they need you more. Promise that you will come back."

The simple request carried the weight of all their lost years, all the separation and longing they'd both endured. Kyra felt her pendant warm against her skin, as if responding to the gravity of the moment.

"I promise," she said, meaning it with every fiber of her being. "Fate didn't bring us together only to tear us apart."

"I love you, Mom," Jasmine whispered. "I always have."

The words broke something open inside Kyra's chest—a dam holding back emotions she hadn't allowed herself to fully acknowledge. She reached for her daughter and hugged her tightly, breathing in the scent of her hair, memorizing the feel of her in her arms.

"I love you too," she whispered back, the words feeling both new and ancient on her tongue. "Subconsciously, I've always known you were out there. I just didn't dare to believe."

53

MAX

Max reviewed Turner's intelligence briefings, studied the maps of Tehran showing the locations of Kyra's sisters' homes, and committed the extraction protocols to memory.

He should go to sleep, but he was reluctant to leave the penthouse and go down to the Guardians' shared apartment.

He wondered whether Kyra was done talking to Jasmine in the living room. He had ventured out of the home office earlier, wanting to get some of the leftovers from dinner, but when he heard them talking and realized that they were sharing a moment, he quietly retreated to the office and went over the maps again.

As a soft knock at his door pulled him from his thoughts, he knew right away it was Kyra, and a moment later the door opened and she walked in, wearing a loose T-shirt and leggings. Her hair was down, framing her face in soft waves, making her look younger, and somehow less formidable.

"Are you still working?" she asked.

"I'm done. I should be heading to bed." He closed the laptop and rose to his feet.

"Yeah, me too, except I don't think sleep is going to happen. I'm too hyped up."

He smiled. "Want me to sing you a lullaby?"

He'd meant it as a joke and was surprised when she nodded.

"I would love that. Jasmine told me that you are a great singer and that I should ask you to sing to me sometime. How about you sing to me now?"

"Sure. Here?"

She chuckled and reached for his hand. "Not here. Have you ever seen the penthouse master bedroom?"

She was inviting him to her bedroom?

They'd shared kisses, touches, but he knew this wasn't about sex. She just needed someone to be with her tonight because her emotions were all over the place.

"Can't say that I have. Do you want to give me a tour?"

She nodded and turned around, tugging him by the hand to follow her.

The master bedroom was right next to the

office, and as she opened the door, his eyes immediately were drawn to the massive four-poster bed that was situated on top of an elevated area in the back of the room. There was also a sitting area with a couch and an armchair and a couple of bookcases flanking the fireplace.

He thought she would lead him to the couch, but she surprised him, heading for the platform and the massive bed on top of it.

The covers were already turned down, as if she'd tried and failed to sleep before coming to find him. The room smelled of her—that indefinable scent that had begun to feel like home to him, mixed with the faint traces of the soap and shampoo she'd used earlier.

"I don't want to be alone with my thoughts tonight," Kyra said. "Usually, before a mission, I'd go over plans, check weapons, review contingencies. But now I have an entire team doing that for me. Everything feels different." She turned to look at him. "Would you mind lying next to me in bed? You can sleep here if you want, but if you want to go back to your own bed, can you do that after I fall asleep?"

"Of course." He toed off his boots and followed her to the bed. "I'll lie over the covers."

He had showered and changed clothes earlier, so it wasn't because he was afraid of dirtying her bed. He was afraid of being too close to her and wanting something he couldn't have tonight.

"As you wish." She climbed under the covers and pulled them up to just under her breasts.

He wished she had pulled the blanket higher up to her neck so he wouldn't have to stare at the enticing swell of her breasts, but he wasn't going to say anything. Instead, he tucked the blanket around her and lay down beside her on top of it.

"For twenty years, all I had was the resistance," she said quietly. "The mission was everything. Success or failure affected people I cared deeply about, but it has never been so personal." She looked up at him, her golden-brown eyes reflecting the soft light from the bedside lamp. "Now I have Jasmine. The girls. And..." She hesitated, then finished softly, "And you."

His heart lurched in his chest. It was a confirmation of the deepening connection that had been growing between them, and he was grateful to her for putting it into words.

He wished he could reciprocate, but telling her he loved her was premature, and he didn't know how else to verbalize what he was feeling.

For a long moment, they lay side by side in silence, their faces turned toward each other.

"Are you afraid?" she asked softly.

"No. We're well prepared, the team is strong,

and the plan is solid. Still, shit happens, you know?"

She chuckled. "Tell me about it. I'm an expert on that."

"I doubt you are as good as me at failing."

She reached across the space between them, her fingers brushing his cheek in a touch so gentle it made his heart inflate. "You found me when I was lost, and you helped bring me back to my daughter. I'd say that you are pretty good at winning."

"So are you."

She sighed. "I'm learning how to live. How to be with Jasmine. With the girls." Her voice softened further. "With you."

Max took a deep breath, knowing that if he was ever going to speak his truth, it should be now, before they faced whatever awaited them in Tehran.

"I know that it's too early to talk about love, but I care about you, Kyra," he said, the words inadequate for the depth of feeling behind them. "Deeply. More than I thought I was capable of." He paused, searching for the right words. "I've lived a long time, known many people, many women, but I've never felt toward anyone what I feel for you. It's like we are connected by some cosmic thread. Like we were meant to be together."

She smiled. "Destined mates?"

"Yeah, and don't make fun of this. It's real."

"I would never make fun of something like that, especially since I feel the same way. It's almost scary, this lightning-fast connection between us. Unlike you, I haven't been close to anyone I can remember, and you are the first man who makes me feel truly alive, who proves to me that I'm not broken beyond repair and that I still have hope of having it all. But those thoughts terrify me almost as much as they excite me."

He was floored by how completely honest and open she was. "Why does it terrify you?"

Kyra was quiet for a long moment, her fingers absently playing with the pendant at her throat. "Because I've lost so much already," she said, her voice catching slightly. "The more I care, the more I have to lose."

Her raw honesty touched something deep in his soul. He understood her fear all too well. Immortality meant accumulating losses, watching humans age and die, seeing history repeat its bloody cycles. Opening yourself to connections meant opening yourself to pain.

"I can't promise nothing bad will happen," he said honestly. "We're immortals, but we're not invulnerable. The mission has risks. Life has risks." He reached out to tuck a strand of hair behind her ear, letting his fingertips linger against her skin. "All we can do is make each moment count."

Her eyes glistened with unshed tears. "How do

you do that?" she asked, her voice barely above a whisper.

"Do what?"

"Say exactly what I need to hear."

He snorted. "No one has ever accused me of saying the right thing. I usually say all the wrong things and step on people's toes."

She smiled. "Maybe we are so much alike that we think the same way, and that's why we resonate with each other."

"That's a very good way to think about it. Another is to trust that the Fates brought us together for a reason. I, for one, don't plan to argue with them."

That drew a soft laugh from her. "The Fates," she repeated. "I've never been one for destiny or fate. I've always believed we make our own paths."

"Maybe the Fates open doors, but we decide whether to walk through them or not."

She considered this, her expression thoughtful. "So, this is a door?" She waved at the small space between them.

"It is, and I'm walking right through it if you let me in."

Instead of answering, Kyra moved closer, bridging the distance between them. Her lips found his in a kiss that was both gentle and certain, but he still wasn't sure whether it was an invitation for more or just an affirmation of her feelings toward him.

He cupped her face, returning her kiss with equal tenderness, letting her set the pace.

When they parted, Kyra's eyes remained closed for a moment, and when she opened them, the quiet certainty in them made his heart race.

"Whatever happens tomorrow," she said softly, "I'm glad we have tonight, even if it is only to hold each other tight."

"Me too," he said, kissing her forehead.

"Would you sing to me now?"

He started humming a tune, an old Scottish love ballad that he had forgotten the lyrics to. But as he hummed, the memory of them returned, and he started singing softly.

Kyra let out a breath and closed her eyes, and after a few moments her breathing slowed and deepened.

He kept singing, marveling at the sound of the steady beat of her heart against his side, and the warmth of her body seeping through the blanket between them.

It struck him that in all his centuries of existence, all his adventures and battles and conquests, few moments had felt as perfect as this one. Not because it was dramatic or passionate, but because it was real. Because it was Kyra, with all her strength and fragility, choosing to share this moment of vulnerability with him.

COMING UP NEXT
The Children of the Gods Book 94
DARK REBEL'S FORTUNE

After decades as a freedom fighter with nothing to lose, Kyra has finally found what's worth living for—a daughter she can't remember, a family who needs her protection, and a connection with Max.

But her struggle is far from over. As she races to save what remains of her stolen past, the stakes have never been higher. With the truth finally within reach, will Kyra's fortune bring triumph—or tragedy?

JOIN THE VIP CLUB

To find out what's included in your free membership, flip to the last page.

NOTE

Dear reader,

I hope my stories have added a little joy to your day. If you have a moment to add some to mine, you can help spread the word about the Children Of The Gods series by telling your friends and penning a review. Your recommendations are the most powerful way to inspire new readers to explore the series.

Thank you,

Isabell

Also by I. T. Lucas

THE CHILDREN OF THE GODS ORIGINS
1: Goddess's Choice
2: Goddess's Hope

THE CHILDREN OF THE GODS
Dark Stranger
1: Dark Stranger The Dream
2: Dark Stranger Revealed
3: Dark Stranger Immortal

Dark Enemy
4: Dark Enemy Taken
5: Dark Enemy Captive
6: Dark Enemy Redeemed

Kri & Michael's Story
6.5: My Dark Amazon

Dark Warrior
7: Dark Warrior Mine
8: Dark Warrior's Promise
9: Dark Warrior's Destiny
10: Dark Warrior's Legacy

Dark Guardian
11: Dark Guardian Found

12: Dark Guardian Craved
13: Dark Guardian's Mate

Dark Angel
14: Dark Angel's Obsession
15: Dark Angel's Seduction
16: Dark Angel's Surrender

Dark Operative
17: Dark Operative: A Shadow of Death
18: Dark Operative: A Glimmer of Hope
19: Dark Operative: The Dawn of Love

Dark Survivor
20: Dark Survivor Awakened
21: Dark Survivor Echoes of Love
22: Dark Survivor Reunited

Dark Widow
23: Dark Widow's Secret
24: Dark Widow's Curse
25: Dark Widow's Blessing

Dark Dream
26: Dark Dream's Temptation
27: Dark Dream's Unraveling
28: Dark Dream's Trap

Dark Prince

29: Dark Prince's Enigma
30: Dark Prince's Dilemma
31: Dark Prince's Agenda

Dark Queen
32: Dark Queen's Quest
33: Dark Queen's Knight
34: Dark Queen's Army

Dark Spy
35: Dark Spy Conscripted
36: Dark Spy's Mission
37: Dark Spy's Resolution

Dark Overlord
38: Dark Overlord New Horizon
39: Dark Overlord's Wife
40: Dark Overlord's Clan

Dark Choices
41: Dark Choices The Quandary
42: Dark Choices Paradigm Shift
43: Dark Choices The Accord

Dark Secrets
44: Dark Secrets Resurgence
45: Dark Secrets Unveiled
46: Dark Secrets Absolved

Dark Haven
47: Dark Haven Illusion
48: Dark Haven Unmasked
49: Dark Haven Found

Dark Power
50: Dark Power Untamed
51: Dark Power Unleashed
52: Dark Power Convergence

Dark Memories
53: Dark Memories Submerged
54: Dark Memories Emerge
55: Dark Memories Restored

Dark Hunter
56: Dark Hunter's Query
57: Dark Hunter's Prey
58: Dark Hunter's Boon

Dark God
59: Dark God's Avatar
60: Dark God's Reviviscence
61: Dark God Destinies Converge

Dark Whispers
62: Dark Whispers From The Past
63: Dark Whispers From Afar
64: Dark Whispers From Beyond

Dark Gambit
65: Dark Gambit The Pawn
66: Dark Gambit The Play
67: Dark Gambit Reliance

Dark Alliance
68: Dark Alliance Kindred Souls
69: Dark Alliance Turbulent Waters
70: Dark Alliance Perfect Storm

Dark Healing
71: Dark Healing Blind Justice
72: Dark Healing Blind Trust
73: Dark healing Blind Curve

Dark Encounters
74: Dark Encounters of the Close Kind
75: Dark Encounters of the Unexpected Kind
76: Dark Encounters of the Fated Kind

Dark Voyage
77: Dark Voyage Matters of the Heart
78: <u>Dark Voyage Matters of the Mind</u>
79: <u>Dark Voyage Matters of the Soul</u>

Dark Horizon
80: Dark Horizon New Dawn
81: Dark Horizon Eclipse of the Heart
82: Dark Horizon The Witching Hour

Dark Witch
83: Dark Witch: Entangled Fates
84: Dark Witch: Twin Destinies
85: Dark Witch: Resurrection

Dark Awakening
86: Dark Awakening: New World
87: Dark Awakening Hidden Currents
88: Dark Awakening Echoes of Destiny

Dark Princess
89: Dark Princess: Shadows
90: Dark Princess Emerging
91: Dark Princess Ascending

Dark Rebel
92: Dark Rebel's Mystery
93: Dark Rebel's Reckoning
94: Dark Rebel's Fortune

PERFECT MATCH

Vampire's Consort
King's Chosen
Captain's Conquest
The Thief Who Loved Me
My Merman Prince

THE DRAGON KING
MY WEREWOLF ROMEO
THE CHANNELER'S COMPANION
THE VALKYRIE & THE WITCH
ADINA AND THE MAGIC LAMP

TRANSLATIONS

DIE ERBEN DER GÖTTER
DARK STRANGER
1- DARK STRANGER DER TRAUM
2- DARK STRANGER DIE OFFENBARUNG
3- DARK STRANGER UNSTERBLICH

DARK ENEMY
4- DARK ENEMY ENTFÜHRT
5- DARK ENEMY GEFANGEN
6- DARK ENEMY ERLÖST

DARK WARRIOR
7- DARK WARRIOR MEINE SEHNSUCHT
8- DARK WARRIOR – DEIN VERSPRECHEN
9- Dark Warrior - Unser Schicksal
10-Dark Warrior-Unser Vermächtnis

LOS HIJOS DE LOS DIOSES

EL OSCURO DESCONOCIDO
1: EL OSCURO DESCONOCIDO EL SUEÑO
2: EL OSCURO DESCONOCIDO REVELADO
3: EL OSCURO DESCONOCIDO INMORTAL
EL OSCURO ENEMIGO
4- EL OSCURO ENEMIGO CAPTURADO
5 - EL OSCURO ENEMIGO CAUTIVO
6- EL OSCURO ENEMIGO REDIMIDO

LES ENFANTS DES DIEUX
DARK STRANGER
1- Dark Stranger Le rêve
2- Dark Stranger La révélation
3- Dark Stranger L'immortelle

The Children of the Gods Series Sets

Books 1-3: Dark Stranger trilogy—Includes a bonus short story: **The Fates Take a Vacation**

Books 4-6: Dark Enemy Trilogy —Includes

A BONUS SHORT STORY—THE FATES' POST-WEDDING CELEBRATION

BOOKS 7-10: DARK WARRIOR TETRALOGY
BOOKS 11-13: DARK GUARDIAN TRILOGY
BOOKS 14-16: DARK ANGEL TRILOGY
BOOKS 17-19: DARK OPERATIVE TRILOGY
BOOKS 20-22: DARK SURVIVOR TRILOGY
BOOKS 23-25: DARK WIDOW TRILOGY
BOOKS 26-28: DARK DREAM TRILOGY
BOOKS 29-31: DARK PRINCE TRILOGY
BOOKS 32-34: DARK QUEEN TRILOGY
BOOKS 35-37: DARK SPY TRILOGY
BOOKS 38-40: DARK OVERLORD TRILOGY
BOOKS 41-43: DARK CHOICES TRILOGY
BOOKS 44-46: DARK SECRETS TRILOGY
BOOKS 47-49: DARK HAVEN TRILOGY
BOOKS 50-52: DARK POWER TRILOGY
BOOKS 53-55: DARK MEMORIES TRILOGY
BOOKS 56-58: DARK HUNTER TRILOGY
BOOKS 59-61: DARK GOD TRILOGY
BOOKS 62-64: DARK WHISPERS TRILOGY
BOOKS 65-67: DARK GAMBIT TRILOGY
BOOKS 68-70: DARK ALLIANCE TRILOGY
BOOKS 71-73: DARK HEALING TRILOGY
BOOKS 74-76: DARK ENCOUNTERS TRILOGY
BOOKS 77-79: DARK VOYAGE TRILOGY
BOOKS 80-82: DARK HORIZON TRILOGY
BOOKS 83-85: DARK WITCH TRILOGY

BOOKS 86-88: DARK AWAKENING TRILOGY

MEGA SETS
THE CHILDREN OF THE GODS: BOOKS 1-6
INCLUDES CHARACTER LISTS
THE CHILDREN OF THE GODS: BOOKS 6.5-10

PERFECT MATCH BUNDLE 1

CHECK OUT THE SPECIALS ON
ITLUCAS.COM
(https://itlucas.com/specials)

**FOR EXCLUSIVE PEEKS AT UPCOMING RELEASES &
A FREE I. T. LUCAS COMPANION BOOK**

JOIN MY *VIP CLUB* AND GAIN ACCESS TO THE VIP PORTAL AT ITLUCAS.COM

TO JOIN, GO TO:
http://eepurl.com/blMTpD

Find out more details about what's included with your free membership on the book's last page.

TRY THE CHILDREN OF THE GODS SERIES ON <u>AUDIBLE</u>

2 FREE audiobooks with your new Audible subscription!

FOR EXCLUSIVE PEEKS AT UPCOMING RELEASES &
A FREE I. T. LUCAS COMPANION BOOK

Join my *VIP Club* and gain access to the VIP portal at itlucas.com
To Join, go to:
http://eepurl.com/blMTpD

INCLUDED IN YOUR FREE MEMBERSHIP:

YOUR VIP PORTAL

- Read preview chapters of upcoming releases.
- Listen to Goddess's Choice narration by Charles Lawrence
- Exclusive content offered only to my VIPs.

FREE I.T. LUCAS COMPANION INCLUDES:

- Goddess's Choice Part 1
- Perfect Match: Vampire's Consort (A standalone Novella)
- Interview Q & A
- Character Charts

If you're already a subscriber and you are not getting my emails, your provider is sending them to your junk folder, and you are missing out on important updates. To fix that, add isabell@itlucas.com to your email contacts or your email VIP list.

**Check out the specials at
https://www.itlucas.com/specials**

Made in the USA
Middletown, DE
23 April 2025